PASSION IN PRAGUE

JENNIFER SKULLY

Redwood Valley Publishing

© 2025 Jennifer Skully

This is copyrighted material. All rights reserved. No part of this publication may be reproduced, stored in a retrieval system, or transmitted in any form or by any means, electronic, mechanical, recording or otherwise, without the prior written permission of the author. This is a work of fiction. The characters, incidents and dialogues in this book are of the author's imagination and are not to be construed as real. Any resemblance to actual events or persons, living or dead, is completely coincidental.

PASSION IN PRAGUE
A ONCE AGAIN NOVEL

Book 13

Prague, the city of spires, music, and moonlight—and the most enchanting place to fall in love...

Elise never thought she'd find love again. Divorced for years, lonely, and carrying a secret that has kept her from ever finding love again, she arrives in the beautiful city of Prague for the final leg of a whirlwind European trip. What she doesn't expect is Kent—a widower with a tender heart, a passionate touch, and a family whose approval he doesn't want to lose.

What begins as a spark in one of the world's most romantic cities quickly blazes into something deeper. Days filled with historic castles, fascinating river cruises, charming cafés, and delicious dining on Czech cuisine give way to nights of breathtaking intimacy. Passion burns between them, slow and sultry as a waltz on the Vltava River. For the first time in decades, Elise feels truly cherished and desired.

But Kent's daughter, still grieving her mother's passing, doubts Elise's place in his life. And worse, Elise's secret past could cost her everything. For their love to last beyond the cobblestone streets and velvet nights of Prague, they'll have to trust not only in each other, but in forgiveness and the future they're daring to claim.

Set against the spellbinding backdrop of Prague's winding streets and glittering river views, this later-in-life, sexy second chance holiday romance will sweep you away—and prove that love is always worth the risk at any age.

ACKNOWLEDGMENTS

A special thanks to Bella Andre for this fabulous idea and to both Bella and Nancy Warren for all the brainstorming on our 10-mile walks. Thank you also to my special network of friends who support and encourage me: Laurel Jacobson, Kathy Coatney, Shelley Adina, Jenny Andersen, Jackie Yau, and Linda McGinnis. As always, a huge hug of appreciation for my husband who helps my writing career flourish. And to Wriggles, whom we have renamed Princess. Because she wants what she wants exactly when she wants it. Just like a princess!

1

Elise Martin woke with the sunrise, the clock on the bedside reading six-thirty. She relished the early mornings. And even more so today, when she awoke to the sights and sounds of early September in Prague, the capital of the Czech Republic.

She stretched away all her body's kinks, then climbed out of bed, though not bounding the way she would have when she was twenty. Still, she considered herself to be in reasonably good shape for fifty-five, and she weighed just about the same as she had when she was in college.

The boys would be up soon, demanding her attention. She nannied eight-year-old Marek and six-year-old Luca, the young sons of renowned pianist Tomás Novak and his partner Amanda Woodward. His three-month European concert tour over the summer ended here in Prague, his birthplace, though he and the family lived in San Francisco.

She stood still by the bed for a moment, listening to the baby monitor on the bedside table. But there wasn't a sound, not even a rustle or a giggle. Which meant she had a little more time to herself to get ready for the day.

She thought the boys were a bit old for a baby monitor, but Amanda had insisted, saying that Luca suffered from nightmares. And indeed, he sometimes did.

Elise gathered clothing to take with her into the bathroom. The elegant bedroom, with its four-poster bed and thick duvet, also featured a seating area with two comfortable chairs that probably cost a fortune, a delicate dresser which looked like a French antique, and plush Persian rugs beneath her bare feet. The bathroom matched the bedroom in luxury, with a soaker tub, a separate shower, and gold-plated faucets and taps.

The Novaks traveled in style, staying at five-star hotels, but since they often visited Prague to see Tomás's family, they'd purchased this river-front row house near Old Town. Tomás and Amanda had remodeled, updating the kitchen and bathrooms, building a beautiful veranda that overlooked the Vltava River and the famous Charles Bridge, as well as adding a balcony to their bedroom suite upstairs. The house, with five bedrooms, had room enough for Amanda's father, who would arrive today, and Sarah, Amanda's childhood friend, flying in tomorrow for the wedding.

Though Tomás and Amanda had two children together, they were only now getting married. And they'd chosen Prague for the ceremony.

After her shower, she heard the boys' voices on the monitor and dressed quickly. Luca barreled into her as she left her second-floor bedroom, which was across the hall from the room the boys shared.

"Breakfast," he said, his lips in a pout. "I'm hungry."

She ruffled his blond hair. "Then you could have asked Cook to prepare your breakfast."

Luca grimaced. "But I want you."

The household included a cook, a driver, and a twice-weekly cleaning service. Elise didn't even have to change her own sheets.

When the family arrived at the row house three days ago, Cook had insisted they use her title rather than her name. Elise hadn't asked why; it was the woman's choice. She didn't live in, but went home every night after all the dinner dishes were done and returned early in the morning to prepare breakfast.

Elise took the boy's hand. "Let's go down and see what Cook will make for us."

Though she'd cared for the two boys over the last three months, Elise wasn't their regular nanny. Back in the San Francisco Bay Area, her friend Cynthia had the job. However, Cynthia had knee replacement surgery that kept her from accompanying the Novaks on the concert tour this year. There was no way she could run after the boys until she'd recovered. Elise had agreed to fill in for her, and it hadn't been a hard sell.

An elementary school teacher, Elise had retired two years ago. The chance to travel through Europe had been irresistible. Cynthia would be fine, but she needed a few months of rest and physical therapy after the surgery and would take over again once the family returned to the Bay Area at the end of September. The added benefit for Elise turned out to be the opportunity to travel in luxury and see so many major European cities—London, Vienna, Paris, Berlin, Amsterdam, Rome, Barcelona, and more.

And now they were in Prague.

Approaching the kitchen, Elise heard Marek, Luca's older brother, chattering away at Cook. He was the more outgoing of the two boys, a spirited child, full of curiosity and energy. He also had a natural inclination for mischief, often pushing the boundaries set by his parents, and by her. His infectious grin endeared him, even when he was up to no good. Luca, on the other hand, was a sweet-natured but shy boy with a gentle disposition. He had an appealing innocence, often clinging to his older brother. Cautious around new people, it took him a couple of weeks to warm up to Elise. But after three months, his affectionate side shone through.

Cook—a plump, older woman with graying hair and a ready smile—was preparing a breakfast feast of cold cuts, cheese, sliced bread, tomatoes, cucumbers, and boiled eggs. Fried eggs, bacon, and hash browns weren't part of a typical European breakfast. Although the boys sometimes insisted on some sweet American-style cereal.

The Novak family lacked the formality preferred by many wealthy people, and they ate at the kitchen table, which was large enough for all of them. The dining room was used only for dinner parties with the likes of symphony conductors, cabinet ministers, and patrons of the arts.

Cook set out all the breakfast offerings only moments before Tomás entered.

"Good morning, my poppets," he said in a deep, brilliant voice before kissing both boys on the tops of their heads. His barely noticeable accent had a British cast to it.

Tomás's artistry on the piano never failed to make Elise cry. She'd often taken the boys to his matinee concerts and always felt herself carried away by the music. Though at times he played pieces that weren't her taste, she loved when he played Rachmaninoff's rhapsodies and Chopin's nocturnes. The orchestral pieces he accompanied on the piano were divine. Now that the concert tour was over—he'd played his last concert in Prague's famous Rudolfinum—he pleased himself on the piano in the living room, filling the house with everything from classical to old standards like "Summertime" and "Fly Me to the Moon" and even "Over the Rainbow."

Elise could sit quietly and listen to him all day.

"Good morning, Elise." Before he took a seat, he added, "I hope you slept well."

"I did, thank you, Tomás." Here again, with names, they didn't stand on ceremony. A handsome man on the shorter side—he was only five eight—Tomás Novak had presence. His hair, the same russet color as Marek's, was short, clipping away the curls both boys had. His long, elegant fingers produced piano perfection, and in his mid-forties, he was at the pinnacle of his career.

"Tuck in, boys." Tomás plopped bread, meats, and cheeses onto his plate. The boys did the same. So did Elise.

While Tomás had been born in Prague, he'd been educated at Cambridge. He still used some British idioms, even though he'd lived in San Francisco for the last twelve years.

He was also insistent that the boys be bilingual, learning the Czech language from a tutor. Neither Cynthia nor Elise spoke the language.

Before adding slices of hard-boiled egg to her open-faced sandwich, Elise spread mayo on her bread, sprinkling it with paprika, something both the Czech and the Hungarian people loved. In only three days, she'd come to relish the taste as much as she enjoyed the European-style breakfast.

Amanda Woodward flew in, her elegant peignoir floating behind her, her long blond hair cascading gracefully to the middle of her back. The boys squealed, jumping up for hugs and kisses.

Where Tomás was hardy, Amanda appeared much more fragile. Marek took after his father in both looks, russet-colored hair, and demeanor, while Luca favored his mother with his delicate features and tousled blond curls.

She took a seat next to Tomás, who sat at the head of the table, and picked a half piece of bread off the plate, adding one slice of meat, one of cheese, and no condiments.

Amanda was terrified she wouldn't fit into her wedding dress after all the scrumptious dinners she'd attended honoring Tomás while on tour. Always a bit high-strung, she'd become even more so as their big day approached.

Though having been together for ten years—and with two children—Amanda and Tomás's wedding would take place in two days. They'd planned to be married shortly after Luca was born, but Amanda's mother had been gravely ill, and cancer had taken her five years ago. Then there was the pandemic. Now they were using this visit to Prague, where all of Tomas's family lived, to finally have the wedding. Especially as it was the end of Tomas's European concert tour.

"I slept horribly last night," Amanda said with great drama.

"I know." Tomás brushed her cheek with a kiss. "You tossed and turned all night."

Before she took a bite of her open-faced sandwich, Amanda smiled at the boys and clapped her hands. "Are you excited to see *Dědeček* today?"

Elise had learned that *Dědeček* meant grandfather in Czech. Luca clapped his hands, crying, "*Děda, Děda, Děda*." Which was the shortened version the boys had used since they were very young.

Elise had to admit she was a bit intimidated about meeting Kent Woodward, Amanda's father. An important architect in the San Francisco Bay Area, as well as all over the country, he'd recently retired. She knew some of the buildings he'd designed, and his work was both brilliant and innovative.

What would he think of her? She, a nanny, a former schoolteacher, while he was a renowned architect, with his works written up in magazines and videos made about his unique structures. His work not only shaped cityscapes but also influenced architectural trends.

Of course, she'd wondered the same thing about Tomás, a

world-famous classical pianist. But right from the beginning, he'd treated her almost like one of the family, never as a servant.

Mr. Woodward, however, was an unknown quantity.

With both Amanda's and Tomás's attention focused on wedding preparations, then the wedding itself, and finally the honeymoon, when Elise would be left alone with the children —and Kent Woodward if he stayed after the wedding. Who knew how it all could turn out?

The man was not the type to have ever made an unforgivable mistake in his entire life. She, on the other hand... Her mistakes didn't bear thinking about now.

He'd most likely leave right after the wedding, when Tomás and Amanda went off on their honeymoon at a *chalupa* —which, Elise had been told, was a large holiday cottage—in the Krkonoše Mountains outside Prague.

But even more, the wedding meant the end of Elise's European adventure. After the honeymoon, the Novaks would return to San Francisco, Cynthia would once again be the boys' nanny, and Elise had no idea how she'd fit into the family's lives now that she'd grown fond of them all.

The arrival of Amanda's father seemed to signal the end of the fantasy life she'd been living for the past three months.

"Elise." Amanda's voice jerked her out of her thoughts. "Could you pick up *Dědeček* from the airport? And take the boys with you. He'll love seeing them as soon as he walks out of customs. Jakub will drive you." Jakub was the family's driver while they were in town, with two cars for their use, the large sedan Jakub drove them around in and a smaller personal car that Tomás and Amanda took out when necessary.

Elise smiled. "Of course."

But her insides felt tremulous. It was the last thing she wanted to do.

The flight had been long, and Kent was glad he'd booked a business class pod so he could sleep. Now the time change didn't bother him. He made it through customs, and with his suitcase in tow and computer bag slung over his shoulder, he stepped into the arrivals hall.

Searching for Amanda, he saw the boys first, just as they saw him and raced across the lobby straight at him. They clung to his legs like limpets. He dropped his bags to kiss the tops of their heads. "Hey you two, boy, have I missed you."

They were two bright spots in his world. Though he'd retired this year at sixty-five, which seemed to be a good age for it, he sometimes regretted the decision to keep working. He should have retired long ago, before Gail got sick, before the cancer took her from him. They'd often talked of all the trips they would take when he retired, all the cruises, all the new places they would see together. He was sure she would have loved Prague, but they'd never made it.

The only things that had carried him through the last five years without Gail had been his work and his grandsons.

Amanda had pressed him to retire, wanting him to come on tour with them so he could spend time with the boys. He'd been too late to accompany them this year, but next year, he would make it a priority. His daughter was right; he needed time with the boys. And he believed they needed him.

Even though Tomás was an amazing father, and they saw their Czech grandparents once a year, they needed an accessible grandparent. He took them for a day out when he could, a hike, a picnic, the zoo or the Exploratorium or any of the lovely places to visit around the Bay Area. But he wanted more time with them.

He looked up then, hoping to see Amanda, but expecting the chauffeur.

And he met the strikingly blue eyes and warm smile of the most stunning woman. Her blond hair, streaked with silver and cut short to frame her beautiful face, glittered in the sunbeams through the skylights.

She literally stole his breath.

Holding out her hand in greeting, she said, "I'm Elise, the boys' nanny."

For a moment, drinking in her perfection, he could neither open his mouth nor take her hand in his.

Until finally she dropped it back to her side.

He covered his misstep with a wide grin, his hands on the boys' heads. "And I'm Kent Woodward." He smiled, feeling idiotic since she already knew who he was.

She smiled in return, as if she hadn't noticed his foolishness. "The boys have been on tenterhooks, knowing you'd be coming today."

Her voice was like a piece of music that Tomás might play, her tone soothing. He was sure it calmed the boys when they got too wild, which they definitely could.

As their gazes met and then clung, a spark shot through him. With the widening of her pupils, he was sure she felt the spark too, even as the boys jabbered about everything they wanted to do while he was here.

Then she waved a hand. "Jakub has the car outside. Amanda is so eager to see you."

The boys ran ahead, turning to walk backwards, tourists and businesspeople and families skirting around them.

Elise hurried to catch up, taking both their hands and corralling them.

He was happy to walk behind, his gaze following her slim figure in a tunic sweater over black leggings and low-heeled boots. Definitely not the dress for a matronly nanny in her fifties. After hearing about her from Amanda, he was expecting someone dowdy and ancient-looking.

She was anything but. And that the outfit suited her perfectly. Sexy, even tantalizing.

The boys peppered him with questions as Jakub, the driver, appeared and led them to the car. Kent tried to manage their enthusiasm while keeping his composure in front of Elise. Every time their eyes met over the boys' heads, a surprising spark flared inside him.

Jakub opened the back door, then turned to load Kent's bags in the trunk. Elise ushered the boys inside, where the car's wide back seat would easily fit the four of them. After the boys clambered in, Kent touched Elise's elbow, politely helping her inside.

Tiny electric shocks seemed to go off in him at the contact.

Once the car was rolling, Elise said, "Amanda sends her regrets for not picking you up. She had the final dress fitting scheduled for today."

He had an illogical desire to take her hand, raise it to his lips, and kiss the back of it. But he said only, "I figured she'd have a very busy schedule before the wedding."

"Look at me, Děda!" Marek cried. The moment Kent's eyes were on him, the boy made funny faces. Not to be outdone, Luca imitated him.

Both Kent and Elise laughed. She had a pretty laugh—sweet and light—that seemed to touch him on the inside.

When the boys finally settled down, Elise included them in the conversation. "We went to many of Papa's matinee performances, didn't we?"

Marek rocked in his seat with excitement. "And we went backstage, and they had all these yummy treats for us to eat."

Next to him, Luca rubbed his stomach in agreement.

Elise chuckled. "Is that what you remember the most—the treats?"

Marek, with all the seriousness of a boy coached in advance, said, "Papa plays as if music is like magic."

Elise's voice softened. "Whatever Tomás played was the most beautiful music in the world. He just kept getting better and better."

Kent was extremely fond of Tomás. Ten years older than Amanda, he'd helped her settle into motherhood and stood by her side while she grieved her mother's passing. Caring for the boys had helped him too. Kent asked, "Are you two looking forward to your mama and papa's wedding?"

They both shrieked in unison, "Yes, yes, yes!"

Elise smiled indulgently. "You're very excited about being ring bearers, aren't you?"

That sent the boys into another round of gleeful shrieks.

With their noise giving him cover, Kent leaned closer and asked, "How's Amanda doing?"

Despite having Tomás to cling to through that awful time, Amanda had struggled to move on from her mother's death.

A pang of guilt jolted through him as he thought of his late wife—especially because of that flutter of excitement in his belly over another woman, a sensation he hadn't experienced in years. The unexpected meeting with a beautiful woman had made his heart leap. But thinking of Gail and Amanda turned that flutter of excitement into a quiver of guilt.

Gail was diagnosed with cancer eight years ago, just after Amanda gave birth to Marek. Tomás and Amanda had put off their wedding plans, and Amanda had been at her mother's side through her illness. Kent had taken as much leave as possible, but massive projects had demanded his input. That too was another source of guilt. Then, five years ago, they'd lost Gail. Along with his own grief, he'd had Amanda to think of. Even with her two boys to look after, she'd struggled with depression.

In the last couple of years, Amanda's depression had kept him from pursuing any new relationships, though he felt he might be ready. He'd dated a few times but kept that from Amanda, knowing how deeply her mother's loss still affected her. He could only hope that now, with her decision to finally go through with the wedding, it was a sign she was ready to move past her pain.

He still grieved for his lost wife, but he knew Gail would want him to go on. And now, at sixty-five, with only a limited number of years left, he didn't want to spend them alone.

The thought made him glance at Elise again as she lovingly interacted with the boys. She made them laugh and squeal with delight, even coaxing more from Luca, who was naturally shy.

Yes, she was good with the boys. She was also beautiful and sweet.

Suddenly, he was torn—caught between the unexpected possibilities of this Prague visit and the complicated emotions surrounding his family's grief. He had to focus on Amanda's wedding, on the family, on Amanda herself.

As difficult as it seemed, he had to put aside the tantalizing attraction he felt for his grandchildren's captivating nanny.

2

Tall and temptingly lean, with distinguished silver hair, Kent Woodward was too handsome, too nice, too loving with the boys—and just too much.

He reminded her of the man who'd once been in her life long ago. A man who had seemed so nice and so perfect. At least in the beginning.

But God, she didn't want to think about Nick.

Kent had actually helped the driver carry in his bags. A man of his stature would normally have let the help do the work, but he hadn't treated Jakub as if he was mere *help*. Just as he hadn't treated her like the help.

Then he carried Luca in his arms, took Marek's hand, and ushered them both into the Novaks' spacious, luxurious home.

As soon as he saw Amanda, Kent let Luca slide to the floor and opened his arms. His daughter flew into them, and there could be no mistaking the tight, loving hug between them.

Stepping back, her hands still resting on her father's arms, Amanda said, "Tomás just ran out for a few things I needed.

He'll be back any moment. He's so looking forward to seeing you." She rubbed his arms, her excitement palpable. "I'm so sorry I couldn't meet you, Daddy. I've been so busy before the wedding."

Kent shook his head, and Elise saw the smile in his eyes. Brushing a wisp of blond hair from Amanda's face, he said, "No worries." Then his piercing blue eyes, so much like his daughter's, swept over Elise. "Elise took exceptionally good care of me."

She couldn't tell if the smile was for her or for Amanda. But it heated her from the inside out.

She should have added *too dangerous* to the list of adjectives she'd applied to him.

Amanda stepped back and waved a hand airily. "Thank you so much, Elise. You can take the boys now. I'll get my father settled in."

"No, no," the boys cried in unison. "We want to stay with Děda!" Then together: "Please, please!"

Marek grabbed the handle of Kent's suitcase, trying—and failing—to lift it.

Elise said, "Come along, boys. Let Mr. Woodward have some time with your mother and get all unpacked."

They whined at her words.

Then Kent looked at Elise, and she felt as if he could see straight inside her—as if he sensed her attraction.

"Please call me Kent," he said. His gaze held hers too long before he added, "And I appreciate how well you treated me on the way here."

It felt as if their eyes locked for an eternity. Then Elise noticed Amanda's eyebrows rise slightly, as though she'd caught the long look and attached some significance to it. Her gaze flicked between them, first her father, then Elise, then back again.

Elise didn't know how long that silent interchange might

have gone on if Marek hadn't grabbed his grandfather's hand. "Come on, Děda! We'll help you take everything upstairs."

Kent smiled, slinging his computer bag off his shoulder and handing it to Marek. It plopped to the floor immediately. Luckily, a rug cushioned the impact.

But Marek was stoic. He lifted the bag again, pulled the strap over his head to steady it, and began marching up the stairs—leaning heavily to one side under the weight.

Amanda smiled, but Elise didn't think it reached her eyes. Amanda wanted time alone with her father, but the boys were intent on not letting her have it. Then again, once they were in bed tonight, she'd have all the time she wanted.

Amanda waved an imperious hand. "Boys, run along. Your grandfather can see you later. Elise, why don't you go to the kitchen and get a snack for them?" she said, as if she wanted to get rid of the bothersome nanny. She wasn't generally high-handed and—like Tomás—she treated Elise almost like family.

Still, Amanda had definitely seen that *look*. Maybe she'd even detected some sort of connection that wasn't actually there. But she certainly hadn't missed the flare of interest in her father's eyes. Elise would have stepped away right then if Luca hadn't raised his arms to her. "Carry me," he said, softly pleading.

Amanda opened her mouth—to say what, Elise had no idea—but Kent interrupted. "Let Elise carry our boy." He smiled at his daughter. "After all, I have to carry my suitcase."

Rather than risk sounding snippy before her father, Amanda headed up the stairs after Marek, who was still struggling with the computer bag. Elise hefted Luca into her arms. He clasped his legs around her waist, and she supported him beneath his bottom. He was already too heavy for this, but she carried him anyway.

Picking up his suitcase effortlessly, Kent mouthed, *thank you*, then followed Amanda up the stairs.

"I'll help you unpack," Amanda said after Elise took the boys to the schoolroom.

It was obvious his daughter wanted some alone time. Or, more likely, she'd wanted to occupy Elise elsewhere. He hadn't missed the way she'd looked from him to Elise, assessing, assuming.

She got as far as unzipping his case and pulling out the travel cubes. Then Amanda threw herself into the overstuffed chair, and Kent took over.

"Oh my God, Daddy." She slumped deeper into the chair. "The wedding preparations have been monstrous," she moaned.

He loved his overly dramatic daughter to pieces. But she was prone to exaggeration. "You should have told me. I could have come earlier."

She waved a hand in the air. "It's just this tour. It was taxing beyond belief. A new city almost every other day. You know how that disrupts the boys."

She hadn't addressed his slight scolding, but he didn't say it again. Amanda seemed to get a kick out of the drama. "At least you had Elise to help."

She rolled her eyes. Dramatically. "Don't get me wrong, Elise is great."

"She seems very capable. Not a young, flighty au pair."

"There's at least that. I didn't have to worry about her taking off with some hunky Frenchman when we were in Paris," she said with a groan.

"The boys seem to adore her."

Amanda followed that with a huff. "She's just so..." She fluttered her fingers. "I don't know."

He hung his shirts in the armoire. "Has she done something wrong?" He made a production of his unpacking, so it wouldn't look like he was hanging on Amanda's every word.

She sighed. With groans and moans and sighs, she was gearing up. His daughter, if there was trouble, needed to make it sound intense. Since her mother died—no, maybe even since the boys were born—Amanda seemed to thrive only in crisis mode. To use an old cliché, she'd make a mountain out of a molehill.

"She just takes over," Amanda groused.

Kent hesitated to ask if that wasn't exactly what Amanda and Tomás had hired her to do.

"I barely get time with the boys," she continued the complaints. And yet, instead of coming to meet him at the airport, Amanda had sent Elise.

But he said, "It'll be okay if you tell her to back off."

"Oh no." Her eyes went wide. "Tomás would have a fit. He likes to leave the kids with her. We had so many parties and balls and dinners to attend. And we've got the honeymoon. We'll be gone for ten days."

Kent mollified her by saying, "Then why don't you let me observe her with them over the next few days? After that, I can talk with Elise, if you'd like."

He didn't say that he would love to observe her. And have a very long talk with her. Many endless talks, in fact.

But Amanda sat bolt upright. "No. Don't do anything." Again, her hands were fluttering, this time so quickly they were almost a blur. "We've only got a few more weeks with her. Then Cynthia will be back and the boys will be at school during the day."

Though he assumed Elise was around Cynthia's age, their regular nanny was much more matronly, her dresses drab, her gray hair messy as if she'd never put a comb through it. But her looks didn't matter. She was an excellent nanny and so good with the boys. Amanda adored Cynthia, who drove the boys to their private school, picked them up, helped with homework, took them to the park, got them off to bed, all the endless activities of two energetic boys.

"Don't upset the applecart, Daddy. I can put up with Elise for another few weeks. I just wanted you to know what she was like. Bossy."

He laughed. He probably shouldn't, but the description sounded ridiculous.

Amanda couldn't seem to resist saying, "I know how you dislike bossy women."

He didn't like the term. It was demeaning. He preferred assertive and commanding, all traits which were admirable in a man and should be admired in a woman.

Elise was a smart, attractive, caring woman only a few years younger than he was. She was exactly his type.

Yes, Amanda had definitely seen that glance between them downstairs. He wouldn't call it flirty, yet it was like a bolt of electricity had shot through him. And when Elise's eyes had widened slightly, he'd known she felt the electricity too.

It was obvious Amanda was trying to steer him away.

His daughter wasn't ready for him to date. She wasn't even ready for him to flirt.

And he was afraid she never would be.

THE NEXT MORNING, THEY HEADED TO PRAGUE'S OLD Town Square—Kent, Elise, and the boys.

After breakfast, while Elise took the boys upstairs to dress, Amanda had pulled him aside and asked him to entertain them for the day. While they were his delight, he hadn't wanted to leave his daughter alone to handle all the last-minute wedding arrangements. But despite her obvious tension, she'd insisted she didn't need him.

Tomás had gone with Jakub to pick up Sarah, Amanda's maid of honor, from the airport. Kent hated leaving Amanda when she was so stressed, but she would have Sarah, her childhood friend from San Francisco, to help manage the chaos and provide emotional support. Probably even more than Kent could, which would be why Amanda asked him to take the boys out. She needed girlfriend time now, not Dad time.

So he'd done as Amanda requested.

His daughter just hadn't expected him to take Elise too. That was obvious in the way Amanda had tried to find excuses to keep Elise at the house. Yet none of them were rational, and Tomás had overruled her before he left for the airport.

Now here they were.

The house Tomás had purchased was close to Old Town Square, so they walked. Kent's first destination was the astronomical clock, which he'd read about. The streets of Prague were narrow, some barely more than alleys—the city was a maze of alleys—but everywhere the mouthwatering scent of fresh-baked goods floated in the air.

Marek and Luca ran circles around him and Elise. "Can I have a *koláč*? Can I have a *koláč*?" they chimed in unison, eager for the sweet Czech pastry filled with jam or other tasty fillings.

Kent and Elise played good cop, bad cop. Kent would have given in, but Elise said, "You just had breakfast. Let's wait until later. Then you can have hot chocolate *and* a koláč."

Kent winked at her, and she smiled in return. Odd how her smile could make his heart turn over.

As they made their way through the alleyways to the square, the boys bounded ahead, with both Kent and Elise keeping their eyes on them.

At well past ten o'clock, all the shops were open, and Elise groaned as they passed one that seemed to glow red. "Thank God the boys didn't notice this one. They would've asked me what it was, and I don't even know how to explain it."

Kent glanced inside the door at the strange contraption displayed there. Then he laughed, reading the shop's sign. "Good God—it's the Sex Machines Museum."

With another smile, Elise blocked the sight with her hand, laughing as she marched on.

He couldn't help laughing with her. "What the hell was that thing in there?"

Softly, she said, "I believe it was a woman's erotic chair."

Kent gasped, feigning shock. "Is that a—?" He didn't finish the question.

Elise, still smiling—though now her smile seemed entirely erotic to him—answered, "Yes, it is. A chair with a massive you-know-what in the middle. Personally, I think sitting on it looks more like torture than pleasure." Then she called out, "Boys, don't get so far ahead!"

The boys stopped in their tracks and waited.

Kent had to agree with Elise. The thing was massive. But he couldn't help laughing and catching her hand. "So big isn't always better?" he couldn't help asking.

She blushed at the erotic talk, even if it wasn't explicit. "Not when it's *that* big."

They caught up with the boys, with no more time for discussion. Yet that brief conversation stirred him. He couldn't help imagining how big was *just right* for her.

Was it a subtle signal when she'd brought the museum to his notice?

He'd felt that zing of connection between them—the one

he was sure Amanda had sensed. But had Elise felt it in the same way he did?

As the alley opened up onto the square in front of the town hall and the astronomical clock, the boys once again ran ahead into the gathering crowd, taking all Elise's attention as she watched out for them. They had missed the show at ten o'clock, but with the eleven o'clock hour still fifteen minutes away, people were already milling in the square. Tourists drank coffee and ate pastries at the surrounding restaurants, and a tour group made their way into the throng as their guide explained in English about the clock.

"Shall we push our way through so the boys can see?" Kent asked.

"Yes," Elise agreed. "I'm sure no one will mind, since we have the boys."

Indeed, people let them through so the children could stand up front. The astronomical clock loomed above them, its intricate details catching the morning light. Kent gave the boys a bit of history, his voice brimming with enthusiasm—not just for them, but for himself as well.

"The clock is called the *Orloj*, and it was first installed in 1410, which means it's very, very old. It's mesmerized people just like us for over six hundred years. There's even a legend that if the clock ever stops, misfortune will fall on the town. So the people make sure it's always working."

He wondered if it had stopped during World War II. Or in 1968, when the Russians marched into Prague. But he didn't want to ruin the magic of the moment with dark questions.

"The *Orloj* doesn't just tell time," he continued. "It marks the position of the sun and moon in the sky, tracks astronomical movements, and even shows the signs of the zodiac."

The boys hopped about in excitement. "When does the show start? When does it start?"

He checked his watch. "In just a few minutes."

Finally it began, first with the ringing of a smaller bell. Then two small doors above the clock opened to reveal figures marching in procession as the clock tolled the hour.

"Look up," Kent told them. "Those are the twelve apostles."

Tourists raised their phones, taking videos and pictures. Kent was too entranced with the boys' reactions to pull out his own phone.

"And those four—" He pointed to the figures on either side of the clock itself. "—tell the story of Vanity with his mirror... then the Miser clutching his gold. And on the other side, the Turk, who represents pleasure." And lust, though Kent didn't say that, but it did remind him of that conversation with Elise outside the Sex Machines Museum. "The skeleton ringing his bell is Death, reminding us that time never stops."

Luca gasped. "That's scary," he said, his eyes wide.

Kent crouched down to meet his grandson's gaze. "Yes. But don't worry. After death tolls his bell, the golden rooster crows—announcing the start of a new day. The rooster symbolizes dawn, the triumph of life over death."

He wondered if the boys were too young for that explanation, and he added gently, "It's the clock's way of saying life always goes on."

Both boys watched with rapt attention. When Kent looked at Elise, she wasn't gazing at the clock at all—she was looking at him.

Over the boys' heads, he felt their electric connection spark again.

With the way she drew in an unsteady breath, he was sure she felt it too.

ELISE HADN'T EXPECTED HIM TO BE SO FLUENT IN HISTORY. Handsome, yes. Charming, absolutely. But eloquent in a way that made the past come alive? That was unexpected. And surprisingly attractive.

As the bell finished tolling the hour, the boys were already bounding away from the astronomical clock, darting through the crowd around the tower. Elise and Kent could do nothing but follow across the cobblestones. In the center of Old Town Square, still-blooming flowerbeds encircled the sculpture of a tall robed man surrounded by people lying at his feet.

That was the children's destination. They raced across the square toward an elderly woman feeding pigeons at the base of the monument, the birds' cooing rising above the noise of the tourists.

Standing far enough back not to disturb the boys' fun, Elise folded her arms, studying Kent. "You know an awful lot about the clock."

His gaze stayed on the boys, since they might bolt at any moment. "I like history. I love helping people fall in love with it too." He smiled. "And naturally I love looking at all the architecture." He pointed across the square. "That church, for instance, is in the Gothic style. Its twin towers have a large spire surrounded by smaller spires. Very ornate." He pulled out his phone and tapped for several seconds. "It's the Church of Our Lady before Týn."

He pointed past the monument, where the boys were still happily watching the woman and the pigeons. "That building is Rococo." He glanced at his phone. "It's the Kinský Palace, which is now the National Gallery. Look at all the statues along the roofline. And the decorative motifs over the windows."

She had fun testing him. "What about that church over there?"

He turned to follow her line of sight. "Baroque. It's also a very elaborate style. See the domed spires and the columns?"

"It's beautiful. Both churches are."

With another look at his phone, he said, "That's St. Nicholas Cathedral." Then he added, "The monument where the boys are feeding the pigeons is the Jan Hus Memorial. Jan Hus was a religious reformer, and the people at his feet are his followers. And that—" He pointed to the tall column opposite the memorial. "—is the Marian Column, a statue of the Virgin Mary on top."

With a laugh, she asked, "Does your phone really say all that?"

He turned his screen to her, smiling. "I just asked for all the things we could see right here in Old Town Square."

Then he jutted his chin at the boys as they dashed through the pigeons, scattering them. A crowd had formed around them, people taking pictures as if they were the tourist attraction rather than the memorial. The old lady gave them each a handful of seeds, and to their delight, the birds once again flocked to them.

"But they're the most endearing sight in the square, don't you think?" He looked at Elise then, with laughter and a charming twinkle in his eye.

Something seemed to shift inside her as she met his gaze.

Maybe this trip to Prague could be about more than sightseeing. Maybe, just maybe, there was something more to discover here in this romantic city. Especially after that rather risqué conversation outside the Sex Machines Museum. She couldn't believe she'd said those things to him and blushed all over again. And yet, the banter had been such fun.

But instead of confessing what she felt, she said, "You're so good with the boys. It's clear they adore you."

His smile deepened. "After losing my wife, they're the light of my life." A sudden shadow passed over him. The sky was a clear, brilliant blue—no cloud in sight—so the darkness came from within. "Children are why you carry on," he murmured. "They keep you going."

"I'm so sorry for your loss," she said softly. "And for Amanda's."

Still not looking at her, he reached out a hand. Elise laid her palm against his, his warmth flooding into her.

He squeezed her fingers. "Thank you." A sigh escaped him. "It's been a long time. Years." He looked at her again, a faint shadow still in his eyes. "At the risk of sounding like a terrible person, Amanda has had a much harder time moving on than I have. I tried to clean out her mother's things a couple of years after we lost Gail, and Amanda was so horrified, I just couldn't do it. I still haven't done it. It felt like I'd committed a crime even thinking about it."

She felt the pain in his words. The guilt. For a moment, they simply watched the boys in silence. The elderly woman gave each child another handful of seeds, and the pigeons clustered around them like a gray-and-white storm.

"I'm sure it was very hard on Amanda," Elise said gently. "With two little boys, one of them still a baby, and without her mother to lean on for all that advice." Then she added, "But maybe for you, it was more about relief that your wife wasn't suffering anymore."

They turned to each other at the same moment.

"Yes." He breathed in deeply, let it out. "I feel like I did all my grieving before she was gone. But you can never tell your daughter that her mother's death was a relief."

Elise finished for him. "It wasn't relief that she was gone. It was a relief that she wasn't in pain anymore. But you probably still feel guilty about that too."

He ran a hand through his hair, his gaze drifting back to the boys. "Yes." The word came out fractured, choked. He closed his eyes as if looking inward. A sheen of moisture dampened his lashes. Finally, he looked at her again. "Thank you. No one's ever understood that." He gave a soft, self-deprecating laugh. "Or maybe I just never told anyone. Thank you for letting me get that off my chest."

This time, she squeezed his hand.

His smile returned, the weight of his confession seeming to lift from him. "Shall we go get the boys their treat? And a coffee for us?"

Feeling warm inside, she said, "I'd love that."

He was handsome and smart and compassionate. He loved history, loved his grandsons, his daughter, his wife. He was a loyal, honorable man who would do anything for his family.

She could see herself falling for him if she wasn't careful.

3

The brief conversation with Elise had somehow lightened Kent's spirit, as if her words helped shed some of the weight of the past. Perhaps it was also easing the burden of his inadequacies—his worry about how to do right by Amanda. He could only imagine Elise had been an excellent teacher, giving her students exactly what they needed. She had the gift of making people feel capable.

They watched the boys racing through the flock of pigeons, tossing seeds and making the old woman laugh. She didn't even scold them when they startled the birds into flight with their shrieking charges. Perhaps that was the whole point of the feeding—to give the children delight.

They might have spent the entire afternoon there, but Kent finally called out, "Boys, let's get a hot chocolate and some *koláče*."

Leaving the birds and the woman behind, the boys rushed to join Kent and Elise.

At a café on the square, they ordered coffees for themselves and hot chocolates for the boys, along with an assortment of *koláče*, the famous Czech pastries. Kent chose a different filling for each so they could share. The boys, however, weren't fond of the nutty sesame or the slightly tangy *tvaroh*—the soft cheese filling that resembled cottage cheese, though tasted sweeter. Instead, they devoured the pastries filled with raspberry and apricot jam. Kent and Elise shared both the *tvaroh* and the poppyseed, its earthy sweetness pairing well with their coffee.

The boys chattered with excitement—about the astronomical clock, the birds, the wedding tomorrow where they would be ring bearers. Marek bobbed in his seat, thrilled at the idea of being the center of attention, while Luca seemed far more subdued, as if afraid he might make a mistake at a crucial moment.

Elise squeezed his hand. "You're going to be marvelous," she told Luca, before smiling at Marek. "Both of you."

Back at the house in the late afternoon, after Elise had helped the boys dress for the rehearsal, Kent cornered Elise alone in the hall outside her room. She tried to beg off attending, saying, "But I don't have a part in the wedding, and I'm not family."

"You've been with the family for three months," he countered, because he wanted her there. "You've taken care of the boys. And after the rehearsal, we'll all have dinner at Tomás's parents' house. You can't stay home alone while everyone else is out enjoying themselves."

"But—" she started.

Kent put a finger gently to her lips, a jolt of electricity zipping through him at the contact. "Consider yourself my plus one."

Her cheeks flushed and her pupils flared, as if she'd felt the spark. "There are no plus-ones for a rehearsal dinner."

"There will be so much food at Tomás's parents' home," he cajoled, "that you'll absolutely need to come and help eat some of it. Or they'll be stuck with leftovers for days."

She finally relented. "All right. Thank you. I'll just get changed."

When Elise came down the stairs to join the family for the ride to the church, she wore a peacock blue dress that set off her eyes. Amanda sucked in a breath, and Kent quickly stepped in. "We can't leave Elise all alone while we're out having fun."

Amanda arched a brow. "She'd probably enjoy the time off from the boys."

"But it's a good thing she's coming," he insisted. "She can keep an eye on them so you can concentrate on the family."

Amanda gave him a look. "I'm sure you could have done that. Besides, their cousins will probably do all the entertaining that's needed."

The discussion ended there, though Kent wondered once they were at the church—especially when he'd seated Elise in the pew he would eventually take with the boys—if Amanda had once again sensed the electricity between them. Beside him as they waited for their walk down the aisle, his daughter bristled with frantic energy as Sarah started the march.

After Elise's encouragement that afternoon, the boys performed perfectly, even little Luca walking with confidence.

Then it was Kent's turn to take his daughter's arm. In this mock ceremony, he gave Amanda away, but tomorrow, he would do it for real. Though she'd already belonged to Tomás, and he to her, for almost ten years, the moment still felt significant. Returning to the pew, he squeezed in between Elise and the boys without looking to see if Amanda watched him.

Elise leaned in. "She's the most beautiful bride."

Kent nodded. She was. His daughter was the image of her mother—lissome, beautiful, regal.

After the ceremony, they all drove to Tomás's parents' home in a nearby district.

Though not large, the Novak's house was elegantly decorated. A belief in tradition showed in every detail. The dining table gleamed, set with china for twenty. The Novaks had clearly expected Elise's presence, with a place setting for her too.

Guiding her to a seat, he took the chair beside her. Filip, Tomás's father, gray-haired, stocky, and stoic, filled the wineglasses. Tomás's mother, Hana, still spry though in her late seventies like her husband, poured grape juice for the children—including Luca and Marek's five cousins.

Filip raised his glass and, in heavily accented English, declared, "*Na zdraví!* To finally having our beautiful Amanda as our true *snacha*." Kent assumed that meant daughter-in-law or something like it.

Tomás's younger brother, Petr—the baby of the family, with their sister Dagmar between him and Tomás—rose next and lifted his glass. "It's about time you did your duty, brother."

Everyone laughed. They likely all knew the delay in vows had come more from Amanda than Tomás.

Kent rose then, holding up his glass. "To the most amazing man my beautiful daughter could have brought into our family. Though we welcomed you years ago, I know how much Amanda's mother longed for this day. I believe she's smiling down on us now."

Tears glittered in his daughter's eyes, and she stood to hug him.

But Gail wouldn't have wanted this celebration to turn maudlin, and with his arm around Amanda, his glass high, he toasted, "To family." Then he couldn't resist adding, "And to new beginnings."

That toast was especially for Elise. Even if no one else knew it.

The Novak family was a loud, boisterous bunch., and the dining room swelled with laughter, clattering silverware, and overlapping conversations, everyone talking over everyone else. Scents of roasted meat and garlic lingered in the air, competing with the fruity tang of red wine. They dined on *vepřo knedlo zelo*, which Tomás's mother Hana translated as pork, dumplings, and sauerkraut, all of it complemented by a deliciously rich gravy. She claimed the dish was a national treasure, and Kent had to agree.

Sarah, Amanda's maid of honor, looked a bit overwhelmed, her wide brown eyes darting from one relative to another. Since the age of ten, their friendship had never wavered, despite their unique personalities, Amanda outgoing, Sarah reserved and shy. Amanda, appearing radiant and serene as if none of her earlier anxiety had existed, kept Sarah involved in the conversation so she wouldn't feel the sudden urge to bolt.

It was clear the family adored Tomás—the eldest son, the older brother, the famous uncle—and they were terribly proud of his world renown.

Beside Kent, Elise whispered, "They all speak English so well. Even Hana and Filip."

"They were taught from a young age," he said. "And Hana and Filip became fluent right alongside the rest. Tomás told me that for long stretches, even a whole week at a time, he and his siblings were allowed to speak only English in the house."

"I wish we were so diligent in the US." Elise sighed. "If we started children in first or second grade—third at the latest—we'd have a bilingual nation."

"But which language?" he countered. "Spanish? Chinese? And then there are all the different dialects of Chinese. The US is a melting pot, so how could we choose just one language?"

She laughed, low and warm. "So true. The parents would have to choose."

After a day together, she seemed to feel more at ease with him. They talked about his work, her students' antics, the sights they'd seen that day, and how the boys had loved it all.

"Next time we take the boys out," Kent said, "we'll have to visit Prague's Dancing House. It's a hotel—I think they'd love it."

Elise hesitated, pulling back slightly. "I thought you were leaving after the wedding."

He shook his head. "I have an open-ended ticket." At first he'd thought only about an extra day or two with the boys, but now Elise added inducement to stay longer. Maybe even through the honeymoon.

Tomás and Amanda would be gone for ten days, retreating to a large, beautifully appointed cottage in the Krkonoše Mountains just a couple of hours' drive from Prague. After the grueling concert schedule and wedding preparations, they deserved the time away, leaving Elise in charge of Marek and Luca.

She gave Kent a sweet smile, though it didn't quite reach her eyes. "The boys will love having you all to themselves."

They had to lean close to hear each other over the din. He wondered what her guarded look meant, but then she added, "Some alone time with you will be good for them."

He laughed—not as loudly as the others, but enough to draw a glance from Amanda. Entranced with Elise, he barely noticed. "But you'll be there. They're a lot to handle, and I'll need your guidance."

The boys had never been a problem when they were with him. Like any children, they could become irritable when overtired, but he knew the signs.

"Naturally," she said with a smile. "They're my charges until we all return home."

He couldn't stop his answering smile—or the strange flutter in his chest over the thought of the extra days spent in her company along with the boys.

ELISE LAY AWAKE IN BED, STARING AT THE DARKENED ceiling. She should have been thinking about the boys and how she would handle them during the wedding and reception tomorrow, especially with dignitaries, important guests, and extended family present.

Instead, she thought about Kent Woodward.

The day had been glorious. He was knowledgeable, warm, attentive to the boys, a wonderful conversationalist—and so handsome her heart had raced from morning until night. And he wanted her help with the boys during the honeymoon.

Which meant they would have what felt like unlimited time together.

Don't get attached.

That irritating voice in her head was insistent. She had no intention of attaching herself. That didn't mean she couldn't enjoy a bit of flirtation. But she wasn't foolish. They came from different worlds. He was a well-known architect. She was a retired schoolteacher. Once this trip ended and Cynthia resumed caring for the boys, Elise would never run in his circle again.

Besides, she didn't want anything permanent. After her disastrous first marriage, she couldn't go there again. Not after what Nick had done. And especially not after what she'd done. The memory pressed like a stone on her chest, making her gulp for air.

But Kent seemed genuine, kind, and attentive. That was the problem. She didn't deserve a man like him.

But something a little more casual?

A smile curved her lips in the dark.

Flirtation subtle enough the boys wouldn't notice? That might be very fun indeed.

THE WEDDING EXTRAVAGANZA SURROUNDED ELISE IN A glow of light and sound. Gold filigree shimmered from wall sconces, candlesticks, and ornate columns. Even the priest's robes glimmered with gilded thread. The wedding march thundered in the vaulted ceiling, reverberating through the stone walls, while stained glass windows poured colored prisms over the polished marble floor. The scent of beeswax candles and roses drifted through the ornate church, mingling with the faint sharpness of incense clinging to the air.

Amanda's handsome father escorted her down the carpeted aisle, her gown's train sweeping gracefully behind her. The pearls sewn into her dress shimmered like droplets of light, catching the glow from the candles.

Kent was resplendent in a black tuxedo that contrasted beautifully with his silver hair. Elise had never seen a more striking father of the bride. He smiled at her as he passed. Before the ceremony began, he'd seated her in the front row —ostensibly so she could watch over the boys once they handed off the rings.

Marek and Luca, who had proudly carried the rings, were already fidgeting. Normally, ring bearers took their seats in the congregation after passing over the rings, but Amanda had wanted the boys up by the altar to watch her come down the aisle. Tomás rested a steadying hand on each boy's shoulder as Kent walked with Amanda.

Elise thought she heard the faint catch of tears in Kent's voice as he gave his daughter to her groom, the love of her life. Then he took each boy's hand and led them down to the pew, stepping past Elise to sit on her other side, while the boys hugged close to the aisle. It was her job to take care of them, and she felt like an imposter sitting in the family row.

Amanda and Tomás faced each other at the altar—she radiant in white, he tall and striking in his gray tux. Sarah, the maid of honor, glowed in sapphire blue, a perfect complement. Petr, Tomás's brother, stood up as his best man.

In a low voice, she murmured to Kent, "She's even more beautiful than yesterday at the rehearsal." She didn't add how handsome he had looked with his daughter on his arm.

Kent nodded, his gaze shining, and said in hushed tones, "Her mother would have been so happy. I feel she's here with us now."

Elise's eyes misted. "I'm sure she is."

As the bride and groom gazed so fondly into each other's eyes, reciting their beautiful vows while their two adorable little boys perched in the pew beside Kent, unexpected tears blossomed in Elise's eyes.

Unbidden memories washed over her. It had been so long since she'd stood before an officiant. Like any young woman in her early twenties, she'd dreamed of a wedding like this—wearing a dress she'd chosen with care, her father giving her away, her mother in the front pew, dabbing at her eyes with a lace hanky.

But she'd had none of that. She and Nick had waited in a courthouse while a weary judge finished sentencing prisoners, then married them with a few austere words, his secretary serving as witness. No flowers, no music, no family. Just the smell of old paper and disinfectant wipes and the company of strangers. She should have known even then it would never last. Nick hadn't had it in him. And after she lost the baby, neither had she.

As if sensing her sudden distress, Kent discreetly slipped her a folded handkerchief. Elise patted under her eyes, careful not to smudge her makeup. She sniffed once, then willed the memories away. That had been thirty-five years ago. She refused to let the past ruin the day.

The ceremony stretched on—chants echoing, the priest's voice rising and falling like waves—while Elise kept the boys occupied so they didn't wriggle into distraction.

Finally, the bridal party began the joyful march down the aisle. Marek and Luca, forgetting all sense of protocol, bolted from their seats and rushed their parents before Elise could stop them. Tomás caught Marek's small hand with an indulgent grin, while Amanda—half laughing, half exasperated—took Luca's. Together, the family made their way out of the church amid phones raised high to capture the perfect couple with their perfect children.

Kent looked at Elise, his smile soft. "Don't worry. We couldn't have stopped them unless we threw ourselves across the aisle." It was nice that he made it their mistake, not just hers. His eyes lingered on her, concerned. "Are you okay now?"

She nodded, returning the hanky. "Thank you. I don't know what came over me." With a weak laugh, she added, "I always cry at weddings." In truth, she avoided weddings when she could.

As Kent folded the handkerchief away with quiet grace, Elise surprised herself by smiling—and even laughing. "And I didn't blow my nose in your handkerchief."

He chuckled. "That's what they're for."

She wrinkled her nose. "That's what tissues are for. And I forgot to bring any."

Kent offered a smile as he rose and offered his arm to escort her out.

Outside, bells pealed overhead, the late afternoon sun turning the church's stone facade a warm honey color. Tomás, Amanda, and the boys climbed into the waiting limousine for the reception. Elise longed to beg off, a dull headache pressing behind her eyes, her emotions still raw. But she had charge of the boys, and she knew they'd clamor for their parents' attention unless she corralled them.

When Kent helped her into one of the sleek cars lining the curb, she admitted softly—if only to herself—that she didn't want to go, but didn't want to be left behind either. It was, as her students used to say, pure FOMO. Fear of missing out.

And she didn't want to miss the possibility of a dance with Kent Woodward.

4

The crowded ballroom glowed with chandeliers, the air thick with the aromas of roasted beef, pork, and duck, garlicky goulash, and buttered rolls. Dishes were accompanied by both bread and potato dumplings, and it all started with a traditional wedding soup, a beef broth with liver dumplings that looked like small meatballs. The buffet groaned under platters of delicacies, the champagne flutes fizzed, and Amanda shone in her pearl-accented gown, her train pinned up by Sarah's careful touch.

The dinner had been devoured, the toasts made, and on the dance floor, the newlyweds swayed into their first dance. Tomás, elegant as ever, led Amanda with practiced ease, his hand firm at her back. The music of strings and piano curled around them—trust Tomás to hire a chamber music ensemble instead of a DJ—and they looked every inch the fairytale couple.

Kent's throat tightened. He hadn't expected to choke up, not after more than a decade of seeing Amanda and Tomás together, raising their children side by side. Yet something about this moment—his daughter radiant, her husband's strong arms around her—pierced him with beauty and a bittersweet pang, as if, having lost his wife, he was now somehow losing Amanda too.

Beside him, Elise plucked the handkerchief from his pocket and slipped it into his hand. Her gaze warmed him. "Just in case," she said.

She'd broken the spell, and he was grateful. He didn't want to sink into maudlin grief. Not today. Today was about what he'd gained, an admirable son-in-law, two grandsons who filled his heart, and all the family gathered close.

"You're right," he murmured with a smile. "I wouldn't want to burst into tears in the middle of the father-daughter dance."

"You'll be fine." She laughed softly and leaned over to kiss his cheek. There was nothing sexual in it, and yet he felt his skin heat with the sweetness of it.

Soon the signal came. Guests rose, applause swelled, and Kent left Elise with his grandsons while he stepped onto the floor, cutting in for his dance with Amanda. The parquet floor gleamed beneath their steps, and violins swelled as he took her into his arms.

"You're so beautiful," he whispered.

Amanda sighed, her smile tired but content. "Thank God it's all over. Now we get to enjoy ourselves."

"It was the most beautiful wedding I've ever seen."

With a mischievous smile, she tilted her head. "Even more beautiful than yours and Mom's?"

He chuckled. "I'll admit I had a bit of a hangover at mine. They just kept refilling my beer mug at the bachelor party."

Amanda rolled her eyes. "That's why I told Tomás not to have one. He just went out with his brother."

Kent thought of last night after they'd left the Novaks, with Amanda curled on the sofa where she and Sarah watched a sappy romance movie. He smiled. "I'm so happy for you, sweetheart."

Her expression trembled, sadness flickering in her eyes. "I wish Mom could've been here. We should've gotten married right away, even with the diagnosis."

"She might have managed, but the planning would've exhausted her."

"I know. I just... wish." Her sigh suddenly seemed close to tears.

He swallowed hard, grief pressing tight again. He wished too—wished with everything in him. To chase it away, he said lightly, "Your boys were adorable at the altar."

She brightened, her smile returning. "They were so good. Even when Elise let them run down the aisle after us—it was actually perfect. Everyone loved it."

"She didn't exactly *let* them. They were off like rockets before either of us could move."

Amanda laughed. "True. But it worked out."

When Filip cut in to dance with Amanda, and Tomás danced with his mother, Kent turned to Sarah and swept her into the steps. Soon the dance floor filled with family—children darting in between skirts and trouser legs, Marek and Luca squealing with their young cousins, the music spreading joy to every corner of the hall.

Across the room, Elise sat alone at their table, hands folded in her lap. He'd made sure to seat her at his table along with the boys, since Amanda had chosen not to have Marek and Luca at the head table. That would have spelled chaos.

Looking at Elise, Kent's chest tugged. Surrendering Sarah into Tomás's arms—because he definitely had to dance with his wife's maid of honor—Kent crossed the floor and held out his hand to Elise.

"I can't," she protested softly. "I'm not family."

"Don't make me dance with Tomás's father," he teased. "Come out there with me."

She relented, slipping her hand into his. The warmth of her touch sank deep, anchoring something he hadn't realized was drifting.

Then she was in his arms. And nothing had felt so right in a very long time.

Floating around the dance floor in Kent's arms felt glorious. The parquet gleamed under the chandeliers, and the subtle scent of the fragrant food mixed with perfume and champagne.

Elise couldn't remember the last time she'd danced like this—with a man who excited her the way Kent did. She felt beautiful. Cherished. Desired.

Around them, couples swirled in glittering gowns and tailored tuxedos, laughter and conversation lifting above the soft lilt of the chamber music. For Elise, the moment shimmered with unreality—like stepping into someone else's dream.

As Kent expertly twirled her around the room, one song blended into another and other couples shifted partners—everyone except her and Kent.

"You're a wonderful dancer," he murmured, his breath brushing her ear, sending tingles racing through her body.

Elise accepted the compliment. "Thank you. And you're amazing."

He rewarded her by holding her a little tighter.

God, what she wouldn't give for an entire night in his arms like this.

The music changed then, to a faster, more modern beat, and the younger guests rushed onto the dance floor, skirts swishing, shoes tapping. The boys naturally joined in, dancing with their cousins all in a group.

Kent pulled back, though his fingers stayed locked with hers. "I really don't think I can dance to this." With a smile, he tucked a strand of hair behind her ear in an intimate gesture. "I like it much better when I can hold you close."

Heat rushed to her cheeks, loving what he said, as he led her back to their table.

"Hana and Filip are certainly tearing it up out there," Elise said, pointing at the floor with a jut of her chin.

Hana's gown flowed like liquid silver, and Filip grinned as if the two had been born for this. Their steps had the easy rhythm of people who'd once jived to Elvis and Ann-Margret and never forgot how to let the music move their bones.

Soon the children joined them, hands linking, circling each other in laughter.

"They exhaust me," Kent groaned.

Elise laughed, the champagne bubbles tickling her tongue. "Oh, come on, you know you can do it."

He took her hand, squeezed her fingers, then lifted her knuckles to his lips, brushing a tender kiss there. Looking at her through his lashes, he murmured, "We both could." His smile widened, and he didn't let go of her hand. "But I'd rather stay here with you, when the music makes it seem as if we're alone."

Her heart melted. Oh, how she liked it too.

With a lazy smile that mesmerized her, he asked, "Tell me more about you. I know you're a schoolteacher. What grades did you teach?"

With the innocuous question, Kent kept them to safe surface conversation. "Elementary school. I taught the lower grades, one through three."

"No wonder you're so good with the boys." Admiration

filled his gaze. "But you retired to... travel?" His deep voice rose with the question.

"Yes." The single word wasn't the whole truth. She was just getting old. She'd tried her best on the computer, but her students, as young as they were, had long outpaced her. Kids were like sponges, soaking up knowledge on their devices at home, and they were teaching her. Instead, she told him about the traveling she'd done. "When I first retired, I couldn't resist a visit to the pyramids at Teotihuacan in Mexico. It's a fascinating place. I did a Caribbean cruise as well, to places like San Juan, Puerto Rico. And Aruba. But—" She shrugged.

"Cruising isn't your thing?"

"I think it's better done with someone else."

"You were alone?" He sounded almost shocked.

"Cynthia and I went together. But her knees were just so bad she couldn't really do much." She smiled fondly, since it wasn't Cynthia's fault. "I certainly couldn't have asked her to walk between the two forts in San Juan."

Finally, he asked the inevitable. "Never married?"

Her stomach sank, the same hollow weight it always carried when she thought about her marriage. About Nick. Something she tried not to do often. But she didn't want to lie to Kent.

"Yes. I was married. Once. A very long time ago. He was my college professor." God, how it hurt to admit that. But if she gave him a little, maybe he wouldn't ask for the whole sordid story. "He cheated on me. So my marriage didn't last very long."

She knew she was putting all the blame on Nick, but she couldn't tell Kent the whole truth. That Nick already had a wife. That their affair had broken up his marriage when Elise learned she was pregnant. That she'd been so young, so foolish, thinking love justified betrayal.

She said aloud, "I lost my baby the day I found him with another of his college students." Nick was nothing if not true to form.

The words made her sound as if she'd been the innocent party. And she let it stand, because she couldn't bear to see Kent's admiration turn to disgust—the same disgust she felt for herself. The disgust Nick's wife had heaped on her, and deservedly so.

Kent placed his hand over hers on the linen-draped table. "I'm so sorry."

She managed a wry smile. "Of course, I should have known it would happen. He was charming. His female students adored him." She sipped her champagne, the bubbles catching in her throat. "It was silly of me not to realize I wasn't the only one."

Kent soothed her, his thumb stroking the back of her hand. "That doesn't excuse him."

"No," she said softly. "It doesn't excuse me either. My parents couldn't handle what happened. They never talked to me again. Unfortunately, they passed before we could reconcile."

She could never tell him about the scandal. About why her parents disowned her. About how adamant she'd been that she was in love, that she and Nick were meant to be together. But she didn't need to tell Kent. This was temporary. When they returned to San Francisco, she'd never see him again. For now, she just wanted to enjoy this, to enjoy him.

Again, he said, "I'm so sorry. That must have been very hard."

She shrugged, though the weight pressed down on her. "They were older. Very traditional."

"But I'm sorry they weren't there for you when you needed them."

"I'm sorry too," she whispered.

She couldn't bear it if Kent treated her the same way, which he undoubtedly would if he knew everything. Some things just couldn't be forgiven.

"And you never remarried?"

Kent already knew the answer. Her painful experience had shaped her whole life, her view of love.

Sadness stirred within him. She had never known a lasting love.

When she said quietly, "No, I never did," he wanted to gather her close, hold her, comfort her.

Instead, he gave her a piece of himself.

"The end of something we cherish is always hard."

She seemed to understand what he meant. "But your loss was so much greater. And not through your own folly."

He didn't argue; there was a world of difference between divorce and death. "It was hard," he admitted. Such an understatement. First came the diagnosis. Then the hope the doctors could heal her. And finally, the death of that hope when he realized they couldn't.

This time, Elise laid her hand over his, offering quiet solace.

"I thought all I would feel was relief when she was finally out of pain," he said hoarsely. "But I was also very angry." Before he'd only told her about the shameful relief.

"Of course you were."

"But I had to get past that. For Amanda. I was so deep in my anger that I didn't realize how much she was struggling. She'd leaned so much on Gail, especially once she became a mother herself. She needed a mother's advice, her good sense, her love. I had to put aside my own feelings to help her."

"I'm sure you were the best father to her. And the best grandfather to the children."

He chuckled without mirth. "I suppose that's how I got through it. I couldn't afford to sink. Amanda and the boys needed me. Maybe, in a way, that saved me."

She said nothing, only squeezed his hand, as though she understood completely.

After a moment he added, "But after five years, I'm actually doing much better than Amanda is."

He stopped himself from saying more—from admitting he was ready to move on. That he was interested in Elise. More than interested. He didn't want to scare her off, not after what she'd just confessed.

When Amanda and Tomás were away on their honeymoon, there would be time enough to show Elise what he felt.

And oh, the things he wanted to show her.

Elise lay awake in her bed that night, unable to sleep. The dance music still played in her head, along with the remembered feel of Kent's arms around her. But what truly kept her awake were the ghosts of her past.

She hadn't told Kent the whole truth. Blaming the divorce on Nick, she'd kept all her terrible secrets to herself.

She'd had an affair with her married professor. She'd gotten pregnant. And when she told Nick about the baby, he'd been aghast, even accusing her of getting pregnant on purpose. But they were both at fault. She'd gone on the pill, but he'd begged her to let him feel her flesh around him, and she'd let him take her before the pills were completely effective. While she'd wanted to use a condom for safety, he said they'd be all right, that he'd pull out at the last moment. And she'd let him talk her into it, only one of her many bad decisions.

Nick had wanted her to have an abortion. She'd refused, telling him she wouldn't make any demands on him except to help support the baby. But in her heart, she'd wanted him to leave his wife, and she'd felt no guilt about that back then. Young, in love, and pregnant, she had unrealistic visions of a happy life with him.

But she'd definitely used her wiles on him. His wife was barren. His wife would never give him a child. Didn't he want a baby? Didn't he want to be a father?

Back then, she hadn't realized how persistent she'd been. Now, with the perspective of thirty-five years, she saw clearly how she'd pushed, how she'd manipulated his emotions, how she hadn't cared about his wife. She'd been relentless.

All she'd cared about was her baby. And her baby needed a father.

Yet another bad decision.

Maybe Nick had allowed the fantasy of being a father to overrule his objections, and in the end, he'd asked his wife for a divorce. And so, with Elise two months pregnant, rather than wait for the long process, Nick got a quickie divorce in Nevada. It had been the end of the term, and they'd moved to Las Vegas for the required six weeks. Then stayed the rest of the summer, because Nick had signed an affidavit with the divorce papers stating he would remain in the state. And they'd married. In the fall, however, he went back to teaching, leaving her alone, so it would look as if he was still fulfilling all the state requirements.

And there was another of her bad decisions.

Elise never knew how Nick's wife—his ex-wife—had found her. But when she opened the door without looking through the peephole, thinking it was Nick—only later realizing he never would have knocked—she instantly recognized his ex-wife on the doorstep.

With the blasting Las Vegas heat making her feel faint, their confrontation took place right there on the steps of that rented townhouse.

Elise had never used the woman's name, because that would have made the horror of what she'd done even worse. And she didn't use it then.

"What are you doing here?" she'd demanded.

The disheveled woman immediately attacked her with words. "You don't think you're his only whore, do you?"

Her words cut deep into Elise's fears. Nick had cheated with her—why wouldn't he cheat with someone else? Especially now that over five hundred miles separated them.

Slammed with all her doubts, Elise couldn't defend herself when the woman lashed out. "You're despicable. You took advantage of his addiction."

She asked in a squeaky voice, "What addiction?"

The woman laughed. Her hair hung stringy and limp against her scalp. Gray roots had grown out three inches. Angry crow's feet squinted at the corners of her eyes. Her mouth pinched like a witch's.

Again, Elise couldn't defend herself. True, Nick had approached her first, saying he couldn't get her out of his head, that she was so beautiful, so sweet, so desirable. But she'd wanted him. And she'd pushed him to divorce his wife.

The woman snarled like an animal. "There should be a prison sentence for scheming bitches like you."

Her words disjointed, Elise could only say, "I didn't... I'm not..."

All the while her mind screamed at her: *Don't say her name. Don't even think her name. Maybe then it won't be real.*

The woman went on as relentlessly as Elise herself had

once been with Nick. "Do you think you can hold him with that trick of getting pregnant? Do you think you're special to him? Do you think you can ever keep him?" Then she thrust her phone in Elise's face.

There was a picture of Nick sitting on the grass in the quad beneath a tree, an extraordinarily beautiful young woman beside him. He'd only been gone two weeks.

His ex-wife tightened all the screws in Elise's heart. "Where's your happy little marriage now?"

Elise found her voice. "It's not true. He's probably her tutor. It's just a business meeting between professor and student." That was what she'd so badly wanted to believe.

The woman laughed, the shrill sound piercing Elise's skull like an ice pick. "Why don't you check it out for yourself?"

Then Nick's ex-wife left, leaving behind the feckless young woman who had destroyed her marriage.

Elise hadn't been able to stop herself, and she'd driven back to Berkeley, gone to the apartment Nick had rented for the school year. He was supposed to visit her twice a month, but he hadn't come, claiming that the beginning of the term was too busy.

She found the door unlocked—like he had nothing to hide.

Except the sexy student from the picture on his ex-wife's phone riding Nick like he was a bucking bull. Wow. Fast worker. Much faster than Elise had been.

She hadn't confronted him. Hadn't asked him why, or when it started. It might even have begun before they left for Las Vegas, when she was pregnant and feeling sick and so unsexy. He'd shouted something as she ran, but she wasn't sure he even got out of bed to follow her. Leaving rubber on the road, she'd peeled out. She didn't even see the stop sign, her eyes too blurred with tears.

She never saw the car that broadsided her.

Now, all these years later, she didn't even remember the impact.

But when she woke up in the hospital, her baby was gone.

She'd told Kent she lost the baby after seeing Nick with another woman in their bed.

But she'd lost her baby not because of Nick's infidelity but through her own negligence. Because she'd wanted so badly to get away that she'd gotten behind the wheel when she was in no condition to drive.

Elise didn't feel her tears until they trickled down her temples onto the pillow. It was so long ago, but losing her child was still a wound that had never healed. The guilt, good Lord, all the guilt.

She didn't know how she'd survived it. Her parents had cut her off when they learned she was pregnant by her married professor, when they realized she was a homewrecker. And she'd been so drawn into Nick's web that she'd ignored and eventually lost all her friends. There'd been no one to turn to.

A year later, the university fired Nick for unbecoming conduct. That had been the only way they could end his tenure. Whether it was with that same student or another, she didn't know or care. She didn't know or care where he'd gone after that or what he was doing.

Eventually, she'd pulled her life back together, finished her education, became a teacher, built a new life. She loved teaching, loved the children, and she learned to enjoy life again.

And when her body felt about to burst with carnal needs, she'd satisfied them with casual liaisons. Yet she never allowed herself a long-term relationship. Never allowed herself to have a child.

That had been her punishment.

But now, for the first time in thirty-five years, she wanted a man for more than just a night or a week or a month.

It wasn't love. She hadn't fallen in love with him.

But being in his arms had given her a taste of what she'd missed all these years.

And that made Kent a very dangerous man.

5

Amanda's best friend Sarah had to get back to work, and the next morning she left for the airport even before the boys were out of bed to say goodbye. Elise didn't know how the woman had managed to get up so early after all the revelry of yesterday's wedding. She hoped Sarah had booked a lie-flat pod, where she could sleep all the way to San Francisco.

In her bedroom, Amanda was in a tizzy packing for the honeymoon. "There wasn't a moment to do it before," she complained to Elise. And Elise couldn't help but offer. "Would you like some help? You just throw everything on the bed, and I'll fold and put it all in the suitcase."

Amanda took Elise's face between her hands and kissed her forehead. "Bless you. Otherwise, Tomás will be screaming at me for not being ready to go."

Tomás would never scream at Amanda. Elise had never met a man more patient, except perhaps Kent. But she folded and laid everything in packing cubes to keep things organized, while Amanda ran around the room taking things out of drawers, putting them back, and appeared close to tearing her hair out.

Kent had looked into the bedroom one time, seen the chaos, and backed out, saying, "I'll leave you ladies to it. I'll just get the boys up and downstairs for breakfast." And he vamoosed.

"They love their děda," Amanda said, smiling as she came in from the bathroom with a loaded case of toiletries.

Elise had to add, "He's very good with them."

Amanda tried to shove the cosmetics bag into the case. "I'm surprised Dad decided to stay. I thought he was going home right after the wedding, like Sarah."

Elise couldn't be happier he was staying, but she didn't say that to Amanda. "I'm sure he wanted extra time with the boys while you're gone."

Amanda murmured an answer, concentrating on how much more she could fit in that bag. Elise pushed more clothing into another packing cube, squished it down, then zipped it. And then she dealt with the dresses Amanda wanted to take.

Elise didn't say anything. The ten-day honeymoon in the mountains without children was a retreat from the world. Perhaps they were planning to drive to a nearby town where she might wear those dresses. But did she need so many? It wasn't Elise's place to ask. She simply zipped the dresses into the garment bag.

Amanda plucked some sexy lingerie from her drawer and plopped it into another packing cube. Now *that* was what she needed on her honeymoon. As Amanda managed to zip the suitcase while Elise knelt on it, she said, "I'm worried about him. My dad."

Elise had no idea what to say. She didn't feel good about encouraging Amanda to talk about her father, not when Elise felt such an attraction to him.

But her silence didn't stop Amanda. "I think sometimes he's lonely. Unfortunately, he could fall prey to any scheming woman who comes along."

Though Amanda didn't look up, Elise wondered if this was a warning. She didn't want to contradict Amanda nor agree wholeheartedly, and hoped what she said was somewhere in the middle. "He appears to be a very intelligent man. I'm sure he'll spot a schemer fairly quickly."

"But men don't always think with their head." Amanda tapped her temple.

Elise pursed her lips to keep from asking which head Amanda thought he might be thinking with. It was an obvious joke, and the conversation was making her uncomfortable. What was she supposed to say? That he was a grown man who could take care of himself? Or asking what the harm was in having a little fun? But she said nothing.

Especially since she didn't want to betray her own interest in Amanda's father.

They'd shared so much last night—serious things like her marriage and his wife's death and his worries about Amanda.

But there had also been the dancing, his arms around her, his body flush against hers. She'd felt a stirring of desire, and she was almost positive he had too. And now, here was Amanda, warning her about scheming women.

Did Amanda think Elise was one? But if she did, why would she go off on her honeymoon and leave Kent and the scheming woman in charge of the boys?

No, Elise had to be imagining things. She said what an older woman, perhaps even a mother, might say. "You need to think about yourself now. And Tomás. And the wonderful honeymoon you have ahead of you."

Just then, as if he'd been waiting outside to hear his name, Tomás walked through the door. "Are you ready, sweetheart? I'd like to get on the road."

As if they hadn't been discussing her father, Amanda beamed at her husband. "I'm ready, darling."

Tomás hefted the suitcase off the bed, Elise followed with the hanging dress bag, and Amanda grabbed her purse.

The boys were already racing around the foyer, Kent watching them, a delighted smile on his face.

Marek and Luca cried out in unison, "Can we go? Can we go?"

Tomás answered tongue-in-cheek, "Little boys cannot go on Mama and Papa's honeymoon."

Like twins, even though they were two years apart, they put their hands together in prayer. "Please!"

Kent stepped forward then, putting one hand on each of the boys' heads. "Don't you want to stay with your děda? I've got so many fun things planned for us."

They immediately whirled to face him. "What?" Marek cried out. And Luca hopped on his toes, his hands still in prayer mode.

"It's all a surprise." Kent put his finger to his lips. "Which is why I can't tell you, because that would spoil the surprise, right?"

They dashed through the dining room, the living room, and back out to the foyer again, shrieking, "Surprise, surprise, surprise!"

They were adorable.

At last Elise said, "Why don't you kiss Mama and Papa goodbye, wave them off, and then you can start thinking about your surprises."

Even she didn't know what Kent had planned. Or maybe that was just a way to excite the boys and give them the impetus to let their parents go.

With the big car loaded, they all stood out front and waved as Tomás and Amanda drove away down the road.

When they turned the corner, Kent said, "Let's go finish your breakfast, boys."

His grandchildren rushed back inside the house, as if the food might be gone if they didn't get there fast enough.

Kent looked at Elise and smiled. Not an ordinary smile, but a sexy, mischievous, even wicked one that sent a thrill through her. He smiled as if he remembered dancing with her in his arms last night, as if he remembered how good she felt against him, as if he were thinking about how good he could make her feel.

The heat in his eyes said so much more than words ever could.

Alone at last, Kent thought. Of course, they weren't truly alone—there were the boys and Cook. While the boys ate their breakfast, Elise helped him pull together a picnic lunch to take with them. Cook had tried to do it for him, but he'd thanked her politely and said he had something special in mind that he wanted Elise's help with, though that was just an excuse to have Elise by his side.

So Cook busied herself cleaning up the morning's breakfast dishes while the boys chattered like magpies, never needing an answer. He and Elise sliced freshly baked bread, slathered it with butter, piled on meats and tomatoes and cucumbers, and placed waxed paper between each open-faced sandwich. With every touch—as they passed a knife, or a plate of sliced tomatoes—their fingers brushed. His temperature rose. His skin heated. And he heard every quickened breath she took.

He knew she felt the attraction too.

After last night, after everything they'd shared about

themselves, after all the dances where he'd held her in his arms, he could actually scent her desire. And his pheromones were an exact match for hers.

With the sandwiches packed, along with a few treats for the boys, they headed out, clambering into an Uber for the first leg of the morning's journey. Kent could have driven Tomas and Amanda's second car, but trying to find parking for every stop he had planned sounded nightmarish.

Elise sat in the back seat with the two boys, while Kent took the front and leaned back to look at them.

"Where are we going, Děda?" Marek demanded.

Kent caught Elise's eye and smiled. "It's a surprise. I can't tell you until you see it."

The Uber pulled up to the curb at their first stop, and they all climbed out, Kent slinging the insulated bag with their picnic over his shoulder. The boys' eyes went wide, and their mouths dropped open.

"What is it, Děda?" Luca had to know.

Kent let his smile grow as wide as the boys' eyes. "It's the Dancing House." He swept his hand in front of him, as if he were a host presenting to his latest guests. "Do you see how it looks like a woman dancing with a man?"

Then he glanced at Elise, remembered dancing with her last night. His heart seemed to turn over in his chest when she said, "It's like Fred Astaire and Ginger Rogers."

The boys just gave her a look that said *huh?*

Kent asked, "Haven't you heard of them?"

Both boys shook their heads slowly, once one way, once the other.

They stood across the street to get the full view of the building.

Kent said, "This used to be an apartment building that was bombed during the Second World War, and nothing was rebuilt here for a very long time. Fred Astaire and Ginger Rogers were very famous dancers back in that era. The Dancing House was nicknamed Ginger and Fred for a while." He looked at Elise. "I'm glad you know who they were."

She laughed, and he felt the sound deep inside, felt it filling him up. "I always used to watch the old movies on TV when I was a kid," she admitted. "I loved the musicals and watching Fred Astaire and Ginger Rogers dance."

Just he had loved dancing with her. Then he told the boys all about the building—who had designed it, the history, the controversy. "Some people hated it, while others loved it. The president at the time thought it was amazing. But other people thought it was too modern with all the old historic buildings in the city." He looked at the boys. "What do you think?"

Marek frowned. "It's weird."

Kent laughed as he planted a kiss on Marek's head. "It is weird. But it's also beautiful, don't you think?"

Luca stared at it thoughtfully. Finally, as if he were an ancient man who'd thought a long time, he said, "I like that it's different from everything else. Sometimes being different is okay."

Kent went down on his haunches and hugged the boy, because he knew Luca sometimes thought he was different. "I agree," he said with a smile. "Different is good."

Then he stood again and looked at Elise. "What do you think?"

She looked at him rather than the building and said softly, with what might have been a hint of seduction, "It makes me want to dance."

It was exactly what Kent wanted to hear.

After the Dancing House, they headed to Charles Bridge. The ancient stone structure crossed the Vltava River, connecting Prague's Old Town with the castle district of Malá Strana, also known as Lesser Town. At night, as he'd enjoyed every night since he'd arrived in Prague, the golden light of gas lamps illuminated the bridge, with Prague Castle perched majestically on the hill as its backdrop.

Now, it teemed with tourists taking pictures of the baroque statues lining the bridge, the fortified gate towers on either end, and the street performers captivating their onlookers.

"The bridge was built around the year 1400 under commission from King Charles IV," he told the boys.

"Is that why it's called Charles Bridge?" Luca asked. Marek was less patient with the history lesson, shifting foot to foot and gazing at the street performers.

"Yes." Kent ruffled Luca's hair. The bridge was a masterpiece of medieval Gothic engineering. Kent appreciated the massive sandstone blocks and the elegant arches. "There are sixteen arches supporting the structure and its 516-meter span." He leaned down to get both boys' attention. "As the only means of crossing the Vltava River until 1841, it was the most important connection in the city. This bridge has witnessed centuries of history, from royal coronation processions to daily commerce."

And now it played host to this endless parade of tourists and artists.

The boys ran ahead, joining the crowd around the street performers. Dressed in period costume from the Renaissance era, they sang songs and played old-fashioned instruments—the lute with its rounded body and intricate rosette, a cittern with its wire strings catching the sunlight, and a small drum that provided rhythm for their melodies. The sweet, plucked tones of the stringed instruments carried over the chatter of the crowd.

Elise drew close as they watched their little charges. "I love that you know something about everything."

He grinned. "You mean I'm a know-it-all?"

She bumped her hip against his, a thrill shooting through him at the familiar contact. "Absolutely not," she declared in a schoolteacher voice. "But you love architecture and history, and you love to share it with the boys."

With a chuckle, he jutted his chin at the two. "I think they're far more interested in the players than in my history lesson." But he didn't care. He'd keep on giving them little tidbits.

"You're instilling in them a love of learning."

She couldn't know how much her words meant to him.

The boys rushed back, begging for coins to throw into the performers' baskets.

Kent shared a smile with Elise at their enthusiasm. "I don't think they care what's being played," she said. "They just love the costumes and the excitement."

He agreed. The back of his hand brushed hers as they walked, and he felt a whole different excitement, one that thrummed in his blood and turned his skin hot and his body hard. Thankfully, his jacket covered the effect her touch—such a simple touch—had on him.

He couldn't remember when he'd last felt this enticed, this lusty. Elise made him feel young again. He wanted to stop right there in the middle of the bridge, put his hands on her shoulders and turn her to him so he could see the effect *his* touch had on *her*. But he followed the boys, hiding his feelings for now.

Later, he told himself. Later, he'd show her exactly what was happening inside him.

Stopping at a cart, Kent bought a spiral of *trdelník*—the sweet chimney cake vendors sold from carts throughout the city—and broke off pieces for the boys, watching them delight in the cinnamon-sugar pastry, crispy on the outside and soft on the inside.

They moved on to more street performers—two children dancing to Michael Jackson's "Thriller," emulating his moves with surprising precision. And the boys cried for more coins.

Their exuberance was infectious. The day excited him too. Being with Elise thrilled him, and his grandsons' antics filled him with joy.

A tour boat passed under the bridge—the Vltava was deep enough for river traffic—and the boys raced from one side to the other, watching it emerge. Marek hoisted himself up, leaning over the stone balustrade to see the boat better. And Luca tried to do the same.

Both Elise and Kent rushed to grab the boys before disaster occurred. Their hands brushed and their forearms slid together as they each pulled a child down to safety.

Electricity shot through Kent, and it wasn't just the momentary fear as he saw his grandsons in peril. It was her.

When their eyes met over the boys' heads, her pupils were wide, her nostrils flared, her breathing quickened. It could have been due to the close call. But the flush on her cheeks told him it was more—it was the same thing he felt.

She scolded gently, "Luca, Marek—" Her voice held a harsh edge. "—you both know better than to climb up on a bridge like that. You could have fallen. You worried your grandfather acting like that." She looked at him.

He saw so many other words in her eyes, things she wanted to say just to him.

Without even being asked, his grandsons turned to him. "We're sorry, Děda," Luca said in his sweet, childish voice.

And Marek, the older one who should have known better, added, "We're really sorry."

Kent bent to hug them both close to his chest. "You almost gave me a heart attack."

They had, for just a moment, but now his heart was beating hard for Elise, as he looked at her over his grandsons' heads.

His daughter and her husband were gone. The boys would go to bed by eight.

And the rest of the evening was his to share with Elise.

6

They stopped for macarons, hot chocolate, and coffee on the opposite side of Charles Bridge in Malá Strana. The cobblestone streets and red-tiled roofs of Lesser Town seemed to come right out of a medieval painting, as did the storefronts, even with their electric signs.

Elise still felt that jolt of excitement through her body. It wasn't just the heart stopping moment with the boys. Kent's touch out there on the bridge had seared her like lightning. And when she'd met his gaze, she knew he'd felt it too.

He was still feeling it. She recognized that in the looks he gave her, his blue eyes turning as hot as the center of a flame.

She was playing with fire. This was her employer's father. Their attraction could turn disastrous. Except that her employment would end in just a few short weeks. Cynthia was almost fully recovered, and when they all returned to San Francisco, it wouldn't be long before she took over as the boys' nanny again.

Did a little flirtation now really matter?

If Elise wanted another nannying job, however, Amanda could refuse to give her a reference if she thought there'd been hanky-panky. Especially if she thought Elise was a "scheming woman."

Seated outside the café, with noisy tourists ambling by, she looked at Kent once more as he regaled the boys with tales of his travels to faraway places where he'd worked. They listened with rapt attention.

"Istanbul is a beautiful city right on the Bosphorus Strait, where it meets the Sea of Marmara. You see those beautiful Turkish tiles everywhere." He leaned close to the boys. "Even my hotel bathroom was tiled in fantastic colors."

Both boys looked at him wide-eyed. Marek said, "We didn't go to Istanbul on this trip with Mama and Papa."

Kent ruffled the boy's hair. "Maybe next time. When you're at my house again, I'll point out the tiles on the patio that I bought at a Turkish bazaar."

Luca, with his hands stuffed under his bottom, bounced on his chair. "Tell us about the blue city, Děda!"

Obviously, the boys had heard these tales before, but neither of them seemed to care. Kent, with an adorable sparkle in his eyes, said, "It's called Chefchaouen, the blue city in Morocco. All the buildings are painted blue." He leaned close, lowering his voice as if he were revealing a great secret. "And there are cats everywhere." Then he settled back in his chair again. "Your grandmother Gail wanted to feed them all. But our guide told her it was a bad idea—we would soon have had a parade of cats following us."

Elise couldn't help the smile that welled up from deep within her. "Isn't it a herd of cats? Or a flock? Or a band? What do you call a group of cats?"

Kent crossed his arms over his chest and chuckled, his gaze roaming over her face as if he needed to memorize her. "It's a clowder of cats. Like it's a murder of crows."

She returned that infectious grin. "A clowder! How on earth did you know that?"

"Because I'm a know-it-all," he told her with a wicked grin.

After their macaron break, they strolled through the shops, buying small bags of candy the boys picked out from enormous barrels. A shop full of stuffed animals caught Luca's eye, and inside they found everything from bears and dogs and cats to frogs and alligators and turtles. And even T-Rexes.

Marek pretended he was too old to want a stuffed animal, but he eyed the pterodactyl swinging from the ceiling. While Luca cuddled the abominable snowman called Bumble from *Rudolph the Red-Nosed Reindeer*, Marek circled beneath the pterodactyl.

Kent bent down to Marek as the boy stared up at the stuffed animal. "I can see that hanging in your bedroom back home, can't you?"

Marek tried to appear nonchalant, which for a little boy meant shuffling his feet and shrugging his shoulders. Then finally he murmured, "There's going to be a field trip to see dinosaur skeletons at the museum this fall."

While Elise had homeschooled the boys during their European tour, back home they would return to their private school.

Kent rubbed the boy's shoulder. "Then you'll need to study up on pterodactyls. And what better way to start than having one flying in your room?"

"Yes, Děda, I think you're right," Marek said in what he probably hoped was a very mature voice.

In a small voice, Luca asked, "May I have Bumble?"

The look Kent gave his grandson was lit like a sunbeam shooting down from the skylight, enveloping the boy in light and warmth. "Of course."

Kent had a clerk retrieve a long pole to bring down the pterodactyl. The boys held their toys to their chests as Kent paid. They thanked him without being prompted and left the shop, walking with him between them, holding his hands while they clutched their prizes in the other.

It was so... Elise didn't have words for it. He adored these boys and never talked down to them. He lavished them with stories and listened with genuine affection to their childish chatter. This was no act—he loved them with every cell of his being.

She couldn't help the warmth that spread through her chest at the sight of this beautiful man and his grandsons.

They wandered through the town until the boys, despite their hot chocolate and macarons, announced they were hungry again. They stopped for a late lunch in a nearby park, feasting on the open-faced sandwiches they'd prepared. Afterward, the boys begged to play hide-and-seek with their děda.

Elise stayed seated on the grass to watch over their things, her eyes following the giddy boys as they tried to catch their grandfather. Kent didn't make it easy for them, ducking behind trees and benches, sometimes crouching low with a mischievous grin. The boys didn't want an easy win anyway, and their shrieks of triumph when they finally spotted him made Elise's heart squeeze. Watching him like this—so patient, so playful—charmed her even more.

Later, they strolled along the river path, the boys rushing back every few minutes to relay discoveries. A flock of swans swayed on the current, white feathers glowing against the late afternoon light. One swan nested on a mound of reeds, clearly guarding her eggs. The boys beamed with pride when they reported they'd only watched from a distance and left her otherwise undisturbed.

By the time they took an Uber back home, signs of fatigue were written all over the boys—grumpy smiles, pouty lips.

Cook had prepared a delicious dinner of goulash and dumplings, gravy thick and rich with paprika and onions clinging to the tender meat. Elise smiled; everyone talked about Hungarian goulash, but to her, that version was more soup than stew. This goulash was hearty and full-bodied, made even better by the fluffy white potato dumplings that soaked up the sauce like sponges. This was true Czech comfort food.

After dinner, they spent two happy hours building LEGO castles and playing *Člověče, nezlob se!*, a Czech board game similar to the English game Sorry!. Cook popped in to see if there was anything else they needed, then left for the night. Finally, the boys, earlier than usual after the day's activities, yawned, their eyelids heavy.

Kent murmured, "It's been a long, exciting day. Shall we put them to bed?"

Together, they helped the boys into their pajamas and stood watch while they brushed their teeth. Luca still needed a stool, but Marek was tall enough now to reach the sink on his own. Once tucked into their twin beds, they rallied one last time, crying out in unison, "Story, story!"

Elise laughed and backed toward the door. "I think they want Děda to read to them."

Kent's eyes twinkled knowingly, as though he saw through her attempt to slip away, but he obliged, picking up a book. Elise lingered just outside the room, leaning against the wall.

His voice carried, warm and full of animation. He quacked like a duck, meowed like a cat, and barked roughly as a watchdog, drawing giggles and questions from the boys—stall tactics to keep sleep at bay. But eventually, their chatter faded until only his voice remained.

He was so good with them, such a wonderful grandfather. Such an amazing man.

Then came the soft slap of the book closing, a rustle as he rose to kiss the boys one last time, then the gentle pad of his footsteps across the floor.

Elise didn't retreat. She was there when he stepped into the hall and closed the door quietly.

"You're so good with them," she said softly.

"It's love," he answered, eyes twinkling again. He brushed her elbow, guiding her down the stairs. "Would you like to enjoy the night air outside and have a drink?"

It had been a gloriously warm day, and the September night felt unseasonably mild. Still, Elise tugged on a sweater and grabbed the baby monitor before joining him.

By the time she stepped outside, Kent had wheeled a small drinks trolley onto the veranda. From their high vantage point, the castle gleamed on the hilltop, golden against the indigo sky, while Charles Bridge arched over the silver ribbon of river, its gas lamps glittering like a string of fairy lights.

"What can I pour you?" Kent asked.

"White wine, thank you." She accepted the glass, recalling how often Tomás and Amanda had shared an evening drink with her after the boys were in bed. She doubted they would mind if she indulged now.

Kent sat on the chair beside her. "I'd say that was a successful day with the boys."

She laughed. "They were very well behaved. Most of the time." She winked.

His smile deepened, eyes crinkling with warmth. "I've seen those other times too." He tapped his glass lightly against hers. "But you're extremely patient with them."

She inclined her head in acknowledgment. "Thank you. I love those little boys."

They chatted idly, but Elise wasn't truly listening. Her mind replayed the sound of his voice as he'd read to Marek and Luca, the playful way he'd slipped into character, the boys' laughter filling the room. Her heart melted all over again, and part of her longed to melt into him.

She didn't realize when their conversation trailed into silence, only that she suddenly felt Kent's gaze on her. His eyes traveled over her face, lingering on the curve of her lips.

A quiet, scintillating energy hummed in the air, an unspoken invitation that curled deep inside her. If he asked, she might take his hand and follow him.

But that temptation was far more than mere flirtation. It was dangerous, and too complicated for her work, for her life.

Pulling her sweater tighter, she rose. "It's getting chilly. Thank you for a lovely day and a lovely evening." She was grateful when he stayed seated. "I'll see you in the morning, and we'll plan tomorrow's activities." Then, already turning, she added, "Good night."

"Sleep well, Elise." His words floated after her in the quiet night.

Something in the way he spoke her name sent a quiver down her spine. And as she walked away, she admitted to herself that she was in danger of wanting far more than flirtation.

KENT HAD WANTED TO BEG ELISE TO STAY LONGER WITH him on the veranda last night. But he knew that if she had, he wouldn't have been able to stop himself from touching her. Even kissing her. Yet he'd sensed her hesitancy. He was family. She was an employee. Not that it mattered to him—but he had to respect her apprehension, even as he thought he saw regret in her gaze too.

Back in his room, he'd taken a cold shower, but his sleep had been restless with dreams of her. He'd found release in his morning shower, making him feel like a lusty, hormone-laden teenager. He hadn't felt the need to touch himself like that in years. His libido had been strong as a young man, and now, at sixty-five, he felt it all returning for Elise. But with her, he didn't crave just release. He craved *her*.

Maybe that was what she'd seen in his eyes last night. Maybe that was why she'd left.

At eight o'clock, Tomás's mother Hana called. Kent felt like he'd been awake for hours.

In her pleasantly accented voice, she said, "Filip and I wondered if we might have the boys visit us today. With all the wedding preparations, we've had so little chance to see them."

He'd already planned the day's activities. But since he lived near the boys in California, and Hana and Filip saw them only once a year, he tossed aside his plans. "Of course. They'd love to spend time with you, Hana. Give us an hour to get them dressed and fed, and we'll bring them over."

She sighed, warm and grateful. "Thank you, Kent. That would be nice."

When he hung up, he realized this change was self-serving—it gave him a whole day with Elise. A day to show her Prague, and perhaps ease some of the hesitancy she'd shown last night.

Then he remembered to call Cook and tell her they wouldn't need her today, though of course he would pay her. They argued good-naturedly, she saying it wasn't necessary, he insisting. In the end, he won.

An hour later, they ushered the boys into Hana and Filip's elegant home. Marek and Luca rushed into their grandparents' arms, and the two showered them with kisses. Kent was glad he hadn't been greedy with their time.

"We have so many fun activities planned," Hana said, her voice sweet as the boys hugged her legs. She glanced at Kent and mouthed, *thank you*.

Elise offered politely, "I can stay for the day, if you'd like me to help."

Kent nearly said no, but Filip beat him to it with a gentle, "We can manage them. But thank you."

Was that a sigh of relief he heard from Elise? He hoped so.

In the car, after arranging to pick the boys up after dinner, Kent said, "Since you have the day free, why don't we do the things I'd planned with them?"

She hesitated, her luxurious hair blowing in the slight breeze. "I should probably prepare some lesson plans."

It sounded like an excuse, and he was having none of it. **"You're not going to make me go sightseeing on my own, are you?"** He wanted to take her hand, kiss her knuckles, her fingertips—but he restrained himself.

Finally, with a small smile, she said, "All right. That would be wonderful."

His heart leapt like a Lipizzaner stallion in mid-air.

The day was warm, and she wore a pretty sundress that bared her arms. He wanted to touch, to stroke, even to kiss her smooth skin. What would she say if she knew all his thoughts?

Kent found parking a couple of blocks from Prague Castle, where they joined the throng of tourists. Elise stopped to photograph the soaring spires of St. Vitus Cathedral rising above the walls. Guards in blue uniforms flanked the gates, ramrod straight, their sternness reminding Kent of Buckingham Palace.

They walked through the courtyards, past pale Renaissance facades, then into Vladislav Hall, its ribbed vaulting soaring like stone wings. He craned his neck. "The ceiling—it's extraordinary, isn't it? Built in the fifteenth century."

Outside again and crossing the courtyard, they paused as a sleek black car bearing a diplomat's flag glided past, a reminder that the castle was also the seat of government.

But it was the cathedral that took his breath away. Its

Gothic towers rose like spears into the sky, its bronze doors framed with gilded reliefs. Inside, light spilled through the jewel-toned stained glass, dappling the stone walls in pools of color.

Elise tipped her head back, eyes closed, and a shaft of sunlight fell across her face.

As she slipped her hand into his, he thought she was as beautiful as the cathedral itself.

ELISE FOUND IT HARD TO BREATHE. PART OF IT WAS THE beauty of the place, but it was also the warmth of Kent's hand, the memory of that almost-kiss she'd seen in his eyes last night.

She shouldn't want more. But she did.

It could be casual, she told herself. Just until Amanda and Tomás returned. She'd done casual before. But Kent Woodward made her long for more.

Not that she deserved *more*. Not after her devastating marriage.

She slipped her hand from his, and they continued through the castle complex. Kent eagerly pointed things out. "See that Romanesque rotunda? And there—Baroque, far more ornate. St. Vitus itself is High Gothic, of course." He named others, including the Basilica of St. George, Romanesque and severe, and the Loreto, with its baroque exuberance.

The architecture intrigued him, and she loved the mellow tones of his voice more than the words themselves.

By the time they finished, it was lunchtime. They found a café tucked away on a side street, near St. Nicholas Church—which was not the same as St. Nicholas Cathedral in Old Town—and shared a variety of *chlebíčky*, open-faced sandwiches with a spread of potato salad or garlic cheese and topped with ham or smoked salmon or egg slices. Instead of sitting across from her, Kent slid into the corner seat beside her. His thigh brushed hers, his hand grazing her ear as he tucked a loose strand of hair away.

The only way she could stop herself from trembling at his closeness was to talk. "Did you research Prague Castle and the other sites beforehand?"

He grinned boyishly. "I like to know what I'm looking at."

She laughed softly. "Nothing wrong with that. I did a little research before taking the boys to different sites while we were on tour. We managed the Vatican, the Louvre, and Gaudí's Sagrada Família in Barcelona."

His eyes lit. "Tell me what you thought of Gaudí's masterpiece."

She smiled. "Is this a trick question?"

"No trick."

She remembered the cathedral with its forest-like columns inside and its exterior statues that seemed to be melting. "It felt whimsical. Almost surreal. The columns were like trees. It was almost like walking through someone's dream."

"That was his design," Kent said. "He wanted it to feel like a forest. He died before it was finished, of course, but they're completing it in his style."

"I'm so glad they're going to finish it."

Her answer seemed to please him deeply. He reached for her hand again, squeezing. "So—you loved it?"

"I did," she whispered. It felt like a confession.

After lunch, he suggested, "How about a stroll through the park?"

"I'd love that."

They returned to the car and drove to Letná Park. Though the park wasn't far from St. Nicholas Church, they would have needed to walk back to the castle again for the car. The scenery was worth it. Chestnut and maple trees blazed with autumn color. They sat on a bench overlooking the Vltava, watching ducks paddle in a pond below, Prague's red roofs and bridges spread out in the hazy light as time slipped past.

She couldn't remember their words—only his laughter, the way he leaned close to point something out, the soft peck of his kiss on her cheek.

For dinner, they chose street food from a stand, *klobása*—a slightly spicy sausage, smoky and dripping with juice. Grease ran down her chin, and she laughed, handing the rest to him. "We can't let it go to waste."

"Guess I'll need extra treadmill time," he joked.

"You're perfect the way you are," she said before she could stop herself.

His gaze flared with heat. "Funny. I was just thinking the same about you."

She flushed, heart racing. If not for the sausage in his hand, she thought he might have kissed her right there.

But a flock of schoolgirls swirled past like noisy sparrows, and the moment dissolved.

Elise glanced at her watch. "We should get the boys. After a day like this, they won't want to go to bed."

"They'll be exhausted," Kent said with a glint in his eye. "Want to bet on it?"

A laugh bubbled out of her. "It's a bet. What do I get when I win?"

His gaze burned hotter. "How about I tell you what I want after *I* win?"

With that look, she absolutely hoped he'd win.

7

Kent won the bet when the boys fell fast asleep not long after they'd arrived home. As they tiptoed from the room, Kent murmured to Elise, "A glass of wine on the veranda again?"

The day they'd spent together exhilarated him, a faint thrill still rushing through his veins. And guilt? Over what Amanda would think? He refused to let those thoughts into his brain. But he noticed Elise's hesitation in the way her eyes dropped and her gaze lingered on the tile floor.

He couldn't lose her. Not now. "That's my prize for winning the bet—a relaxing glass of wine with you and some delightful conversation."

Finally, she looked at him. "All right." She swallowed as if still unsure, but then she added, "That would be lovely."

Relief washed through his body, leaving his knees weak. He hadn't realized until this moment how badly he'd wanted her to say yes. He'd anticipated it all day long.

"Just let me get the boys' monitor."

"I'll raid the wine fridge," he told her when she returned

to the hallway with the compact device. "Will you put together some cheese and crackers for us?"

She preceded him down the stairs, the sway of her hips making it hard to think of anything else. On the bottom step, she turned slightly, looking up at him. "There's some brie. Do you want me to heat it up?"

"That sounds delicious," he said, though what he really wanted to say was that *she* was delicious. "Any preference on wine?"

She shrugged a shoulder, continuing toward the kitchen. "Something sweet to complement the brie."

Nothing could be sweeter than she was. "I saw the perfect bottle."

While she puttered at the counter, softening the brie in the microwave, he rummaged through the wine fridge until he found the right one. "I'm sure Tomás won't mind us drinking this," he said, holding up the bottle, though she was too far away to read the label.

Sliding the brie onto a plate, Elise added crackers, then pulled out two stemless glasses. She carried the tray to the veranda, and after he turned off the kitchen lights, he followed with the wine and the corkscrew.

The way he felt right now, he'd follow her anywhere. Especially if she led him up to her room.

Kent pulled a small table in front of the two chairs near the balustrade and set the bottle on it. Elise laid the tray beside it, the baby monitor sitting next to the plate of brie. There wasn't a sound from the boys' room.

Without turning on the veranda's bistro lights—better to see the radiance of ancient Prague before them—they settled into the chairs with a view of Charles Bridge, Castle Hill, and the glowing spires of St. Vitus Cathedral they'd visited today. The lights of the bridge glittered in the water while Castle Hill sparkled against the night. Voices drifted up from the street below, and accordion music wafted over from a nearby tourist boat on a dinner cruise.

"What wine did you choose?" she asked.

"A German Gewürztraminer." He poured. "It's a sweet wine. I think you'll enjoy it."

He handed her a glass. She sipped, then smiled. "Oh, that is delicious."

Spreading softened brie on a cracker, he offered it up. "Eat this, then follow it with a sip."

Without giving her the chance to take it, he held the cracker to her lips. Instead of biting, she took the whole thing, her mouth brushing his fingertips. Heat flashed through him.

Then she sipped the wine and moaned softly, her eyes closing. The sound shot straight into his body. He couldn't help imagining what she'd sound like with him buried deep inside her.

But it was just a drink. Not a seduction.

Or maybe it was.

They talked—about her teaching years, her favorite students, her most troublesome ones. She asked about the buildings he was most proud of. Their conversation flowed as easily as the wine. Then he ventured, "Now that you've done some nannying abroad, would you like to do more?"

She sipped thoughtfully, gazing at the shimmering lights of nighttime Prague. "Only if I could do it like this—three or four months abroad, then home to my life. I don't want to be a full-time nanny like my friend Cynthia."

He nodded. Cynthia was wonderful with the boys and loved the job, claiming she was building a nest egg. He wondered if Elise had already built hers. Teachers were notoriously underpaid, but she'd told him she'd worked at an elite private school. Her salary must have been better.

Finally, he asked the question that had been burning

inside him. "I can't figure out how a woman as beautiful as you could remain unattached all these years after your divorce. Men must have been hitting on you left and right."

ELISE'S BREATH CAUGHT. FOR A MOMENT, SHE THOUGHT SHE might choke on the sip of wine she'd just taken. Beautiful? Men hitting on her?

The flattery, the intimacy of the night, the stars overhead, Prague's golden glow, the sweet wine on her tongue, and Kent's warmth beside her—it all pressed against her.

She took another sip to fortify herself before saying, "One marriage was enough."

It hadn't been only Nick's cheating. No, her guilt had roots deeper than that—her choices, her mistakes, her young infatuation with a married professor. That was the part she could never confess to Kent—that she'd broken up Nick's marriage. She was a horrible woman, a home-wrecker. And if he knew how she'd lost her baby? He'd never respect her again.

"So you never found anyone with whom you'd want to try?" he asked softly.

She shrugged, trying to shake free of the memories. He'd asked if she'd ever remarried, and she'd said no. But this was slightly different. "I've just always felt it's better to keep relationships casual. I've never dated the same man for very long." She hesitated—should she, shouldn't she?—then she just said it. Because of the dark. The intimacy of the night. Just because... "It's... well, like a man, a woman has needs."

Would he let that slide? Or comment on it?

"I respect a woman who admits that." He sighed and looked into his half-empty glass. "When my wife hit menopause, sex no longer interested her. I thought most women were like that."

Elise laughed lightly, brushing aside any awkwardness over the topic. "That's definitely not true for all women. Even after menopause." She met his gaze steadily. What consequences could the truth have other than embarrassment? "I still love sex. In fact, I like it more than I ever did."

Instead of shock, she saw only interest spark in his eyes.

He feigned mock horror. "But how can that be if you don't trust men and relationships?"

She couldn't believe she was having this conversation, yet with him it felt natural. Maybe it was his ease, or maybe her attraction had melted her walls. Or maybe she just felt free with him. And she laughed softly. "I was born at the very end of the sixties, the era of free love. I'm absolutely fine with casual sex."

KENT HAD TO SET DOWN HIS GLASS BEFORE THE WINE bubbled right back up.

He'd never met a woman who could say such things so casually. He'd had a few flings before his marriage, and a few after he lost Gail—because a man had needs too. But no woman had ever captivated him like this. He wanted to touch her, kiss her, take her up to his room and make her feel anything but casual.

But he said, hopefully without too much strain in his voice, "Well, if you're interested in casual sex, I'm totally up for that."

Her answering smile was so damn seductive. "In more ways than one?"

Oh yes, he was up. Hard and heavy. Maybe she could even scent the pheromones he was certain were rolling off him.

Elise had hinted—somewhat blatantly—and Kent had taken her up on the invitation.

But could she?

If it had been the beginning of the concert tour, with Kent spending the entire three months with them, the danger would have been far worse. But Amanda and Tomás were away on their honeymoon. Only a couple of weeks remained before they all returned home. Would Amanda even figure it out?

Elise didn't allow herself to think for another moment. Their chairs were so close that all she had to do was lean over. He'd already turned toward her, as if waiting for an answer.

Her lips on his were answer enough.

He tasted so good, like sweet wine and warm, sexy male. Cupping the back of her head, he held her there as he opened his mouth and deepened the kiss.

A fleeting thought almost destroyed the moment, that kissing this man was better than any kiss she'd ever shared with Nick. Even that very first one, which had been little more than a quick grope in his office—cut short when a student knocked on the door.

She banished Nick from her mind. Kent's tongue felt delicious against hers, his hand warm on her head, fingers tangling in her hair, a deep groan welling up from inside him.

Then, almost without pulling away, he whispered against her lips. "Come here."

She was already moving, sliding onto his lap, looping her arms around his neck.

He was hard beneath her bottom, and she felt decadent and utterly desired. Gripping her backside, he pulled her closer against his chest, against the rigid length beneath her.

She wanted to straddle him, to feel him pressed against her core through the thin cotton of her panties.

The night air was cool against her overheated skin, carrying the faint fragrance of linden trees and the rich aroma of coffee drifting from a nearby café. In the square, the bells of the astronomical clock marked the hour, the notes weaving through their kiss.

His hand roamed her side, sliding up until he cupped her breast. As he flicked her nipple, the bead tightened, begging for more, and she moaned into his mouth. He shifted under her, as if he wanted her to feel exactly what she was doing to him.

She was suddenly so hot—not a hot flash, but purely, sexually hot. Her imagination ran wild, with her hitching up her dress, pushing her panties aside, and taking him inside her. Even here on the veranda, where anyone on a boat passing by might see them if they glanced across the water. Or would they be invisible without the veranda's bistro lights on?

Kent was already tugging at the hem of her dress as if he had the same thought, the same desperate need. And his kiss consumed her.

It took her a few moments to recognize the sounds cutting through her haze.

The baby monitor.

Luca.

He cried out in a nightmare. Her mind screamed the terrible thought: *not now, please!*

But no one heard her plea. Especially not Luca, who cried out, even more stridently.

She was breathing hard. So was Kent.

Her words came out in a gasp. "It's Luca."

Kent's eyes were dark, almost black with desire. Or maybe that was just a trick of a streetlight from below.

She scrambled off his lap, because if she didn't, she might stay there despite Luca's terrified cries.

"It's another nightmare," she said in the same breathless voice.

As if he felt nothing about their aborted interlude, he asked, "Does he have them often?"

"Once or twice a week. Especially if he's had too much sugar—which he probably did today over at Hana and Filip's house."

Luca's next cry galvanized her, and she crossed the veranda, flipping on a kitchen light so she didn't bang into anything, and made her way upstairs to the boys' room.

True to form, Marek had slept through it all. She sat on the edge of Luca's bed, stroking his hair as he tossed and turned. Shaking him awake would only shoot terror through him—he needed a gentler touch.

"Wake up, sweetheart. You're having a bad dream."

And the dream of Kent that had entranced her only minutes before faded away.

Maybe that was a good thing. Kent Woodward could prove to be a terrible distraction.

But an oh-so-delicious distraction as well.

KENT STAYED DOWN ON THE VERANDA, AND NOW HE HEARD her sweet voice through the baby monitor: "Wake up, sweetheart. You're having a bad dream."

He would have rushed upstairs with her, but his entire body still throbbed. He wanted her so badly he almost couldn't breathe. If she'd let him, he would have taken her right there on the veranda, not caring one whit about being seen.

He hadn't left any lights on down here, and they would

have been nothing more than shadows. But still, they might have been seen.

And he wouldn't have cared.

His gut knotted with desire. And yet her soothing voice over the monitor calmed him.

"Do you want to tell me about it, sweetheart?"

Luca's words were nothing more than a mumble.

But Elise answered, "That sounds terrible. But now you're awake, and you know it wasn't real."

Another mumble, then her voice again: "I know, I know. But see how the dream is already fading?" She never called it a nightmare. Just a dream. A *bad* dream. "There, there," she murmured. "I'll stay and stroke your hair until you fall asleep."

She was so good with the boys. It amazed him that she'd never had children of her own. Her husband's actions must have been truly terrible, perhaps far worse than she'd said, leaving her unwilling to try again. He desperately wanted to know her entire history, but unless she offered more, he wouldn't ask.

He listened to her crooning to his grandson, soft, sweet sounds that soothed both boy and man. Downing the last of his wine, he gathered the baby monitor and the bottle, set the glasses on the tray, and carried it back to the kitchen. He washed everything and put it away, all the while listening to her voice.

It quieted even the savage ache of desire inside him.

Baby monitor in hand, he climbed the stairs again.

He stood in the bedroom doorway, with the hall light behind him. She looked over her shoulder and whispered, "I need to stay until he falls asleep again."

"Of course," he said. "I'll put the monitor in your room."

She fluttered her fingers in silent thanks.

In her bedroom, after setting the monitor on the bedside

table, he thought about stretching out on her bed to wait for her. But the night's interlude felt over.

There was always tomorrow.

He wondered what he'd do if he fell for her completely... and she wanted nothing more than casual.

8

They were enjoying another delicious breakfast Cook prepared of cold cuts and cheese for open-faced sandwiches topped with cucumbers and tomatoes. The scent of strong coffee mingling with the yeasty warmth of freshly baked bread made the kitchen feel like a corner café.

Elise wanted to eat like this every morning back home. It was so hearty she could easily skip lunch—especially if breakfast came later in the morning.

While the boys prattled on, Elise couldn't help glancing at Kent, remembering last night's delicious kiss. His gaze caught hers, and in the sunlight streaming through the windows over the sink, his eyes glittered with unspoken memory. When his smile deepened, she knew he was thinking about the same thing. Or maybe he remembered her shameless confessions—that she still loved sex, perhaps even more than before menopause, and that casual relationships suited her just fine.

She flushed at the thought. How had she let herself say such things? And yet, she was glad she had.

Her mind drifted back to the taste of his mouth, the

strength of his body, the low rumble of his groan. Despite herself, color crept into her cheeks.

Of course he noticed. His gaze never left her face. When his mouth curved into that maddeningly kissable smile, Elise's heart gave a telltale leap.

She reached for another piece of bread—just as Kent's phone rang. He tapped the screen, then grinned. "Hello, my beautiful married daughter who is calling me while on her honeymoon." He let the teasing words hang.

Amanda's sweet voice rushed in. "I just wanted to know how you filled the day without the boys yesterday. Hana told me they'd had the boys over."

Guilt pinched Elise's stomach. Yesterday had been full of teasing, hand-holding, and stolen glances. And that kiss. Amanda would not have approved. But Kent's tone was calm, almost neutral. "We visited Prague Castle. I don't think the boys would have been terribly interested, so I thought I'd get that out of the way while they were with Hana and Filip."

Amanda chuckled, though Elise thought she heard a trace of weariness in her tone. "You're right. They'd have been bored silly and started complaining halfway through."

Elise's nerves eased a fraction. Then Amanda said, "Let me talk to my little darlings."

"They're right here," Kent replied, turning the phone so Amanda could see her boys.

Mother and sons chattered away, the boys talking over each other, eager to share everything they'd done and how much fun they'd had with their Czech grandparents.

As the prattle filled the air, Kent's mouth quirked into a half-smile. Elise flushed again under his sidelong glance, certain he was thinking of the moments they'd shared when the boys weren't around. His gaze was invitation enough. Tonight, his eyes promised, they'd do everything all over again. And more.

God help her, she didn't think she'd be able to say no.

UNDER THE TABLE, KENT'S BODY RESPONDED TO HER, HARD and aching. Her pupils had dilated, like a wild creature scenting danger—or desire. She wasn't prey, not by a long shot, but he still wanted to devour her.

Last night had only whetted his appetite. He wanted more.

Amanda's soft, almost tearful voice cut into his thoughts. "You aren't having too much fun without me, are you, my darlings?"

"We miss you," the boys chorused.

And Marek bounced in his seat so hard the chair squeaked, nearly knocking over his juice. "We're going to Prague Zoo today! They've got a giant Komodo dragon and baby gorillas and even polar bears! It's the best zoo in the whole world—I read it online!" His words tumbled out in one long, breathless rush.

Beside him, Luca patiently waited his turn. When Marek finished, Luca's voice, as always, was quieter and more deliberate. "I want to see the LEGO museum. They've built a replica of the entire Charles Bridge out of LEGO... and the Millennium Falcon from Star Wars." His lips curved in a small, hopeful smile. "It's supposed to have thousands of pieces."

Kent had already looked up both places. The zoo was world class, sprawling and wild, and the LEGO museum was practically designed for his grandsons. He smiled, imagining the boys at the zoo, Marek racing from enclosure to enclosure, dragging everyone along, while Luca lingered over every detail, studying the animals and asking questions about what they ate and how they lived.

In between those moments—if he was lucky—maybe he could sneak a kiss or hold Elise's hand for just a heartbeat.

Her nostrils flared slightly as she blew out a steadying breath, and he knew she was having the same visions. But Elise narrowed her eyes at him in a silent reminder that their first responsibility was to the children. And she was right.

He dipped his head in acknowledgment.

"Of course," Kent said quickly. "We'll do both—the zoo and the LEGO museum. They're on our list."

Today was for Marek and Luca. For their joy.

That didn't mean he couldn't sneak in one little kiss when the boys weren't looking.

THE BOYS HAD BLOWN KISSES TO THEIR MOTHER, BUT WHEN the call ended, they were raring to go. They'd enjoyed the zoo, each unable to leave without another stuffed animal, both choosing the same one, a sloth, insisting it reminded them of their favorite movie, *Zootopia*—and of the DMV sloths.

Kent chuckled quietly. "I wonder how the DMV handled the insult in that movie."

Elise laughed, the sound bright and musical in the warm morning air, and he seized the chance to slip his hand into hers, holding it just long enough for a shiver to race through his body. "I think they just ignored it," she said, her fingers curling around his.

Kent grinned, feeling a thrill at the contact. "I actually think the line at the DMV was faster when I was there the last time. So maybe it did some good."

They laughed together, but their laughter carried a heat that wasn't entirely innocent. He felt her joy ripple through him, like a heat-seeking missile drawing him closer. He wanted to wrap her in his arms, to taste that laughter on her lips—but the boys turned, calling to one another. Reluctantly, he let go, and Elise stepped back, her cheeks flushed, the sunlight catching on the silvery strands in her blond hair. She wore a flowing, flowery skirt, with a silky blouse that revealed a tiny slice of delectable cleavage his gaze couldn't help traveling to.

The LEGO museum, called the Museum of Bricks, was a smashing hit. Elise and Kent ended up holding the stuffed sloths while the boys darted between exhibits, posing for pictures they wanted as keepsakes. Luca was right about the amazing replica of Charles Bridge, which even had tiny tourists walking across it. The LEGO builders had created masterpieces of the Taj Mahal, the Statue of Liberty, Tower Bridge in London, the Eiffel Tower. There was even a train set the boys found fascinating as the train went round and round on its track. Children of all ages gathered around every exhibit, staring agog at their favorites.

Kent stole glances at Elise, at the curve of her smile, the way her fingers brushed lightly against the soft toy she carried, and his pulse skipped. God, how he wanted her hands on him like that.

By the end of the day, however, he admitted their two young charges exhausted him. He leaned close to Elise, whispering, "I don't know how you do this day in and day out."

She smiled, brushing a stray lock of hair behind her ear. The faint scent of her lotion drifted toward him—warm, subtle, intoxicating. "While working lessons, they have to sit still. Then I make sure they take a nap—even if they both protest. We did some sightseeing, but it wasn't constant."

That small, intimate act—just brushing her hair from her face—felt charged. Kent's throat went dry, his thoughts focused on the curve of her neck, the creamy cleavage in the vee of her blouse, the gentle scent of her reaching out to him.

After dinner, the boys were thoroughly worn out. Baths and teeth brushing completed, then story time, and when Kent finally closed the book, they were asleep. He tiptoed downstairs and found Elise already on the veranda. The sky had deepened to velvety indigo, stars glittering above the rooftops, and a cool night breeze rustled through the hanging flower baskets. She had pulled on a soft, cream-colored sweater, shoulders relaxed, her silhouette framed by moonlight.

From behind her, he said, "I'll get us some wine. We deserve it after today."

Without turning, she waved a hand in silent agreement.

A starry night. A beautiful woman. The Vltava shimmering in the distance, moonlight glinting off its rippling surface. Kent's pulse thrummed with anticipation. The thought of her so tantalizingly near him shot a low heat through him. He knew exactly where this was leading.

Where he *wanted* it to lead.

The baby monitor sat on the table. He prayed Luca wouldn't have a nightmare and the thing would remain quiet.

After pouring the wine, a Riesling because she liked the sweeter wines, he handed her a glass, and raised his own. "Here's to what I hope was a fabulous concert tour."

She looked at him, moonlight catching in her eyes, reflecting the city's lights in a gleam that made his chest ache. Her voice was warm, soft, and seductive: "It's the most amazing trip I've ever taken." She sipped slowly, letting him watch, letting him wonder what she saw when she looked at him.

He didn't read too much into that look, following the conversation instead. "So, what's next for you?"

She smiled, dropped her gaze, and sipped again. "I've definitely caught the traveling bug. I'd really love to sail along the Norwegian fjords. And there are places we visited I'd like to go back to. The whirlwind of this tour left me wanting more. Rome. Barcelona. Lisbon. I think a Mediterranean cruise would be amazing. I'd also love to take a riverboat down the Nile... maybe even skinny-dip in Lake Como under the summer moon, or watch the moonrise over the Australian outback."

Kent laughed softly, though the sound felt low and rough in his throat, stirred by the sight of her reaching for his hand, fingers brushing his just long enough to make him ache. "So many places, so little time."

She withdrew her hand, a teasing smile playing on her lips. "Then I'd better get cracking." She paused, then asked, "What about you?"

Make love with you, he thought before he could suppress it. But the thought lingered, tasting sweeter than the wine in his glass. He said instead, "I'd like to spend as much time with the boys as possible. I don't want to miss watching them grow up."

"Are you thinking about going with them on next year's tour?" she asked, a knowing gleam in her eyes.

He nodded, though it would be so much better if Elise were there. "Yes. I'll do my best to make that happen." His words suddenly reminded him of the past. That had been his refrain to Gail over the years. Always putting things off until later. Until there was no more *later*.

A dam seemed to break within him, and his thoughts spilled out, unguarded. "My wife and I had planned to travel more when I retired." His chest felt tight. "We took a few trips, but maybe only every three or four years."

"What about the trip to Morocco and the blue city? Where your wife wanted to feed the cats? You took her there."

He smiled, thinking about Gail and those cats. She came back with some of the cutest photos and great memories.

"Yes, we did that," he agreed. "But much more often, I was traveling on my own for business. I was always busy—next project, next building. I'm not sure I would have actually retired. Probably I'd always have found another project to do before I called it quits."

"But you've retired now. And sixty-five isn't really that late. Not even full retirement age these days."

"It was too late for Gail." He swallowed the ache in his throat, the memory of a life lost too soon. "Losing someone makes you realize it can happen to anyone at any time. God forbid—it could happen to Amanda, it could happen to the boys."

"They're safe," Elise whispered. Her voice carried across the veranda, soft and intimate, wrapping around him. "So that's why you retired? For quality time with them?"

He nodded, gazing at Charles Bridge and Prague Castle silhouetted against the night. The river reflected a thousand fractured lights. "Yes. I often got commissions out of town—and I'd be gone for months, coming home only on weekends. That kind of schedule made me realize I might not even recognize them when I got back. I want them to know me too. I don't want to be the grandfather they only saw every few months."

"But you were home on the weekends."

"It's not the same. When I'm working, half the time, I'm on the phone, answering questions." He looked at her again, moonlight bathing her features in silver. "I couldn't go along on this tour. It's still my company, but I've been winding down, training people to take my place, so that next year I'm free."

"Good for you. I'm glad you made that decision."

The words kept coming, as if drawn out by her presence. "But it's been so goddamn lonely since my wife died."

"How long were you married?"

"Thirty-five years." He choked slightly with his memories, and yet the taste of her attention felt sweet and sharp in his mouth. "Forty years, if you count from the day we married to now. The last five without her have been a vast wasteland. And before that..." His voice faltered as his mind drifted to the cancer years, three bleak years of struggle, loss, and slow surrender.

She reached out, her fingers brushing his hand, warmth filling him in ways she could never know.

"I'm so sorry," she whispered, voice hushed with compassion.

He closed his eyes and simply drank in the heat of her touch, letting it anchor him.

Then came her quiet question. "And there's been no one special in the last five years?"

"I've dated," he admitted, his voice low as he lifted his gaze to the night sky. He willed her not to withdraw her hand. "But losing her mother has been very hard on Amanda—especially with the boys so young. She needed a mother's touch."

And he needed Elise's touch.

Her next words were equally soft. "She disapproved of your dating?"

He turned his head, studying her. "She thinks it would mean I didn't love her mother."

Searching her eyes, he tried to read what she thought. Amanda's feelings were a shadow over everything—because this wasn't just about him. It was about Elise, too, if what they were doing could even be called a relationship. Right now, they'd shared only one kiss. They were friends. Not lovers. Not yet.

"Doesn't she know," Elise asked gently, "that you can fall in love more than once in a lifetime?"

He held her gaze. "That's exactly what she's afraid of. That I could fall in love again."

"She can't possibly wish you to be alone for the rest of your life. You're only sixty-five."

"That thought isn't even on her radar," he said, the truth weighing heavy. As much as he loved his daughter, he couldn't deny Amanda's flaw. Since her mother's illness—and even more since her death—everything had been about her grief. Her needs.

"Maybe you need to think about yourself. Five years is a long time to be alone." Then quickly, as if regretting her words, she added, "I'm sorry, it's not my business to say anything."

He felt her withdrawing then—not just her hand slipping away, but her very presence pulling back.

And he absolutely could not let that happen. No matter what Amanda thought.

HAD SHE BEEN THINKING THERE MIGHT BE A CHANCE FOR them? Of course she had.

But Kent's words shattered those fragile hopes, sending them scattering like leaves on the wind.

Then he closed his fingers firmly around hers. "Don't go. Please."

Elise lifted her eyes and found his—dark pools in the moonlight, shadowed and filled with a sorrowful plea.

"But Amanda?" she whispered, leaving the rest unsaid.

"Amanda has two beautiful children and a loving husband," he said. "And you and I have only a few days while she's gone."

A shiver raced through her—not from the chill night air, but from the intensity in his voice, his eyes, his touch.

He was lonely. So was she. She'd been lonely since her divorce. So many lost years. As many years as Kent had been happily married.

Last night, they'd joked about casual sex. But there was no humor in this moment. Only longing. Only need.

And she wanted to answer it.

She wanted *him*.

Without question, without fear, she leaned across their clasped hands. Thank God she'd thought to move the chairs closer before he'd come down.

He met her halfway, lips brushing hers, tentatively at first. When she parted her mouth in invitation, he accepted.

The kiss was tender yet delicious. A melding of mouths, a tasting of tongues—exploring, discovering, learning each other's flavor. It carried the sweetness of wine, the heat of hunger, the ache of long-denied desire.

It had been building for days. Perhaps from the very moment she'd met him at the airport.

Her soft moan broke free, unleashing everything they'd both been holding back.

9

She consumed him with just a kiss. And in return, he devoured her.

That old line from *Bridget Jones* flashed through her mind—nice boys didn't kiss like that. And older people certainly didn't kiss like this. Yet she lost herself in his lips, his tongue, and the ferocity of his mouth on hers.

Had she ever been kissed like this?

Never. Not even in the first flush of lust with Nick. And never with anyone else.

Almost without breaking the kiss, Kent pulled her onto his lap. She wound her arms around his neck, surrendering to the hunger. He was hard beneath her, and God, how she wanted him.

They were both breathless when they broke apart. The sharp intake of his breath told her he was as affected as she was. His eyes burned—dark, hot pools in the night—as he whispered, "Come upstairs with me."

Upstairs. To his room. To his bed. The thought set her pulse racing, her body answering with a sharp ache of need.

But there was one minor problem. Better to speak of it

here rather than upstairs. "I don't have any protection." Protection wasn't only about pregnancy. And it was common sense.

She felt his low chuckle rumble against her. "But I do."

She wasn't sure whether to laugh or gasp. "Do you always carry a condom with you? Or did you just think I was easy?"

He caressed her arms slowly, soothing and arousing in the same stroke. "Neither. I was just... hopeful." His voice dropped, that deep, seductive note vibrating straight through her. "I've wanted you from the moment I saw you at the airport. And the longer I'm near you, the more I ache. So I went to a drugstore. I planned this, Elise, because that's how badly I want you. You're all I can think about."

Had any man ever desired her like this—so openly, so honestly?

The evidence of his need pressed against her, rock-hard and waiting. Still, she couldn't help but ask, "Did you... have to take a pill? To be ready?"

Instead of taking offense, he cupped her cheeks in his hands. "I've been in a constant state of arousal around you. No pill necessary."

It was an odd conversation, but having casual relationships had taught her that you always used protection, and that dating older men often meant a little pharmaceutical help. She whispered in wonder, "Most men aren't like you."

He kissed her again, gently this time, his mouth stoking the fire inside her rather than consuming it whole. "I haven't desired a woman like this in a long, long time." As if reading the doubt in her expression, he added quietly, "I dream about you at night." His words fell like a caress: "I have to stroke myself or I'd go crazy." His whisper deepened, rough with need. "Don't make me go crazy now by not touching me."

With his hands still cradling her face, she leaned in until her lips brushed his. "I want you crazy."

She climbed off his lap—more gracefully than she expected—and held out her hand. "Come with me."

The stars sparkled overhead, and the moon painted his features in silver. He rose and pulled her into his arms, kissing her again, tongues tangling, the taste of him filling her. Then he backed away, taking her hand in both of his as he led her toward the veranda door.

Once inside, he wrapped an arm around her shoulders, drew her close, and steered her toward the sweeping staircase. Down the hallway, past the closed doors, and into his room.

She had a brief thought of the baby monitor left unattended on the veranda. But she was sure she'd hear Luca if he had a nightmare.

And then there was just Kent.

He closed the door gently behind them and turned to her. As his fingers found the buttons of her blouse, his voice was husky. "You're so damn sexy with clothes on." He bent to trail his tongue along her neck as he undid one button, then another, until the silk gaped open.

He'd gone to the drugstore. She'd gone to her lingerie drawer. Had she been hoping even then? When she was with the family in Paris, she'd told herself she was buying something pretty just for herself. But maybe the universe had been nudging her. The lacy bra and panties she wore now felt like fate—she'd dressed for this moment.

He cupped her breast through the lace, his tongue tracing the edge. When he pinched her nipple, she groaned aloud. Then her blouse slid from her shoulders to pool on the floor.

She tugged at his polo, lifting it over his taut abdomen, his sculpted chest. When he raised his arms, she stripped it off, letting her palms skim over the hard planes of his chest.

Piece by piece, they undressed, tension ratcheting higher with every scrap of skin revealed.

Unclasping her bra, he lowered his mouth to draw a tight peak between his lips, sucking, driving her wild. She ran her hands down the smooth strength of muscle and the light dusting of hair on his chest that arrowed toward his waistband. Fumbling a little with his belt buckle, she leaned in to take his nipple in her mouth, swirling her tongue, thrilled at the growl of pleasure that rose from his throat.

At last, he stood before her in just his boxer briefs, and she in only her panties.

A hot flush swept over her. Fifty-five. Naked before a man she wanted more than her next breath. She'd imagined feeling self-conscious, worried about the lines on her skin, the softness of her body. But his eyes, hungry and reverent, banished every shred of doubt.

She reached out, stroking his hard length straining against the thin cotton. He seemed to swell even more at her touch, the tip rising above the elastic. She thought of his confession, that he'd touched himself thinking of her. It was so incredibly sexy.

And she was so wet. So hot. So needy. Like never before.

"You're beautiful." He groaned as she stroked him.

She stepped closer, molding her body to his. "And I love the feel of you in my hand."

Tipping his head back, a growl vibrated up from his chest, as if her touch pushed him to the edge of control. When he looked at her, his eyes burned hot, almost indigo in the dim light.

"I'll never need a pill with you," he said, his voice rough.

She chuckled softly. "Which probably means you don't need it with anyone."

As he slid his hands up and down her arms, his fingers tensed—not painfully, but with intensity. "It's for you. My fantasies. My desire. The aching need in my gut. It's all you."

God, how she loved that too.

His voice dropped lower, harsher. "You know what I've dreamed about most? Finding out how you taste. Learning how to make you cry... and scream."

He turned her, guiding her down until she fell back on the bed. In one fluid move, he whisked her panties away and tossed them across the room.

She was trembling before he even touched her. "I can't scream," she whispered. "The boys."

She prayed Luca wouldn't have a nightmare tonight.

"Then I'll make you *want* to scream." He bent to her. "So pretty." His gaze fixed on her, he spread her thighs a little wider, his fingers sliding up through her folds. The sudden shock of pleasure made her jerk.

"Grab the pillows," he said.

She pulled one beneath her head, even as he shoved his briefs down and off. In the moonlight spilling through the window, she saw him—tall, proud, thick, impossibly hard— and her breath caught.

For a flicker of a moment, nerves skittered through her. She no longer had the smooth, tight body of her twenties. Gravity had its sway, and life had marked her. Would he notice? Would he compare?

But the heat in Kent's eyes burned away every doubt. He looked at her as if she were the most desirable woman alive.

Desire surged back, hotter than the nerves. She wanted his taste in her mouth.

But Kent was already crawling between her legs, pushing them apart with his broad shoulders. His big hands slid beneath her bottom, lifting her to his mouth.

A cry tore out of her, muffled as she bit her lip. She couldn't—wouldn't—wake the boys.

But Kent had only just begun. His tongue dipped between her folds, flicked over her swollen bud.

She fisted the comforter, her body arching to meet him.

Oh God. It was so good, so dizzyingly good. She couldn't remember the last time she'd felt like this—if she ever had.

She loved sex, but not every man knew what to do. Not the way Kent did. He knew exactly how to touch her, how to lick her, how to make her shudder. His fingers slipped inside, stroking her in time with his tongue.

Her climax rose fast and hard, her thighs trembling uncontrollably. Then it hit—an eruption, an earthquake, a tidal wave crashing through her. She shoved her fist against her mouth to keep from screaming.

He didn't stop, holding her down with his hands and his mouth, pulling every last shiver, every last spasm out of her until she was boneless beneath him.

Never. Never like this.

When she opened her eyes, dizzy and dazed, she saw him rolling on a condom.

And then he was inside her.

Slow at first, teasing, stretching her. Her body clutched at him, quivering, and another climax washed through her even before he slammed home, hard and fast, thrust after thrust driving her higher.

"Nothing," she said, her voice raw. "Nothing ever like this."

He kissed her, tongue fierce and demanding, her own taste mingling with his. She wrapped her arms and legs around him, holding him close, reveling in the way he seemed to know her body, as if they'd been lovers for years.

His pace grew urgent, his features taut with pleasure. She felt him swell inside her, felt the heat as he came, his body jerking, neck straining as he let go.

"Christ," he whispered hoarsely, collapsing on her, kissing her again, holding her flush against him as aftershocks shook them both.

Then, rolling onto his back, he took her with him, still inside her.

"Thank you," he breathed at last.

She tipped her head back, meeting his eyes. "I'm the one who needs to thank you."

His laugh was soft, ragged. "You can't thank me for something that felt this damn good." He raked a hand through his hair, muttering a curse she found strangely beautiful on his lips.

Hesitantly, she brushed her fingers across her bare stomach, self-conscious in the cooling air. "I'm not... what I used to be."

His gaze sharpened. "You're everything I want. You're sexier now than you could've been at twenty-five, because you know exactly who you are." He caught her hand, pressed it to his chest, his heart still hammering. "Never doubt what I see when I look at you."

Her throat tightened. "I don't think I've ever felt like that before."

A low growl rumbled from him. "Then you know how good it was for me." He tilted her face toward him. "I loved my wife. It was always good. But this..." He paused, eyes closing briefly before finding hers again. "You gave me something so precious. You made me feel alive again. Like a man."

She twirled her finger through the soft hair on his chest. "Believe me, you've always been a very sexy man. That's why I wanted to touch you from the very first moment."

"But you've made me *feel* like one again."

"And you've made me feel like a woman," she whispered.

"A beautiful, sexy, desirable woman," he murmured back.

They lay wrapped together, stroking each other with tender touches.

She wished she could stay like this all night.

When he slipped away to the bathroom, Kent feared she'd be gone when he returned, back to her own room. Relief flooded him to find she was still there, and crawling into bed beside her, he wrapped his arms around her once more.

Though he wanted her there until morning, he knew she'd leave before the boys were up. So he relished these sweet moments with her.

He tightened his arms around her. That's what he'd meant about feeling like a man again—not obligation, not duty, not release after too long without sex. But joy. Pleasure. Connection.

That's why he thanked her.

That's why he didn't want to let her go.

Kent woke to the sun rising on the empty spot beside him in the bed. He'd expected her to be gone, but seeing that hollow space, he ached with loss.

After showering and dressing, he headed downstairs and found Elise in the kitchen with the boys. Cook had of course laid out a spread fit for royalty. The boys chattered exuberantly about the previous day at the zoo and the LEGO museum, their voices tumbling over one another like puppies at play. Elise poured them juice, listening, smiling, but her eyes seemed to dart everywhere but his.

Maybe she was nervous about what they'd done last night. Maybe she regretted it. God, he hoped not.

Cook handed him a fresh slice of warm toast, and Kent slathered it with butter, then a generous smear of homemade jam.

Then he couldn't resist a little teasing. "How did you sleep last night, Elise?"

Her gaze snapped to his. For an instant, her eyes flared wide—caught—but then her lips curved into a genuine smile.

"I didn't fall asleep right away," she admitted, holding his gaze. He leaned forward, hungry for her next words, for the playful spark he craved. "My whole body was just whirling with all these..." She paused, milking it. "...wild and crazy thoughts." Then she blinked innocently, raised a prim eyebrow, and delivered the final line with precision. "But once I fell asleep, I lay in the arms of my..." Another pause. "...ever-so-comfortable pillow."

His entire body tightened beneath the table. He wanted to haul her into his lap, kiss her until she was breathless, drag her back upstairs, and relive every wild moment of last night.

"I didn't have any trouble falling asleep at all," he confessed, matching her game. "I felt as if sleep itself was pillowed on my chest."

Which was true—she'd been there most of the night, warm against him—until she'd slipped away.

They might have gone on like that, volleying innuendos right over the boys' oblivious heads, but Kent's phone rang. He glanced at the screen—Amanda. Answering, he set the phone in the middle of the table so the boys could see their mother.

"Hello, sweetheart. How's the honeymoon?"

Her voice floated out, calm and happy, a sound he hadn't heard from her in years. Much more relaxed than yesterday. "It's beautiful up here. So peaceful."

The boys pounced before Kent could reply.

"Mama, we went to the zoo, and Děda bought me a sloth!" Luca's prized stuffed animal sat in the seat beside him like a third breakfast guest.

Not to be outdone, Marek nearly shouted into the phone.

"The monkey house was the best, Mama! They chased each other up and down the trees, and we got to feed them bananas!"

Kent chuckled, remembering how lucky they'd been to arrive right at feeding time.

Amanda's features sharpened. "Aren't monkeys dangerous?" She clearly meant the question for Kent.

"There were handlers with us the whole time," Kent reassured her. "And the monkeys were gentle with the boys."

Elise added smoothly, "It's baboons that can be aggressive. We kept well away from them."

Amanda's pause was noticeable. "You went too?" She didn't even say Elise's name.

"Of course," Elise said quickly. "That gave Kent a chance to enjoy quality time with the boys without having to worry. I was right there watching."

"Oh." Just that. And a slight glower.

For a moment, Kent wondered if Elise should have called him Mr. Woodward for Amanda's benefit. But she'd been calling him Kent all along, at his insistence—even in Amanda's presence. It would have been strange to switch now.

"Okay," Amanda said again, the lines on her face smoothing out. "Thank you for that, Elise. I know how much they love time with their *dědeček*." Then her tone brightened as she returned her attention to the boys. "I miss you both so much. So does your Papa."

"We miss you, too, Mama!" they sang out.

Amanda didn't linger in sentiment. Instead, she rushed on. "Your father and I were talking, and we thought what fun it would be if you came up to stay with us for the rest of the week."

Kent frowned. "But it's your honeymoon, sweetheart."

She laughed lightly. "It's not as if we need one. We've been together over ten years."

True. "But I don't want to intrude," he said firmly. "This is your time."

"I don't expect you to stay here," she insisted. Then added, "And I don't want Elise to stay here either. I want it to be just us. Just family."

What had brought this on? Was it her depression and she needed her boys to keep it at bay? Whatever the reason, he could only agree. "All right. If that's want you really want."

"We do," she said, but he wondered how much was her idea and how much was Tomás's.

And yet, at the snap of her fingers—and the turn of her moods—the week ahead shifted into something entirely different. He would miss doing the fun things he'd planned for the boys.

But this meant seven days alone with Elise. It would be like heaven.

10

They packed the boys' things—clothes, toys, rain boots, jackets. The autumn weather in the Krkonoše Mountains could change on a whim. Amanda had offered their driver, but Kent had waved that off.

"I fancy a mountain drive," he'd said.

The road wound out of Prague, leaving behind its spires, domes, and morning clatter of trams. They were soon surrounded by rolling hills that sharpened into jagged green peaks. The forests flamed with early autumn, trees blazing red and gold against the dark pines. Elise kept the boys entertained in the back seat, while Kent stole glances in the mirror, watching her laugh with them, her hair catching sunlight in flashes.

By the time they pulled up to the chalupa—a sprawling chalet tucked into the forest—the sun was high in the sky, gilding the mountainsides. The wraparound porch stretched wide, the kind that invited evenings with wine and blankets. Flowering bushes framed the steps, still offering their last blooms of the season.

Amanda must have been waiting, because she flung open the door and raced down to meet them. The boys flew into her arms, and she dropped to her knees, clutching them as if she'd never let them go.

Then she hugged Kent fiercely. "Thank you so much for bringing them. I've missed them every second."

Tomás strode down the steps with an easy smile. "She's been talking about them nonstop." He clapped Kent's shoulder. "But I'm sure they had the best time with their děda."

"And with your parents too," Kent added.

Tomás turned to Elise. "Hello, Elise. Thank you for bringing them. You must be hungry. We planned lunch before you head back to the city."

Elise smiled warmly. "That's kind of you. Let me just get their things."

Kent followed her to the car. "I'll help." He tossed a grin at Tomás, who was now engulfed by two wriggling boys.

They set the bags by the inside door, unsure where Amanda and Tomás would want everything. The chalupa opened up before them—a massive fireplace anchoring the living room, high-beamed ceilings, polished log walls. The dining area flowed into a kitchen with a long counter lined with barstools.

It had all the warmth of a hunting lodge—without the grim décor of mounted antlers or glass-eyed trophies. Thank God.

But all he truly thought about was the time he could now devote completely to Elise's pleasure.

OVER A LUNCHEON OF CRISP GARDEN GREENS, FRESH-chopped vegetables, meats, cheeses, and hearty bread still warm from the oven, Amanda peppered the boys with questions about everything they'd been doing. They chattered excitedly, mixing memories of the zoo, the Dancing House, the Charles Bridge performers, the astronomical clock, the old lady with the pigeons, and the LEGO Museum into one breathless list, not bothering to sort which had happened before the wedding and which after.

Luca, usually the quieter one, was uncharacteristically talkative. "And we played with our cousins when they got out of school." He turned pleading eyes on Tomás. "Why don't we see our cousins more often?"

Tomás explained gently, "They live very far away from San Francisco. And the flight out there is very expensive for the family." He ruffled the boy's hair. "But maybe we can come here more often than once a year." He glanced at Amanda, and then, with a wistful smile, he added, "Perhaps when you're much older, you and Marek can spend an entire summer here."

Elise noticed the sudden set of Amanda's jaw. But she only said sweetly, "Don't promise things we can't actually do, Tomás."

Tomás ignored the warning. "Certainly not until you're teenagers," he amended, "but before then, we can still come together as a family."

Amanda's smile relaxed again. "Would you like that, boys?"

Both boys let out joyful shouts, bouncing in their seats until the dishes rattled.

Across the table, Elise met Kent's eyes. Amanda had carefully seated them apart—Kent beside Marek, Tomás next to Luca, Amanda at the head of the table with her sons bracketing her. That left Elise as the odd one out, tucked on Tomás's other side. It was probably for the best. If Kent had been within reach, Elise suspected he'd have dared to slip a hand onto her knee beneath the table. Which would have been bad, since Amanda's gaze today was sharp as a hawk's.

Amanda folded her hands, elbows propped on the table, her expression pleasant. "If you want to fly home now, Dad, that'll be fine, since we'll be gone for another week and you'll be all alone and having to entertain yourself." Elise had the impression Amanda deliberately avoided her eyes. "I'm sure you have business to take care of at home."

Kent polished off a bite of bread, then smiled at his daughter, the lines at the corners of his eyes deepening. "No, sweetheart. I have nothing to do back home. I'm retired, remember?"

Elise's heart stuttered at the memory of last night—his weight on her, his voice breaking into groans of pleasure, the intensity of his eyes as he filled her. She forced herself to glance back at Amanda before heat rose to her cheeks and betrayed her.

Amanda, however, was watching her father closely, though Kent seemed oblivious as he added lightly, "Besides, when you get back from your honeymoon, I want to spend those few extra days with the boys."

"But you can see them back home." A harsher note entered Amanda's voice.

Tomás broke in smoothly, cutting her off. "You're always welcome, Kent. It'll be a flurry packing up when we get home, and both Amanda and I will appreciate you entertaining the boys while we handle things."

"No problem," Kent said. "I can even start the packing before you get back."

Elise knew there would be plenty to do—sorting through the wedding gifts, deciding what to leave for the next visit, what to ship, what to give away, and what to take with them. Three months of traveling through Europe and picking up souvenirs along the way left plenty to deal with.

Amanda turned her smile on Elise. "We'll be heading home soon after returning to Prague, and with my father here, you can fly home now, Elise. Truly, we appreciate everything you've done. You made this trip so much calmer than it might have been."

Her words hit Elise like a wrench to the heart. She and Kent had only one night. She needed more. So much more. She kept her face carefully blank as she opened her mouth to answer—only to be interrupted.

"I'd really appreciate it if Elise stayed," Kent said easily. "She can help pack everything, prepare the wedding presents for shipment, things like that. It will save you both so much time."

Tomás brightened. "That's a great idea, Kent." His eyes twinkled as they shifted to Elise, and for just a moment she wondered if he somehow knew. And was encouraging them.

Amanda's lips pressed into a thin line. "But Elise won't know what to keep and what to let go. What if she chooses incorrectly?" Her tone had the edge of a sulky child.

Tomás brushed it off with a wave of his hand. "Anything in question, she can set aside for us. Whatever we don't want, my parents can distribute to the family." He looked at Elise with a nod of reassurance. "Please, Elise, stay."

Amanda splayed her hands on the table, let out a huff, then arranged her mouth into a brittle smile. "Well then, that's decided."

Elise let out the breath she'd been holding. She didn't dare look at Kent, but her heart raced with joy at the promise of another seven days—and nights—in his arms.

"I HOPE YOU DON'T MIND MY WRANGLING A FEW EXTRA

days in Prague for you." Kent expertly guided the car out of the mountains as they headed back to the city.

"Of course not. I'd love some extra time to tour." Elise hoped he'd done it because he wanted more time with *her*.

He held her hand in the center console between them, and her heart soared when he said, "I did it for myself. I can't get enough of you." He glanced at her, and she thought his eyes flamed with a deep blue light.

She didn't feign innocence. "I'd hoped that was why." She shook a finger at him. "But don't forget we'll need to do some packing."

He raised her hand to brush his lips across her knuckles. "I'll be happy to assist you in *any* way you like."

"You're bad." But an inner smile warmed her.

He released her hand long enough to slip a CD into the player, and the gentle tones of piano music filled the air.

"My Foolish Heart," she said. "An old standard from the fifties."

Kent took her hand again. "You recognize it?"

"It's from a movie with Dana Andrews and Susan Hayward. I loved all of Dana Andrews' films."

He glanced at her, one eyebrow raised. "You weren't even born when he was a big star."

She leaned her head against the seat. "They played the classic movies on those old TV stations. Just like the Fred Astaire and Ginger Rogers movies."

"But didn't you rent all the new movies on video when you were a teenager?"

"Sure, I liked the new movies too. Like *The Breakfast Club* and *Risky Business* and *Sixteen Candles*. But the classics were my favorites."

"I was more into movies like *Bullitt, Le Mans,* and *Jaws*."

She smirked. "Guy movies. And I was only five when *Jaws* came out.

He side-eyed her. "Was that a crack about my age?"

"Absolutely not. Your age is perfect." *He* was perfect. "And I loved *Jaws* when I was older. Who didn't?"

He gave her hand a squeeze. "But this song, you actually remember it from an old movie?"

"To tell the truth, Tomás played it one evening. It was familiar, and he told me what it was. Then I remembered the film." She pointed at the CD player. "That's Tomás's, isn't it?"

"Yeah. Most cars don't come with CD players anymore, but Tomás insisted on having one installed. He could've made a playlist to stream through his phone." Kent snorted. "He's old-school in a lot of ways."

Favorite old standards filled the car. Though Tomás's concerts were classical, he often played music she recognized —from movies, and singers like Nat King Cole.

They listened in contented silence while Kent stroked her hand, lightly trailing his thumb along her skin. He'd given her an extra week in Prague, because Amanda certainly would have sent her home.

But more importantly, he'd given her an entire week with him.

When they arrived back in the city, the house felt empty. No sound from the kitchen, no vacuum running upstairs, no pitter-patter of childish feet.

"Where are Jakub and Cook?" she asked.

A smile grew across Kent's face until it crinkled his eyes. "I gave them the week off."

"Were you planning to go home?" She held her breath for an entirely different answer.

His eyes glowed hot, like banked flames. "I decided that since it would just be you and me, we didn't need them."

"What if Amanda had sent me home?" she teased.

"I would've made sure she didn't. And even if she had—" He raised one wicked brow. "—I wouldn't have let you go."

Her whole body tightened, each breath coming faster.

Kent took the two steps between them. His voice dipped low. "What would you like to do with the rest of the afternoon?"

She gave the only appropriate answer. "This." Wrapping her arms around his neck, she rose on her toes and kissed him passionately—holding nothing back, teasing him, flirting with his tongue—until he pulled her close enough that she felt him hard between them.

Breathing harshly, he pulled back just enough to murmur, "I love your ideas."

Then he led her up the stairs.

Kent relished undressing her. She wore sexy lingerie, as if she'd intended to seduce him. Not that he needed it. Being in the car with her, her scent washing over him, her skin warm beneath his fingers, the unspoken desire simmering between them—it was enough.

"You're gorgeous," he whispered, trailing his fingers over her breasts beneath the lacy bra, down her abdomen to the matching panties.

Her eyes were half-closed with need. "I think you're more beautiful."

He chuckled, hooking his fingers in the elastic and drawing the panties slowly down.

She cupped him through his boxer briefs. They'd stripped down to only their underwear, drawing out the anticipation in a slow dance of undressing, touching, kissing. His gut tightened as she squeezed him, then stroked. Christ, he wanted her. He couldn't remember wanting a woman this much in years. Maybe not even since the early days of marriage when everything felt new, or those first exciting months after

Amanda left for college and he'd felt their sex life renewed for a little while.

With her panties just over the curve of her rump, he bent to suckle Elise through the lace of her bra.

She moaned, tangling her fingers in his hair, urging him lower. Or maybe that was only his desire urging him down to his knees before her. He tugged her panties down her legs, leaving them in a puddle on the rug. The musky scent of her arousal filled him. He licked the jewel between her thighs. She moaned, the sound so delicious he couldn't help delving deeper.

When she widened her stance without prompting, he liked her eagerness. She steadied herself with her hands in his hair while he entered her with two fingers, licking and teasing her with lips and tongue. Her legs trembled and her body quaked as he stroked her G-spot. He'd been in his twenties before he figured out what that was. Now he gave that sweet spot all his attention.

Her breath quickened, her moans sharpened. Then she gasped, "I can't come standing up. Please."

Hand on her belly, he pushed her gently back onto the bed. Without missing a beat, he filled her with his fingers again, licked, suckled—worshiped her. Kneeling between her thighs, her legs draped over his shoulders, he gave her everything he had.

Nothing had ever felt so glorious as the moment her body clamped hard around his fingers, her cries rising to the ceiling, her taste flooding his mouth as she came hard for him.

He couldn't remember experiencing a more wondrous moment in years.

It was amazing. Out of this world. Catastrophic. How many more superlatives could she think of?

Kent lay beside her while she caught her breath, his fingers tracing patterns over her skin. His touch kept her excitement simmering.

Nuzzling her ear, he whispered, "You're so beautiful."

He'd said that last night too. She was sure now it wasn't just a throwaway line. He really thought she was beautiful.

While he tantalized her with those sweet caresses, he whispered tender words. "I love how responsive you are to me. How hard you come for me. The way you abandon all thought and give yourself up to my touch."

She definitely did all that.

With his tongue on her and his fingers inside her, there'd been nothing but sensation.

He was the best. Possibly the best she'd ever known. Better than any of the other men she'd slept with. Better than Nick.

What she'd felt for Nick had been all about obsession. She was young and addicted to her professor. But the sex had been... just sex. It had only seemed incredible because of how she'd felt about him. Thirty-five years later, she knew it had been only fixation and lust. For him, it had been lust, nothing more. He'd lusted after many women before and after her.

But this man was different. Different from any other.

She turned to face him. Then she tickled her fingers down his abdomen, wrapped him in her hand, and stroked him gently. He was already hard. Maybe he had been from the moment they kissed. Or maybe even in the car.

Even as he said, "No," he wrapped his hand around hers and helped her stroke him. "I want to be inside you when I come. And I want you to come again before I do."

She loved how easy their sexual banter felt. As if they

could say anything to each other. "I definitely like the sound of that."

He rolled to his back then, while she kept her hand on him in a gentle caress. He stretched to reach inside the bedside drawer and pulled out another condom packet, tearing it open with his teeth. It was such a manly gesture that it sent her pulse skyrocketing. Then he held out the condom to her. "Put it on for me."

She'd always used a condom during the casual relationships she'd had and knew how to put one on to drive him crazy. If he expected just a simple slide of her hand down his erection, he had things to learn about her.

She bent over him, taking him in her hand, placing the condom precisely. But as she rolled it down—slowly, deliberately, holding tight—she followed with her mouth. Taking his crown between her lips, her hand holding his base, she followed the same path with her mouth.

He'd bought fruit-flavored, and she laughed inwardly as the taste of strawberries filled her mouth. It seemed so out of character for him, and yet he was full of delicious surprises.

He choked out a cry as she engulfed him, her lips brushing her hand wrapped around him. "Christ." Then he groaned, such a satisfying sound.

Keeping the condom secure, she sucked all the way back up. He gasped, his body arching, almost levitating. "Holy mother—" Then he followed with a litany of swear words she loved hearing. Because they said how good she made him feel. And how much better she was going to make him feel.

She loved hearing a man curse in the bedroom when they wouldn't do it anywhere else. That meant a barrier had dropped.

Sliding down again, she swirled her tongue around him all the way back up. Until he grabbed her arms and pulled her away. His breath came in gasps. "Don't make me come now. I want to come inside you."

The desperation in his voice was so gratifying.

Then he tucked her under him. "You are full of surprises."

She quipped, "I aim to please."

He swore again, then knelt back on his haunches and spread her legs around him. Until his tip brushed her core. He smiled— so disarming, so sexy, so devilish. "I might have a few surprises myself."

He took hold of her hips, dragged her closer, only his crown breaching her.

She gasped, because it was so good. Because he'd found just the right spot. And with a gentle glide, he slid over it. Then back out. Slow. Agonizing. Incredible.

He did all the work—short, measured pumps of his hips, never going deep, but hitting that perfect spot every time. The slow pace shot pleasure through her. All the while he looked at her, his eyes half-lidded, his skin glowing, his gaze burning into her.

"Good?" he whispered.

She couldn't answer. She could only moan, "Oh my God." But it was enough.

He grinned like a satyr. "Good isn't good enough. Let's make it ecstatic." Then he put his thumb on the tight bead aching between her legs.

She was so wet he slipped easily, circling, whirling. Her whole body seemed to pulse—her toes, her fingertips, her heart, the very core of her sex. He rose slightly, changing the angle, and the pleasure shot off the scale.

Her limbs trembled, her body shook.

He breathed heavily and groaned. "Christ, I can feel you clenching around me." Then he swore again. Maybe it was the rawness of his words, the way he described what she was doing to her. Or maybe it was the slow, relentless glide inside her, the way he never went deep, the way he teased her with that rhythm. Or maybe it was his thumb, unyielding on that desperate spot.

Whatever it was, her entire body went hot, then rigid. The climax rose slowly, matching his pace, building in her quivering legs, her burning thighs, her belly. Then it hit like an 8.0 earthquake. Her body clamped down on him, squeezing, and Elise actually screamed with the pleasure of it all.

Kent slammed into her then. He wasn't gentle. But she didn't want gentle. She needed his hard, fast thrusts, his pounding rhythm.

The orgasm lasted forever. And she kept screaming.

So good. So perfect. Beyond anything she'd ever known.

Was it a minute? Two minutes? Or hours?

She heard him shout, wanted to look at him, but she couldn't—she could only ride out the pleasure wave. He grunted, groaned, and finally held her tight, grinding hard against her, sending her into another frenzy.

And all she could do was follow him into bliss all over again.

There had never been sex like this. There had never been pleasure like this.

There had never been a man like this.

11

They lazed in bed for long, lovely, drowsy minutes. Kent even thought he might have slept, and it was glorious to wake with Elise's body nestled against his. He trailed his fingers along her arm, hoping she'd stir, hoping he could make love to her again. When she tipped her head back on his shoulder to look at him, he thought he saw the same flame in her eyes.

Until her stomach rumbled. Loudly. He couldn't help laughing, and she joined him.

"You didn't even feed me before you hustled me off to bed." Her voice held a husky, seductive note that shot a thrill straight down to his center.

Suddenly, he was hard again.

"I'm pretty sure you did all the hustling," he said with a chuckle. "But you're right, you're going to need sustenance for what I have planned for the rest of the night."

They scrounged in the refrigerator, finding eggs and a rasher of bacon. Her stomach rumbled again as the first slices began to sizzle.

He leaned close for a kiss. "You really are hungry?"

Her smile was as sultry as her voice. "I'm hungry for a lot of things."

It was full dark when they carried their plates out to the veranda. While he'd scrambled the eggs and cooked the bacon, she'd cut slices of bread, toasted them, and slathered them with butter. She spooned eggs onto her toast and took a large bite. "Mmm," she hummed, chewing with her mouth closed.

The sound was so sensual he got hard again. She made him feel like a horny teenager, and he loved it. But he couldn't help teasing her. "Stop that."

She looked at him with the most innocent expression, one eyebrow raised. "Stop what?" Her voice was pure bewilderment, but she knew exactly what she was doing.

"You won't get to finish those eggs and bacon if you don't stop making those noises," he threatened, heat in his voice and his eyes.

Then she whispered, "Do you think anyone can see us from the river or from the street?"

There was nothing innocent in those words, or in her voice, or in the look shining in her eyes.

"I'd love nothing more than to ravish you out here."

That smile—so sexy, so inviting. "The only problem I see is that sound carries farther at night." She pointed off to the right, where laughter and music floated up from revelers in the square.

"They'll just think we're more revelers."

She batted her eyelashes. "Oh, but I don't want to just make merry. I want you to make me scream."

He'd never met a woman like her. He hadn't come to his marriage a virgin, but his experience hadn't been vast. As much as he'd loved Gail, their lovemaking had been more circumspect. He couldn't remember playful banter like this, even in the beginning. He didn't want to compare Elise to his wife—but Elise seemed to love sex for sex's sake. She asked for what she wanted, even if without words, pressing his shoulder when she wanted him to move lower, digging her heels into her butt when she wanted him to take her harder.

"Oh, how I'd love to make you scream," he whispered into the dark.

She raised an eyebrow and smiled wantonly. He wanted that smile. Needed that wantonness.

"Then we'd better hurry with our eggs and bacon." She ate half a piece of toast, swallowed, and gulped down the rest.

They finished quickly. He even convinced her to leave the dishes in the sink—everything could wait until morning. Except her.

She kissed him in the kitchen with the lights off, wrapped her arms around his neck in the foyer, devoured him at the bottom of the stairs. She walked backward up each step, pulling him with her, stopping halfway to kiss him again, to steal his breath, to set every nerve ending in his body on fire.

In the bedroom, he feasted on her until she screamed. The sound was like a symphony, caressing his ears.

They made love twice more that night, sleeping in between. It seemed impossible at his age to keep going like that, but she brought out the male animal in him. She roused him again at dawn with her hand wrapped around him. He barely got the condom on before he entered her. When she screamed this time, he kissed her, swallowing the sound—not because he was afraid of the neighbors hearing, but because he wanted to indulge his senses with every cry his lovemaking elicited.

The woman made him ravenous. He couldn't get enough of her. And he shocked even himself at how many times he could take her.

After sleeping late in the morning, they showered

together, and he had to taste her again. Then she insisted on taking him in her mouth. This time he gave her everything.

Downstairs in the kitchen, she poked her nose into the refrigerator. "We used all the eggs."

So they dined on the boys' cereal. As much as they loved Cook's breakfasts, the boys still sometimes craved cereal.

Kent wanted to hold her hand while they ate, but they were both right-handed. He wanted to keep touching her, to never let her go. And yet he didn't want to rush things, didn't want to risk ruining this.

"What would you like to do today?" he asked.

"Should we start packing?" She was a nanny again.

He wasn't having it. "We've got a week to get that done." He smiled into his coffee. "I'm going to surprise you with an outing."

"Doing what?"

He wagged a finger in her face. "The operative word was *surprise*."

THEY WALKED HAND IN HAND DOWN TO THE RIVER. ELISE adored his touch. He'd made her body sing last night, but the feel of his hand in hers was tantalizing in its own way—a promise of things to come. Afternoon delight. Starry nights in his bed. Stolen kisses.

When they reached the dock, he led her down the pier to a waiting boat, pulling out his phone to show the tickets.

She clutched his arm. "A boat ride on the Vltava? You're amazing."

Though a sunny day, it was cooler than the past few. The breeze tugged at her hair, and she was glad she'd worn a jacket and her leggings. They took seats at the front so they could see both banks. Prague Castle stood like a sentinel on the hill, the spires of St. Vitus Cathedral glittered in the sunshine, Charles Bridge teemed with tourists, and Petřín Lookout Tower watched over them. Leaning against Kent's shoulder, she lifted her face to the sun's warmth.

"You picked a perfect day." Any day with him would be perfect. She could have burst into song like Barbra Streisand belting out *Don't Rain on My Parade*. But she didn't have the singer's amazing voice.

He squeezed her hand. "I ordered it especially for you."

Deckhands moved among the passengers, handing out blankets, and Kent spread one over their knees. His nearness sent delicious heat spiraling through her.

The green dome of St. Nicholas Church rose above the red-tiled roofs of Malá Strana.

"Baroque," he said. "You can tell by the ornate decoration and the dome. The frescoes inside are incredible." He showed her a picture on his phone.

They passed beneath the magnificent Charles Bridge, people leaning over the balustrade to toss flowers onto the deck. Kent caught a rose and handed it to her, and she buried her face in the scent. "Thank you."

Being with him was... how could she describe it? Like being wooed by the stars.

With all the magnificent buildings they passed, she had to ask. "What's your favorite style of architecture here?"

His smile was a caress. "I love it all. Because we have nothing like it back home. The ancient stones, the history—and then the mix with the new, like the Dancing House. But wait until I take you to the Žižkov Television Tower. Amazing views—but most impressive are the babies crawling up the tower."

Her eyes widened. "Babies?"

"The display is by a Czech artist, David Černý. They're faceless, meant to symbolize humanity's relationship with technology. There used to be an exhibit of them in Palm Springs."

She wrinkled her nose. "I'm not sure I'd like faceless babies."

His lips curved. "You'll have to see them at night."

"I'll trust your judgment." She smirked.

Then he asked, "What do you like best?"

Making love with you. But she kept that to herself. "It's hard to choose. I love everything here." Then she gave him a wide grin. "Especially the goulash."

The boat drifted past Kampa Island. "It's called Prague's Venice, with its canals and mills and medieval houses," he said like a tour guide.

As they floated by Střelecký Island, he got them coffees and slices of *Maroška* cake, and she gobbled up every delicious bite of the honey cake.

Then she sat up straight, giddy with delight. "Look—it's the Dancing House!"

Kent grinned. "We really need to go there at night. It's lit up with all the colors of the rainbow. You'd love it."

Yes, with him, she would.

It was so relaxing drifting along the river. The boat's guide pointed out the spires of a cathedral on a hill above the river. "That is Vyšehrad," the man said, "an ancient fortress which was the seat of many Czech princes."

But of course, Kent was her real tour guide. "What you see is actually the Basilica of St. Peter and St. Paul. It was originally Romanesque, but after a fire and over many years, it was rebuilt in the Gothic style. What you see now is neo-Gothic, so late eighteen hundreds."

"You know everything about architecture, don't you?"

He laughed, the sound filling her heart. "You can't never know everything about architecture. There's always something new to learn. New places to see. New buildings to admire."

She gazed at him for a long moment. "Why did you become an architect?"

He shrugged. "It just seemed natural. I had one of those old Erector sets as a kid. And LEGO blocks—back before they had themed sets. You just built cabins or designed your own thing. I loved it. Sandcastles on the beach. Bridges in my sandbox." He laughed. "Back then, I could never make my bridges stand up. So I started cutting the bottoms out of old buckets, burying them in the sand as tunnels, then covering them with roads for my Matchbox cars."

He must have been an adorable child, just like his grandsons.

Then he asked, "Why did you want to become a teacher?"

She ran her fingers through her hair. "I don't know. I just enjoyed shaping young minds. Movies make it sound like kids hate school, hate their teachers, hate homework. But not all kids are like that. I always found a few who were eager to learn. And that made it rewarding."

"I bet some of your students still email you."

She bit her lip to keep from smiling too broadly. "Yes, some do. I love hearing about how their lives turned out."

"Lives you helped shape."

Then he leaned close and kissed her. A closed-mouth, tantalizing kiss that promised so much more. If there hadn't been children racing around the deck, she might have opened her lips to him. For now, she savored the sweet, tender touch.

THE CRUISE HAD BEEN LOVELY, ESPECIALLY WITH KENT BY her side. After they'd exited the boat and walked down the dock, Elise asked, "Do you want to take a boat to Kampa?"

Kent was already scrolling through his phone. "According to this, Kampa Island isn't really an island. It's separated from the shore by a canal." He pointed to the opposite side of Charles Bridge. "It says here that if we cross over, there's a set of stairs down to the water level. Then we can follow a path to the island."

"Let's go for it." She slipped her hand into the crook of his elbow, loving how natural it felt.

Entwined that way as they crossed Charles Bridge, tourists skirted around them rather than trying to break their link. It didn't matter that it was a weekday—crowds still swarmed the bridge. Finding the stairs easily, they left the throng of tourists behind.

"Thank God most people haven't figured this out." Kent turned tour guide again as they wandered. They paused at the historic Grand Priory Mill along the canal. The wheel no longer powered anything, yet it kept turning, mossy and creaking.

Elise laughed and pointed. "There's a leprechaun sitting on the end of the dock." The statue of a squat little green man with googly eyes puffed on a curly pipe.

Of course, Kent had the answer, knowing a little about everything—though she'd seen him scrolling on his phone earlier. "That is a water demon called *Vodník*." He pronounced it carefully, Vod-neek. "He demands respect." He looked at Elise, a gleam in his eye. "Better kiss me quick before he hexes us."

He pulled her close and kissed her. Not a sweet peck like on the boat, this was deliciously open-mouthed, tongues tangling, pulse racing, skin heating. They broke apart only when they heard voices approaching.

Kent murmured, "Watch out. Vodnik could have used a love hex."

"Like *Love Potion Number Nine?*" she teased, humming a few bars of the song.

He winked as a family arrived to see the water demon, two young children racing down the dock to get their picture taken with him.

Strolling further, they found the Lock Bridge over the canal, hung with hundreds of colorful locks glittering with lovers' promises. "We should have brought a lock," she said with a sad moue.

"Next time," he said, as if there would be a next time.

From there, they found the John Lennon Wall, a mural painted after he'd died and added to over the years. The pictures Elise took included all the other tourists gazing at the artistic wall, but getting a photo with no one in it would have taken forever.

Then Kent found the narrowest street in Prague—Zlatá Ulička, a quirky passage wedged between two buildings and controlled by a traffic light. He pushed the button, and when they got the green, they squeezed in. At first, it was reasonably wide, but as they descended, the alley grew so narrow Elise's shoulders barely fit, and Kent had to turn sideways. At the bottom, it opened onto a stone patio belonging to a small restaurant that faced the water.

"Well, that was exciting," he said.

She patted his arm. "It's all about the adventure, getting there, not what's at the bottom."

The restaurant was closed, maybe for a midday siesta. They pushed the traffic button again and waited, this time for the family from the mill to get through.

The older boy, about Marek's age, grumbled in a clear American accent, "There's nothing down here."

His little brother stared longingly at the locked restaurant door while the parents smiled apologetically at Elise and Kent. Now that the light had changed, Elise and Kent squeezed back up the narrow street. By the time they reached the top, Elise was breathless—not from the climb, but from being pressed so close to Kent the whole way.

They meandered through Kampa Park, coming across a long row of glowing yellow penguins on a narrow pier in the canal.

Elise counted aloud. "There are thirty-four."

She snapped pictures of the penguins with Charles Bridge in the background.

"That's a great one." Kent's approving nod over the photo made her glow.

They also found David Černý's huge sculptures of faceless crawling babies dotting the landscape. They were as tall as she was. "I thought you said they were on the television tower." She gave Kent a look of mock disgust, as if he should have known.

He merely shrugged. "Now you get to see them here too. Think of it as a preview."

The babies unsettled her. Crawling on all fours, their heads smooth except for what looked like a slot or a port where a face should have been, struck her as eerie, Orwellian. "Slaves to technology instead of the Ministry of Truth," she murmured. Perhaps that was exactly what the artist intended.

Walking on, they passed the elegant Liechtenstein Palace with its baroque facade, strolled across Kampa Square, and ducked into the Kampa Museum's courtyard before stopping for coffee at Mlýnská Kavárna—the Mill Café—housed in another old mill with its waterwheel still turning.

Kent held her hand across the table. "I've got a great idea. We could stop at that little produce shop we passed earlier, buy some fruit and bread and have a picnic in the park." He paused, then added, "Or... we could do a dinner cruise."

She laughed softly. "We already did a cruise. I'd love a picnic."

No cruises, no crowds, just the two of them.

Elise smiled, heart tumbling. Nothing in Prague could be more perfect.

THEY DINED ON FRESH BREAD, FRUIT, CURED MEATS, creamy cheeses, and sun-warmed tomatoes with crisp cucumber. But what Kent wanted most to dine on was Elise.

He wanted to give her romance. Between the cruise on the Vltava, their wander through Kampa Island's historic corners, and now this picnic on the grass in Kampa Park, he hoped he was succeeding.

When he kissed a trace of mayonnaise from her lips, she set down her open-face sandwich and leaned closer. Her kiss was sweet, but he felt the banked fire between them as she moaned. Tangling his fingers in her hair, he opened his mouth and claimed her. He could kiss her like this forever.

He might have laid her back on the fragrant grass if they hadn't risked turning their afternoon into a public spectacle.

Against his will, the kiss had to end—or he'd never be able to stop.

Looking almost dazed as he drew away, she pressed her fingers to her lips. "I don't know how you do that to me—make me forget where we are."

He made sure his smile was deliciously wicked. "That's exactly what I want."

They'd had two nights together, and he was sure a million more would never be enough.

The sun dipped toward the horizon. Sitting so close their bodies touched, hands entwined, they watched the sky melt into blues, purples, and molten oranges, light spilling across the river and the towers of Charles Bridge. So entranced, neither thought of taking a photo.

Kent knew it would live in his memory forever, this day, this evening, this sunset. And this woman.

As twilight deepened, the gas lamps along Charles Bridge winked on. Leaving Kampa, they threaded their way through the crowd still lingering on the bridge, then turned to admire Prague Castle glowing against the night sky.

"It's beautiful," she whispered.

But she was even more beautiful. Suddenly, all he wanted was to get her back to the house—into his arms, into his bed.

He leaned close, burying his face in her hair, breathing her in, and whispered against her ear, "I need to make love to you again."

She didn't look at him. She simply took his hand and began walking, tugging him along until he came abreast of her and their fingers laced. Need tightened his throat, and words felt impossible, but he loved knowing she wanted this as much as he did.

Inside the house, they ran up the stairs, shedding pieces of clothing along the way. Her shoes lay somewhere below, his shirt abandoned on the landing. By the time they reached his room, she wore only a bra and panties, and he was down to his boxers. He swept her into his arms as if he were twenty again, and she wrapped her legs around his waist, her heels tapping against his butt. They kissed hungrily all the way to the bed, where he lowered her onto it, followed her down, and braced himself above her.

She sifted her fingers through his hair, held his head between her palms, and murmured, "I need to taste you before we do anything else."

Kissing him once, she pulled back so quickly he knew the taste she wanted wasn't just his lips. He rolled onto his back. "I'm all yours." He meant it in more ways than one—if only she knew.

She kissed her way down, licking one nipple, sucking the

other, then sliding lower across the planes of his stomach as her hands tugged at his boxers. When she freed him, he stood tall and ready.

She didn't devour him right away, though every nerve in him begged for it. Holding him gently, she traced his crown with her tongue. A shudder shot up his spine and fogged his brain. Her mouth closed over him, just the tip, a teasing suction paired with the slow swirl of her tongue. Instinct urged him to roll her beneath him, but the soft slide of her lips, her hand moving with perfect pressure, held him in place. Then she took him deep until he brushed her throat. The sensation nearly undid him. Only sheer will, and his fists clenching in the comforter, kept him from spilling.

If she did that again, he was lost.

HIS TASTE WAS LIKE THE FINEST WINE, THE SWEETEST FRUIT, the truly decadent treat she'd craved all day.

As Elise felt his body tremble, she drew back to the tip, teasing him with her tongue. She didn't want him to finish yet—she wanted him inside her, wanted to go over the edge together. And she let him slip free of her mouth. Reaching for the packet in the drawer, she slid the condom in a practiced tease.

His voice rough with need, he murmured, "You're driving me nuts doing that."

The words sent a fresh jolt of desire through her. She loved that he couldn't hold back what he felt. Straddling him, she guided him to her entrance and whispered, "I need to ride you."

Then she sank down onto him.

12

She was so exquisite astride him, like a conquering Valkyrie.

Could love truly find you twice in a lifetime? Or was this just lust, wrapped in glorious sentiment?

He couldn't be sure—then sensation rocketed through his body, and he could think of nothing else but how she made him feel. The faster she rode, the more of his mind he lost. Grabbing her hips, he rose to meet her, plunging high inside her.

She moaned, then threw her head back and cried out. Convulsing around him, she dragged his own climax from deep inside him. He thrust hard, driving through every mutual quake of their bodies. His release harmonized with hers, seeming to go on and on, until finally she slumped against him, her light laughter warm at his ear. The sound was pure reaction, joy bubbling up from within her.

He held her tightly, the last throes of his orgasm easing into slight jerks inside her. Then he collapsed boneless against the bed, his arms falling away to stretch out to the side.

Her whispered "Oh my God" matched his feelings exactly.

Could this be more than lust?

It was too soon to tell, and yet—he had emotions about her. She wasn't just a woman for a quick tumble, or a few dates ending up in bed. He'd had that in the years since Gail died, moments of mutual satisfaction. But this was different.

This felt like connection.

Still lying on top of him, she clung like a limpet, her weight barely there. And he didn't want to let her go. Not when he was still inside her, not when his body still quaked with aftershocks. Not when she still straddled him.

She laughed softly. "That was so good." She pushed up on her elbows, looking down at him, her hair falling like a curtain of silk around her face. "Where did you learn to do that?"

"That was all you," he murmured, breathless. "I should ask how *you* did *that*."

Her eyes were the sweetest blue, almost guileless, as she whispered, "Thank you."

He finally slid his arms around her, stroking his hands up and down the smooth length of her back. "What are you thanking me for?"

"For the way you make me feel. I haven't felt like this in years. Not since—" She caught herself, shook her head, her hair brushing his chest. "Never mind. It doesn't matter. I just... haven't felt like this in forever."

He wanted to say he hadn't either. Not since those times with Gail when they'd taken advantage of the empty house after Amanda left—loving the freedom of making love in any room whenever the mood struck. But that had been long ago. Since then, there'd been sickness, and loss, grief and loneliness.

"You've banished all the heartache," he said softly.

She dropped down to hug him tightly. "I'm sorry for everything you've lost," she whispered.

Instead of telling her it wasn't her fault, he simply held her, letting her warmth fill him.

They drifted to sleep like that, until he woke again to find she'd slid to the side. He rose to the bathroom, cleaned up, and disposed of the remnants of their lovemaking.

When he returned, she was awake, eyes glinting in the faint light spilling through the curtains. Beyond the window, the Vltava shimmered silver beneath the moon, Petřín Tower lit like a beacon against the sky.

"I'm starving," she said, a teasing spark in her gaze.

For a second he wondered if she meant sex, but then her stomach rumbled and he laughed. "I'm starving too. Let's see what we can find to make sandwiches."

Down in the kitchen, the soft amber glow of a single lamp lit the tiled walls. They found some of Cook's leftovers, and the scent of roast beef mingled with the faint aroma of coffee left from earlier. They shared one sandwich instead of making two, passing bites back and forth. Kent leaned over to kiss away a tiny smear of mustard at the corner of her mouth, then laughed when she caught his lower lip between her teeth.

Without letting her go, he lifted her onto the table beside their crumb-filled plate. She wore only his shirt, the hem brushing her thighs. As he set her down, he slid his hands beneath her, the fabric riding up to her hips.

"What are you doing?" she whispered, pulling back just enough to meet his eyes.

"I'm hungry for more than a sandwich."

He bent, mouth tracing a path down her belly, then lower. Spreading her thighs, he found her slick center, circling the sweet, hardened nub that beckoned him. She tipped her head back, a low groan rising in her throat.

Hooking a chair with his foot, he dragged it close and sat to feast on her. She lay back on the table, legs draped over his shoulders, knees falling open to give him full access. Fingers, tongue, lips—he used them all, making her writhe on the butcher-block top while the city lights glittered through the kitchen window.

SHE'D BARELY FLOATED BACK FROM THE HIGH BEFORE SHE propped herself up on her elbows. He was the best since— well, Kent was the best ever. She reached into the pocket of the shirt she'd stolen and held out a condom.

He laughed, the rich sound filling the kitchen. "I thought you were starving for food," he teased.

"I was. But now I'm starving for this."

She grinned as he took the packet, tearing it with his teeth, something in the gesture purely, wonderfully masculine.

He rolled it on, then pulled her hips forward on the table. She lay back, watching the play of shadows across his face as he slid into her—slow, deliberate, never deep, just teasing with short strokes that drove her mad.

His eyes darkened to midnight blue until she could barely see the iris. "Touch yourself for me," he murmured.

And she did, because he wanted it, because she needed it. The touch magnified every sensation. She clenched involuntarily, drawing a groan from him, but still he kept that slow rhythm, urging her higher while her fingers moved faster and faster. Her climax gathered like a storm, all heat and lightning.

He felt it too, and he took her then, hard and fast, their bodies slamming together, the quake of her release shaking her apart as her cries filled the night. He growled, burying himself deep, pounding once, twice more before shuddering with his own release.

When he collapsed on her, she welcomed his weight, holding him close as though she'd never let go.

※

Kent couldn't quite wrap his mind around how amazing the night had been. Elise was everything any man could want, and somehow, he'd stumbled across her later in life. She'd revived his youthful lustiness. He had no idea who to thank for that—the universe, God, maybe even Gail, who had given him permission to find love again before she passed.

Amanda's permission was still pending. Funnily enough, his daughter was the tougher nut to crack. But he'd get there.

He and Elise showered together, lingering under the spray until the water turned cold, then laughed as they toweled off. After a short trip to a nearby grocery for supplies, they enjoyed a delicious breakfast, stealing kisses across the table —a lovely reminder of exactly what they'd done on that table in the middle of the night—before heading out for the day.

"Where are we going, dear tour guide?" Elise asked, her face splitting into a beautiful smile. Kent wanted to kiss her right then—or better yet, drag her back to the house and have his deliciously wicked way with her again. But he didn't want to tempt fate, just in case the universe frowned on greed.

"Petřín Hill," he said. Beyond Malá Strana—Lesser Town —Petřín offered sweeping views of Prague from its tower, and its gardens promised the romantic ambience he was after.

At the base of the hill, he asked, "Want to hike up or take the funicular?"

She tapped a finger to her lips, considering. "Decisions,

decisions." Then she flashed him another glorious smile. "Let's take the funicular up. We can walk back down."

Kent liked the idea of sitting close, breathing in her scent, letting it remind him of everything they'd shared the night before.

Ensconced in the cable car, he didn't mind the slow climb. Through the windows, wooded paths wound upward through a tapestry of autumn gold and forest green, dotted with benches and stone walls. He could imagine strolling hand in hand back down later.

Beside him, Elise inhaled the fresh air deeply. "I've never thought to ask—have you been to Prague before? With Tomás being from here?"

"I haven't been since Amanda met Tomás," he said. "But I came years ago, just after college. That's why I have to look up so much; I just can't remember it all. I was here working on the restoration of an old hotel not long after the Velvet Revolution."

"Velvet because it was the non-violent overthrow of Communism? 1989, right?"

He held her hand as they remembered the historic moment together.

The higher they rose, the more the bustle below faded, replaced by the quiet woods of Petřín Hill.

"There was so much restoration work happening back then," he continued. "Not just here, but all across Europe. I even worked on a church in Dresden. It was bombed during the war and lay in rubble for sixty years. We found the original limestone quarry, matched the stone, and painstakingly rebuilt everything. I couldn't stay for the entire project, but I went back to see it finished."

Elise squeezed his hand, her touch warm. "That was amazing of you."

"It was a labor of love." He remembered the pride he'd felt as the church rose from ruin.

"When we were in Dresden for one of Tomás's concerts, I wish I'd known. I would've loved to see it."

"I'll take you," he promised.

Maybe she thought it was a throwaway line, because she didn't react to it, didn't ask if he meant it. But he did, with all his heart.

Close to the top, the funicular passed over a crenellated stone wall snaking along the hillside, and Elise pointed. "What's that?"

"That's the Hunger Wall," Kent said. This morning, he'd looked up what there was to see, when he'd thought of bringing her to Petřín Hill. When she raised a questioning brow, he added, "Charles the Fourth built it in the fourteenth century. Legend says it wasn't just for defense, that it also gave work to the poor during a famine. Thus feeding the hungry."

"I didn't know kings could be that benevolent," she mused.

"Neither did I," he said with a grin.

At the summit, Petřín Hill was quieter than Kent expected, though a small line had formed outside the Mirror Maze, its facade like a toy castle.

"Let's climb the tower first," he suggested. They bought a joint ticket for both the tower and the maze.

From below, the sixty-meter Petřín Lookout Tower gleamed against the blue sky, its latticework echoing the Eiffel Tower's grace.

"Lift or stairs?" Kent asked.

Elise tilted her head back to take in all the steps of the open-air spiral staircase—noting the sign that said there were 299 steps—then smiled slyly. "Let's take the lift. We'll walk down."

He slipped an arm around her waist and whispered in her ear, "Do I sense a theme here?"

She hugged him close, her body molding to his. "I'm saving my energy for later," she murmured, her voice husky.

Kent laughed. "I hope that means something really good for me."

"It means good things for us both," she said as they stepped apart, her eyes sparkling.

The more intrepid visitors took the stairs, but the tiny lift was full as Kent and Elise rode with another couple to the top, the elevator grinding noisily the whole way. They stepped out onto the narrow circular platform into a fantastic view of Prague—the Štefánik Observatory, the red roofs of Malá Strana in the late morning sun, the dome of St. Nicholas Church, the pale stone of Prague Castle. The twin spires of the neo-Gothic Basilica of St. Peter and St. Paul at Vyšehrad pierced a sky so clear they could see far into the gentle hills of the Bohemian countryside. Even the crowds along Charles Bridge were visible, tiny figures traipsing along its ancient stones. The Vltava wound through the city, reflecting the sun's golden light, and in the park just below them, laughter and music drifted up from the old wooden carousel.

If they'd been alone, Kent would have kissed her right there. The beauty of the sight—and of her—pressed at his chest. Instead, he slid an arm around her shoulders and held her close as they strolled slowly around the platform, sidestepping other sightseers to drink in the full 360-degree panorama, taking long minutes to appreciate it, to take pictures of every aspect.

"Prague is known as the city of a hundred spires," he said. "Let's count."

"I couldn't even begin to count," she answered, laughing. "There's got to be far more than just a hundred."

The spires of Prague filled the horizon, on churches,

towers, domes, even skyscrapers. Indeed, there were far more than a hundred and far more than they could count.

A group of chattering schoolchildren tumbled out of the elevator, and Kent glanced at Elise. "Got all the photos you want?"

When she nodded, he caught her hand, and together they started down the narrow spiral staircase. His knees creaked, and he chuckled. "You were right not to walk all the way up. It's hard enough going down."

She laughed below him on the stairs, the sound carrying up like music.

Back on the ground, they stopped at the carousel to admire the beautifully painted wooden horses and the laughter of the young children as they rode round and round to the carnival-style music. They read a nearby sign stating that the carousel—which was truly a work of art—was two hundred years old.

The square around the Mirror Maze had grown busier. Elise waited for a gap in the crowd to snap a picture of the Church of St. Lawrence—its modest baroque facade standing out against the sky. The sign explained that it had begun life as a Romanesque chapel before its baroque rebirth. Though it had nowhere near the grandeur of St. Vitus, the small church held its own quiet charm.

"All the churches seem to get reshaped each time a new style comes in," she mused.

"Doesn't everything?" She was reshaping him.

"I guess it does," she agreed. "Let's try the maze. I don't think the line will get any shorter."

The queue buzzed with excited children. The maze's castle facade, complete with two turrets and faux drawbridge, looked like something from a fairy tale. Past the turnstile, red-rope curtains with golden tassels opened to a hall of mirrors, pillars, and arches that fractured every reflection.

Elise gripped his hand. "Don't lose me in here by mistaking me for one of my reflections."

A small girl in a pink jacket hugged a pillar, multiplied into five identical versions of herself in the mirrors. Elise sighed with pleasure as she captured the perfect shot on her camera phone. At certain angles, the reflections seemed endless, corridors of glass stretching toward infinity.

Elise bit her lip. "I need just the right angle with no one but us in it."

Resting his hands on her shoulders, he guided her until the mirrors caught only them, an endless echo of two people standing close. Lifting her phone, she whispered, "You're perfect."

He brushed a kiss against her ear. "You're the perfect one."

Desire nudged at him—a kiss here, surrounded by infinite glass, would feel eternal. But families wound their way through the maze, stealing the moment, and instead he urged Elise through the mirrored labyrinth.

They finally emerged into the central hall, where a diorama depicted a battle on Charles Bridge during the Thirty Years' War. Elise read aloud, "The Swedish army tried to seize the bridge." She tipped her head, teasing, "The Vikings?"

Kent grinned. "Close, but the Vikings were a lot earlier—and mostly Danish and Norwegian." He remembered that the Thirty Years' War had raged in the mid-1600s.

They wandered into the Hall of Laughter. Elise's giggles rang out as warped mirrors stretched them tall as beanpoles, or squashed them short and round. Kent laughed until his sides hurt. When they finally stepped outside, their laughter still clung to the air.

She caught his hand, drawing him near until only inches

separated them. "That was so much fun. I haven't been in a fun house since I was a kid."

He kissed her then, exactly as he'd wanted to for the past hour, uncaring about children or families nearby. He only wanted to linger, tasting her, wanting her, holding her there in the sun.

Over her shoulder, an older couple paused, smiling before strolling away hand in hand, their heads bent together. Kent imagined their kiss had offered the pair a small rebirth—a promise that love and desire never had to fade.

ELISE'S SIDES STILL ACHED WITH LAUGHTER, AND HER LIPS tingled. The Mirror Maze had been delightful, but Kent's kiss eclipsed everything.

Yet there was more to see atop the hill, and plenty of time for kisses later. It was only their second day, but she felt time ticking down until Tomás, Amanda, and the boys returned, ending this idyll.

She wished it could last, but if it did, she would eventually have to tell Kent everything—about Nick, about the reckless things she'd done when she was young. Couples shared their truths, but she couldn't risk changing the way he looked at her.

Pushing away the thought, she took his hand and led him toward the Štefánik Observatory, then on to the Kinský Summer Palace, now a museum of Czech folk culture. Inside, glass cases displayed hand-embroidered blouses, jewel-bright vests, and full skirts heavy with ribbon and lace. She lingered over the Moravian bridal outfit, a crisp white blouse with puffed sleeves, a scarlet bodice embroidered in gold thread, and a full skirt layered with patterned aprons, each hem edged in delicate lace. A crown of silk flowers, tiny beads, and streaming ribbons gleamed behind the glass, as if waiting for a bride to lift it onto her head.

"When I was a little girl," she said, smiling, "Red Rose Tea used to tuck little figurines inside the boxes. I collected the ones dressed in traditional costumes from around the world." She pointed to the Moravian bridal dress. "I remember this one."

"Did you keep them?"

She shook her head. "I wish I had. I looked them up once—people sell them on eBay for ridiculous amounts. Five hundred dollars for what used to be free in a tea box." Her eyes softened with nostalgia. "They kept putting surprises in the boxes for years—animals, sea creatures, and all sorts of different things."

Kent strolled with her down memory lane. "I had G.I. Joes. Then I went through a space phase. I was sure I'd be an astronaut."

"I thought you were always into building—Erector sets, LEGO."

He laughed. "That was my first love. Astronaut dreams lasted only one summer, when we launched homemade rockets in a field."

"I'm glad you're not one-dimensional," she said, bumping his shoulder playfully.

Behind the summer palace, they found a cozy café. Along with steaming cups of coffee, they bought warm savory pies—one filled with creamy mushrooms and sharp cheese, the other with spiced pork, onions, and fresh marjoram.

They carried their treats into the Rose Garden, where autumn blooms nodded in the breeze, a flush of pink and white. Low boxwood hedges outlined the winding paths, and clusters of late roses spilled over their borders—velvety crimson, blush ivory, and a coppery orange that caught the sunlight like flame. The air was fragrant with a soft mingling of honeyed petals and damp earth, touched with the faint tang of fallen leaves. Bees worked lazily among the flowers, and somewhere a fountain burbled, its trickle blending with birdsong from the nearby trees.

Settling on a bench among the scented flowers, the distant sound of bells filled the afternoon. Elise put her hand on Kent's arm. "Listen. The bells are actually playing a song." The sound was beautiful in the garden's quiet. "What is that, do you think?"

Kent, always looking every up—and always finding the answer—took out his phone. "It's Loreto Church. Twenty-seven bells play the song every hour between nine and six."

"They're lovely. Someone has to ring them all like that every hour?"

He kept reading. "No. It's what's called a carillon. Sort of like a player piano, where it plays off a cylinder with little pegs."

"It's amazing. But I haven't heard those bells before, if you say they play throughout the day."

"The church is close by, it's a clear, calm day, and we're up high," he offered as explanation.

As the bells serenaded them, then tolled the hour, they ate their feast, feeding each other bites, laughing when flakes of pastry clung to their lips.

"I'm going to get fat if we keep eating like this," Elise teased, licking away a crumb.

Kent shook his head, eyes warm. "We've been burning plenty of calories at night. And I promise we'll burn off more tonight."

With no one else nearby, she leaned in and kissed him, savoring the blend of buttery pastry and the sweet-spicy scent of his skin.

Voices drifted closer, and she drew back with a smile. "I'll hold you to that."

13

Though the late lunch satisfied her hunger for food, Kent's kiss made her crave more of his touch, his lips on hers, his taste in her mouth. She couldn't wait until they were alone again. And yet there was so much more of the day to enjoy.

They began the trek down the woodland path, passing a few people along the way who were climbing up. The surrounding forest held the music of birds and the chatter of squirrels in the trees. The bucolic atmosphere soothed her, as did Kent's occasional touch on her back—perhaps to steady her. Though she felt in her bones that the brush of his fingers had more to do with needing connection.

She needed it just as much.

He created a hunger that seemed to well up from deep within her. She'd thought about Nick far more in these past few days. It was because of Kent—because she kept comparing her feelings then and now. Though it had been thirty-five years, she remembered clearly those crazy, heady days. With the wisdom of age, she saw they'd been a fantasy, and Nick had been a man she'd built up in her mind, his true self nothing like the figure she'd imagined.

But Kent was no fantasy. He was exactly who he claimed to be. She had no need to invent anything about him.

And that made him irresistible.

At the bottom of the hill, they came to the Strahov Monastery and its famed library. Kent stood mesmerized by the architecture, and he whispered, as if in awe, "Baroque perfection."

Inside, the beauty of the library stole her breath, though the room was roped off to keep tourists from trampling its gorgeous flooring. Ancient books lined the wooden shelves that climbed to the second story. Barely discernible spiral staircases in the corners led to the second level, where the stacks of books reached almost to the ceiling. The balcony's intricately carved balustrade was a work of art in itself. Above it all, the frescoed ceiling—cherubs, saints, and swirling clouds—stole the last of the air she had left.

"It's stunning." The words seemed small compared to its magnificence.

Visitors spoke in reverent whispers. The clatter of a wooden ladder rolled along the floor, then a young woman—a librarian, she assumed—climbed its rungs, stretching up for a book.

As they stepped outdoors onto the monastery terrace, the view weakened her knees. The city and the river lay before them in a sea of red-tiled roofs, the Vltava catching light in a thousand ripples, the city's bridges arching over the water, and its famed spires rising skyward. While the panorama from the lookout tower had amazed and delighted her, this closer view—the warmth of the red tile, the water's sparkle, the green domes of the churches—almost eclipsed what she'd seen higher on the hill.

She slipped her hand into Kent's—or perhaps he'd taken

hers—and they stood like that, hand in hand, for long, precious moments. Then she raised her phone and snapped a picture, though she knew no image could do this view justice.

From the monastery, they wandered the streets and alleys, turning corner after corner to find another historic building, a quiet cloister, a statue bathed in late sunlight. They paused by the river and watched boats drift past, their wakes shimmering on the water. A busker's violin floated across the embankment, its music mingling with the scent of roasted almonds from a nearby stall. The faint perfume of linden trees lingered in the air, and the soft slap of waves against the stone embankment made the whole world feel hushed, as if the city itself were holding its breath. They shared a koláč pastry, its dough rich with sweet cheese and tart fruit, and later stood among the crowd in the Old Town Square, watching the Astronomical Clock once again as it struck five and the carved figures danced their timeless routine.

Kent lifted her hand to his lips. "I fancy a bowl of goulash. How about you?"

When she gave a quick nod, he led her toward a restaurant they saw kitty-corner from the clock. The goulash was thick and fragrant, rich with beef and sweet paprika. Steam rose from the deep bowl, carrying a hint of onion and caraway. The accompanying dumplings were perfection as she soaked up the stew's glossy gravy. Around them, the restaurant hummed with quiet voices and the clink of glassware, and a faint melody of Czech folk music played somewhere in the background. The warmth inside contrasted with the cool dusk beyond the windows, wrapping them in a cocoon of light and spice.

Outside once again, twilight had deepened, lanterns flickering on in the square. Kent took her hand and guided her quickly along the cobbled street. "We should be able to see the Dancing House it all its colors now."

The Dancing House was a mile away, but after the delicious goulash, she felt energized for the walk. They strolled hand in hand, the crisp evening air brushing their faces. The clatter of tram wheels on cobblestones mingled with the occasional laughter of passersby, and the warm fragrance of fresh pastries accented the aroma of brewing coffee drifting from open cafés. The city's lights gleamed on the stones under their feet, and the muted hum of conversation in multiple languages created a comforting chorus.

They stopped on the sidewalk across from the Dancing House, its facade lit up in all the colors of the rainbow, pulsing like liquid light against the darkening sky.

It was mesmerizing, and Kent tilted her toward him. "Do you see how the colors bring it to life?"

Elise thought *he* brought her to life. For years, since she'd divorced Nick, she'd been living a half life. Or maybe this feeling was Prague—the warmth of the old buildings juxtaposed against the crisp night air and the delicate aroma of baked goods.

Kent leaned down and kissed her right there on the sidewalk. It was sweet and deliberate, but beneath it burned an undeniable fire.

After they'd drunk in the colors of the Dancing House, Kent asked, "Shall we go up to the television tower?" Then he smiled. "We can see the crawling babies. But I've also heard it has an amazing view."

"I'd love to see more crawling babies," she said with a slight shiver of apprehension.

They could have walked back to the row house and picked up the car, but Kent hailed a cab instead. The line to enter the Žižkov Television Tower wasn't long. Elise had to admit the enormous babies crawling up the tower were both playful and surreal—as long as she didn't focus on their faceless heads. Soon, they were ascending in the crowded elevator, the city shrinking beneath them.

At the top, the view was breathtaking. Lights sparkled across Prague like a sea of stars. The Vltava wound through the city, its surface reflecting the glow of bridges, street lamps, and illuminated facades. Prague Castle perched majestically on the hill with the twisting streets of Malá Strana below, and Petřín Lookout Tower gleamed in the night, soaring above St. Nicholas Church. Of course, Kent had to look up and identify all the visible landmarks, which Elise wouldn't have done, and yet it was good to put a name to what she could see. The Church of the Most Sacred Heart of Our Lord cast a golden glow across the landscape, and the magnificent plain of the National Memorial on Vitkov Hill stretched out below the taller television tower.

The neon reflections in the tower's glass added a dream-like shimmer to everything. Because of the glass, photographs couldn't capture the scene's magic, but she would carry it all in her mind forever.

Just as she would carry these days with Kent tucked safely in her heart.

KENT MADE LOVE TO HER LONG INTO THE NIGHT, BUT HE savored their days together just as much. He treasured waking with her in his arms, memorizing the curve of her shoulder, the warmth of her skin pressed to his, and the soft weight of the covers over them.

The next day, he surprised her with a tour of the Lobkowicz Palace, their fingers intertwined as they studied painting after painting. He loved art in every form—painting, sculpture, music, architecture—and she seemed to delight in learning alongside him.

In the afternoon, he took her to the Mucha Museum across from the Old Palace Hotel. Elise admired the delicate art nouveau lines, the intricate floral motifs, and the dreamy, elongated figures that the Czech painter was famous for.

"I love the art deco style," she said, tracing a finger just above the ornate designs.

They lingered over each piece, fascinated, and in the gift shop, she bought a book on Alphonse Mucha to study his work further. She added a souvenir pen with a Mucha design to her purchase.

Whenever she used it, Kent hoped it would remind her of this day with him, of all their days together.

Across the street at the Old Palace Hotel, they shared a Czech-style BLT topped with a perfectly fried egg. The aroma of fresh bread, sizzling egg, and cured bacon made his mouth water, though nowhere near as much as she did.

"I'm going to make a BLT this way all the time," Elise declared, smiling. "The egg makes it totally delicious."

And *she* was delicious. She seemed to savor every moment —each kiss, touch, meal, and view. He didn't want any of this to end. His daughter's potential objections lingered in the back of his mind, but he would bring Amanda around. He deserved happiness. Now that Amanda and Tomás were married, it was his turn.

After another night of beautiful lovemaking, the following morning, Kent suggested a visit to the Jewish Quarter. Elise hesitated. "We're ignoring the job we have to do. We've got to go through all the gifts and do some packing."

He pulled her into his arms. "We still have three days." With only three days, he needed to make the most of them. "We can get it done."

"I feel guilty. After all, that's why Amanda agreed to have me stay."

Amanda had wanted to send her home, but Kent refused.

What mattered was time with Elise—whether wandering through the Jewish Quarter, cruising on the river, or organizing gifts. He talked her into a stroll through the quarter's narrow, uneven streets paved in worn cobblestones. They admired its ancient synagogues, the engraved Hebrew lettering on their sandstone facades catching the light, and the Jewish Cemetery, with its moss-covered stones leaning at impossible angles. The sights gave him a profound sense of the city's layered history.

But finally, he allowed her to lead him back to the row house and the job they'd promised to do for Amanda.

Many of the gifts were extravagant, including a high-end espresso machine gleaming in its box, fine china with delicate gold filigree, and other treasures wrapped in colorful paper.

"Do they have an espresso machine at home?" Elise asked.

Kent nodded. "Yes. But they could certainly use one here." He unboxed it, his movements precise so he wouldn't damage it. "In fact, I could go for a cappuccino right now."

Elise gathered the packing material, stuffing it in the empty box. "I'd love a latte."

Together, they set up the machine, following the instructions meticulously.

Then Kent searched on his phone for the best way to make the perfect coffee drink. With the hiss of steam frothing the milk, he inhaled the rich scent of ground coffee as the warm aroma filled the room. They tested, adjusted, tasted—and finally achieved perfection.

Seated on the veranda enjoying their coffees, she asked, "Do you always research everything to make sure you get it just right?"

He laughed. "I guess I do. I love research."

"And did you research how to make perfect love?" she teased.

He leaned close, breathing her in. "Oh no. That just takes

lots and lots of practice." Then he kissed her, a long, sweet, open-mouthed kiss, pulling back to murmur, "I think I need more practice right now. What do you think?"

It was another two hours before they returned to the mountain of wedding gifts. Elise cataloged each item and its giver so Amanda and Tomás could send proper thank-you notes. Late in the afternoon, they called Hana and Filip and invited themselves over, bringing the gifts Kent and Elise decided the newlyweds wouldn't need. Tomás's parents were delighted, immediately assigning treasures to their children.

The couple invited them to dinner, and Hana served *svíčková*, a rich beef stew in a creamy vegetable sauce, accompanied by the traditional bread dumplings. The scent of the cooked vegetables, herbs, and roasted beef filled the dining room. Elise complimented the meal, enjoying the lively conversation. She felt fully accepted, not just as an employee, but as part of this family's world, part of Kent's world.

"Will you continue as the boys' carer once you return home?" Hana asked.

Elise shook her head. "I'm not sure for how long. But Cynthia, their regular nanny, is recovering nicely from an operation, so I'll think she'll be returning soon."

The tour had been a whirlwind, and her time with the family was winding down. But it was Kent who filled all her thoughts, and perhaps her heart.

"Don't you want to do some more traveling?" Kent asked, referring to all their conversations.

Elise could only say, "I don't really know yet." Her mind couldn't stretch beyond the next few days. Soon they would return home, Cynthia would resume her role, and this perfect time with Kent would end.

And then... what?

They'd known each other less than two weeks—a mere drop in their long lives—but the thought of leaving him was unbearable. She had to steer the conversation to something more tolerable and turned to Hana. "Will you and Filip come to the US to visit, do you think?"

Hana shook her head. "It is such a long journey."

Filip interjected, "We will come. Tomás is often here, but we need to see our grandchildren more often."

Kent agreed. "They grow so fast."

"They do," Hana said with a sad sigh. "They're both so much bigger than the last time we saw them. So grown up." She squeezed Filip's hand.

Elise felt a pang—she would never have grandchildren. She had lost that chance long ago, when she'd lost Nick's baby. And when Amanda, Tomás, and the boys returned, it would be only a few days until they all flew home.

Then Kent would be gone from her life as well.

THE FOLLOWING DAY, KENT SUGGESTED A DRIVE TO ČESKÝ Krumlov, an old medieval town with picturesque views and stunning architecture.

He could have spent the whole day in bed with Elise—making love, eating cheese and bread, sleeping, and making love again—but they'd relegated their romantic interludes to the night. Besides, it gave him something to look forward to when they returned to the house.

Reaching Český Krumlov, a two-hour drive from Prague, they parked at the bottom of the hill and strolled up the old cobblestone road to the top. Kent pointed out features as they went. "During the Renaissance, they began painting their exterior walls to look like marble," he said, gesturing toward a building just outside the castle moat. "It was far cheaper, but of course it had to be redone every few years—just like we have to repaint now."

He loved how attentively Elise listened, as if she were drinking in every detail. As if she didn't think he was a know-it-all.

A tabby cat darted out from between two buildings and twined around Elise's ankles. She bent to scratch the cat, laughing softly as Kent snapped several photos.

Though there was evidence of bears in the moat—hence its name, the Bear Moat—the creatures weren't in sight today. Heaps of raw vegetables lay along the walls, downplaying the animals' carnivorous natures.

They wandered through the castle area, then, finding a steep set of stone stairs, they descended into the shopping district. The narrow lanes smelled faintly of woodsmoke and roasted nuts. Elise stopped at a jeweler's window, enchanted by a necklace of moldavite, the greenish tektite born of an ancient meteorite impact in Bohemia.

Standing beside her as she made her choice, Kent couldn't help saying, "Let me buy that for you."

She looked up, eyes wide, almost horrified by the offer and stammered her first words. "N-no, no." Then she took a steadying breath. "Thank you so much for the offer, but I really can't let you do that."

"Why not? I'd love to get you something."

But she was already shrugging her purse off her shoulder and pulling out her wallet, as if she wanted no reminders of their time together once they left Prague. His stomach tightened into a knot. Leaving the shop, he followed her down the hill, watching as she hurried ahead, as if running away. Running from him?

He caught up and took her hand. "I'd really like to give you a gift."

She shook her head, holding up the small bag. "This is the only souvenir I need."

Later they found a rustic tavern serving a platter of Czech delicacies, spiced roast chicken, tender pork, dumplings, tangy sauerkraut, and a little dish of creamy horseradish. The air was redolent with the scent of sweet caramelized onions.

Kent still couldn't let it go. Over a steaming bowl of garlic soup, he asked, "Why won't you let me give you something?"

She kept her gaze on the broth. "I've loved everything we've done together. You don't need to pay me back with a gift."

He wanted to pound the table, but kept his cool. "A gift isn't payment. What we do together is everything I could want or need. A gift is something I want to do, not some sort of transaction." He nearly added that it would be something for her to remember him by, but it sounded too final, as if they'd never see each other again after Prague.

He knew then, with absolute certainty, that he didn't want this to end.

Reaching for her hand, he didn't let her pull away. "I've never felt this way about anyone since my wife."

She still didn't meet his eyes, just stared at their joined hands. Maybe he'd said too much too soon. He softened his tone. "I would shower you with gifts if I could, but I can see you don't want that. But please let me buy one thing for you."

At last, she said softly, "Thank you. Maybe we'll see something else."

He kissed her knuckles. "I'd appreciate that."

Yet he wasn't sure they were past the moment.

14

It was just a gift. Elise didn't know why she'd made such a fuss. Except she kept thinking of it as a farewell present: *Thanks for a wonderful time; here's something to remember me by*.

They were quiet on the drive home. After lunch, he helped her clasp the necklace, and she sat fingering the cool stone—moldavite and garnets edged with silver. It wasn't only what a gift would represent, but also that she'd never told him the truth about herself.

He'd always been faithful to his wife. What would he think if he knew she'd been a home-wrecker, that she'd had an affair with her professor and broken up his marriage when she became pregnant? Nick had married her only because of the baby. And when she lost the baby, she'd lost everything.

She could never tell Kent any of it. And how could you be with someone if you couldn't tell them the truth about yourself—if you couldn't admit aloud what you'd done?

As they returned from Český Krumlov, she tried to leave all those negative thoughts behind. They dined at a small restaurant near the house. The windows glowed with candlelight, and the aroma of roast duck and cinnamon-laced apple strudel tantalized them. Elise let her thoughts quiet, determined not to ruin what remained of their time.

That night she made love to him with all the intensity in her soul, as if it might be the last time.

Afterward, Kent flopped onto his back, breathing hard, drawing her against him. "Jesus," he said on a rough exhale. Then, gathering another breath, he said, "That was so good, I damn near forgot my name." He laughed softly. "Good isn't a big enough word. Magnificent. Stupendous. Miraculous."

She smoothed a hand down his chest, savoring the feel of soft gray hair beneath her fingertips. "Cataclysmic," she added.

He laughed again, sliding his hand along her flank. "Aptly said."

They followed their favorite pattern, padding downstairs —he in sweats, she in his shirt—to raid the fridge. They fed each other tender slices of meat, cubes of cheese, rustic bread, and a sliver of honey cake before heading upstairs to begin again. Until finally they slept.

She woke in the morning light to the delicious feel of his arms around her.

A feeling she wasn't sure she could live without.

With morning came the realization that they had only one full day and night left together. Amanda, Tomás, and the boys would return tomorrow, and Kent felt time closing in on them despite his determination to see Elise again once they were home.

They spent the morning packing what they could, unsure of everything Amanda might want to take home or leave behind.

Having made a picnic in the late morning, they headed to a nearby park. Another glorious autumn day charmed them, with a few white clouds in a sky brushed with blue and the faint scent of rain on the breeze. A hush of leaves stirred in the trees overhead, their gold and russet edges whispering together.

They spread a blanket beneath a chestnut tree whose spiky husks had split, revealing shiny brown nuts. Kent opened the wicker basket and unwrapped bread still warm from the bakery they'd stopped at along the way. They'd packed slices of creamy cheese, smoked sausages, and sweet little koláče with pockets of plum jam.

Elise leaned back on her elbows, the sun painting her face in light, while a pair of sparrows hopped near the edge of the blanket, bold and hopeful. Kent plucked a small wildflower from the grass—a starry blue blossom—and tucked it behind Elise's ear.

As he leaned close, his breath stirred her hair. "You are so beautiful," he murmured, and he felt the warmth of her blush against his skin.

He longed to tell her how badly he needed to see her once they were home. But after yesterday—when even a gift had unsettled her—he dared not risk it. Still, he ached to know if she felt the same.

Later, they wandered hand in hand through narrow lanes and alleyways until they paused before a shop, its windows filled with delicate porcelain figurines. Afternoon light slanted through the glass, glinting off a shepherd girl with delicately rendered features surrounded by three lambs, the painted flowers on her skirt so fine they looked embroidered.

He wasn't sure Elise would have gone inside until he opened the door and ushered her in. Each piece on the glass shelves gleamed like a small treasure pulled from another century. The air inside the shop smelled faintly of lavender polish and old wood, and the floorboards creaked softly underfoot.

"She's gorgeous," Elise whispered, her gaze fixed on the shepherdess.

Holding her hand, Kent watched her face more than the figurine. "Do you like her?"

"She's absolutely stunning." Her voice was hushed, reverent.

The clerk, an older man with silver hair, lines marking his forehead and slanting down by his mouth, wandered closer, his hands held behind his back. "She is Meissen made in the early twentieth century," he said in English, obviously pegging them for American tourists. "Is she not exquisite?"

"Yes," Elise said almost in a whisper.

Kent added, "She's extraordinary."

He and Elise followed the old clerk to the sales counter, where the man pulled out a catalogue to show them how the markings on the figurine indicated its age.

Kent didn't balk or haggle when the old man named the price. "I'll take her."

"You've made a very special choice," the clerk said as he wrapped the figurine in tissue as fine as onion skin, sliding it into a sturdy box. A faint clink of porcelain echoed through the room, as though every piece on the shelves was acknowledging the shepherdess's departure.

Outside, Kent handed the bag to Elise. "She's yours," he said.

She gaped, and her words seemed to tangle on her tongue. "But... I can't... I can't take this. It's too much money."

He tightened his hold on her hand and began walking again, the bag swinging lightly between them. "You agreed earlier that I could buy a gift. This is the one I want to give you."

When she opened her mouth to protest again, he touched

a finger gently to her lips. "Please. I think she looks the way you must have as a young girl."

A laugh seemed to catch in her throat as she looked at him wide-eyed. "Don't be silly."

They had stopped in the middle of the sidewalk, a few pedestrians stepping around them without breaking stride. Kent bent and brushed a kiss against her lips, warm and soft. "Nothing would make me happier than to know this little shepherdess is in your home," he said quietly. "Let me do this. Please."

She looked at him for a long moment, biting her lip, all her indecision reflected in her eyes. But finally, she whispered," Thank you. She's so beautiful. I'll treasure her."

And his heart started beating again.

He wanted to add that he hoped to see the figurine often, to see *her* often. And for more than a few visits or nights in her bed. He would have said as much, but a flicker in her eyes —a frisson of fear that rippled into a faint shiver—held him back.

Maybe once they were back home in San Francisco, she'd be less cautious, less guarded. Instinct told him patience was the only way.

ELISE FELT AN EDGE OF DESPERATION AS THEY CAME together that night. Part of it was the shepherdess, a gift that seemed to signal the end. She'd taken it because he'd wanted so badly for her to have it.

But this was also their last night. Everything would be over soon, and she couldn't get enough of him. She threw off her clothes with abandon, and as their bodies slid together, she kissed him long and passionately, trying to memorize the taste of him.

Trailing kisses down his throat and chest, she drew a nipple into her mouth and bit lightly. He growled, tangling his fingers in her hair.

"Christ, you make me crazy," he murmured.

That was exactly what she wanted. Feathering kisses down the arrow of hair across his abdomen, she wrapped her hand around him and stroked. A guttural groan rose from his throat. Then she lost herself in the taste of him, closing her lips over his crown and taking him the way she'd learned he loved—with her hands and her lips and her tongue. She brought him to full hardness, kneeling between his legs, cupping and squeezing gently until he threaded his fingers through her hair and guided her into the rhythm he craved. He arched, going deep, and she savored the taste of him, the ecstasy she gave him.

Finally, he pulled her up. "You need to stop, or I'm going to lose it completely."

She looked at him, all her yearning clear in her eyes. "I want you to lose it."

But he shook his head. "Not until I'm inside you."

He rolled with her, coming down on top, kissing her so thoroughly she lost her mind. There was only his arms, his lips, his tongue, giving, tasting, wanting.

She thought he'd take her then, and she was so ready, because that was what he did to her, turned her wet and aching. Instead, he copied her, kissing his way down her body, lavishing her breasts, suckling, teasing both nipples as the tension rose between her legs. The need was more than desire —it was a want of him, only him, forever him.

He trailed his fingers down her stomach, slipping between her thighs, playing her in tandem with his mouth on her breast. Her moans became soft cries as he followed the path of his fingers with his lips, down, down, down. He settled between her legs, spreading them with his shoulders, and his mouth found her center. Throwing her head back, she gave a low, strangled cry, sensation rising through her body and shooting back down to where his tongue teased her. Tension built, her legs quivering, and she arched, begging for more. He gave it to her, slipping his fingers inside, teasing as he tasted her. The slow rhythm of his touch deepened every feeling.

Her quivers became trembles. She hooked her legs over his shoulders, toes pointed, calves tight, as if that could stop the shaking. It only shot her higher. Everything pooled low in her body, and then she shattered, crying his name, bucking beneath him as he licked and stroked, forcing her to ride the high until her cries turned to laughter and tears pricked her eyes. It was so good. He was so good.

They were so good together.

She hadn't realized he'd climbed up her body until he kissed her. She tasted herself and him and wished, for a heartbeat, that he'd let go in her mouth so she could remember everything about him—his taste, his feel, his sounds. Yet when he entered her, she knew this was what she needed too—his hardness inside, his body on hers, skin to skin, mind to mind, heart to heart.

KENT PULLED BACK ONTO HIS HAUNCHES, LIFTING HER thighs over his and sliding a pillow beneath her hips. Her climax left her languid beneath him. He whispered, "I want this to be absolutely perfect when I take you."

He'd wanted to give in earlier, but even more he wanted her like this—fully, completely open to him. After rolling on a condom, he entered her slowly, building her up again, keeping a steady rhythm though her body urged him to a faster pace. He caught his breath, controlling himself, holding to the stroke that hit exactly where she wanted. Her moans told him he got it just right. Tonight felt sweeter, hotter, perhaps because of the faint sense of desperation between them—fuel to the fire.

He stroked her thighs, his thumbs gliding along the inside. "Touch yourself for me," he whispered.

He knew what she liked—the sweet, hot touch on that tight little bead—but he wanted to watch her. To hold that sight forever in his mind. She wasn't prudish, not about taking him in her mouth, not about letting him make her come with his tongue, not about caressing herself while he watched. Her body clenched around him, and he gritted his teeth to keep from simply taking what he wanted. The slow rhythm might kill him. But he kept to it for her.

She gripped his arms, her body trembling again. Inside, her muscles worked him. He hissed a breath, trying to maintain control. Her legs tensed and released, and she mirrored that on the inside, driving him almost to the brink. Breath coming in short gasps, her cries fell from her lips. Eyes squeezed shut, all her focus centered on his body inside her and her fingers circling faster, harder, brushing him.

The sight ratcheted his tension higher. He waited for the perfect moment.

When her climax slammed through her, she clenched around him, lost in sensation. He took her hard then, grinding against her, prolonging her release, making it last. Bracing on his hands as her nails bit into his biceps, he rode her cataclysm with her. Until her body dragged his release from him, muscles straining as he threw his head back, giving voice to the roar rising within him.

Never like this. Never before. Only now. Only with her. Only ever with her.

Kent held her nestled against him. She felt boneless, unable to move. All she could do was whisper, "Thank you."

His voice came as a guttural rumble against her ear. "What are you thanking me for?"

"For the best last night ever," she sighed.

He was silent for a long moment, then said, "Best night ever. Not the last night ever."

She summoned the energy to tip her head back and meet his gaze. "Amanda will be home tomorrow."

"Aren't you going to sneak into my room late at night and lie with me after the kids go to bed?" he teased.

She tried to laugh, but it caught in her throat. "That wouldn't be appropriate."

He met her gaze steadily. "Then I guess I'll have to sneak into your room instead."

She shook her head, her cheek brushing the hair on his chest, a delicious stroke against her skin. "I work for Amanda and Tomás. I take care of the boys. It's not right for the nanny to be diddling the grandfather."

He laughed, and she loved that laugh. "I always thought it was the roguish duke who diddled the governess," he said with a grin.

She smiled with him. "Yes, but the governess is always some young, beautiful ingenue. She's not fifty-five years old."

She didn't know why she needed to remind him they weren't young—that they were in the last third of their lives. But he only pulled her closer, his arms tightening.

"Thank God you're not an ingenue," he said. "I'm pretty sure an ingenue wouldn't do the delicious things you do to me."

She trailed her fingers down and wrapped her hand around him. "You mean like this?" She squeezed.

He groaned. "I love the way you use your mouth on me too."

She wanted to taste him again—and she would, in the long night they still had. But she also knew she had to draw a line. "We can't do this with them around. You won't feel comfortable."

"I'll feel perfectly fine."

She sighed. "But I won't."

He slumped back against the mattress, muscles going slack. "All right. But you know you're killing me."

And she thought, with all her heart, that it would kill her too.

Then he said, almost as if he were musing. "When we get home, soon you won't be working for Tomás and Amanda anymore."

There was an unspoken question there. She had to stop it before it grew. "You know that won't work." She avoided his gaze, dipping her chin.

Of course he'd ask, "Why won't it?"

All her thoughts tumbled around in her mind. She couldn't tell him the awful things she'd done, the mistakes of her youth. If they kept seeing each other, it would become more than sex—she felt it already, and feared he did too. One day he'd want to know everything. And she'd have to tell him the truth, have to see his expression change as he learned about the past, the cheating, the home-wrecking, the price she'd paid when she lost her child.

She almost shook her head, silencing the voice that begged *no, no, no*.

All she could say was, "That really won't work for me."

DAMMIT, HE SHOULD HAVE WAITED TO ASK. HE'D *KNOWN* that. And yet she felt so good against him. It felt so right. But those last two words—*for me*—felt as if they sealed his fate.

They told him she didn't want what he wanted. She wanted only what they had now—the romantic days, the sexy nights. *For me* meant no relationship.

Kent knew he couldn't live with that. He pulled her into his arms and kissed her with all the passion and need inside him.

Somehow, some way, he would make her see they were meant to be together.

15

The house was neat and clean. They'd finished packing all the personal items they'd determined the family would want, taken care of all the gifts, shipped several packages home, and Kent had gassed up the car they'd been using. There was nothing much left to do on their last day. His daughter, Tomás, and the boys would be home sometime in the afternoon.

He'd made love to Elise in his big bed one last time in the early morning.

He wanted to take her again now, but the clock was ticking on their time left together, and he could feel her getting twitchy.

"Let's go for a walk," he suggested, wanting to break the tension.

They stepped out into the crisp fall air. The sweetness of *trdelník*, the crispy chimney cake, from a nearby vendor's cart perfumed the air. Leaves in shades of amber and gold crunched underfoot, and a gentle breeze carried the distant hum of Prague's streets.

He hadn't planned what he would say to Amanda when he told her he'd fallen in love with Elise. Somewhere in the night, holding Elise in his arms while she slept, he decided that telling Amanda once Elise no longer worked for her was the best course of action. That time couldn't be that far away. Elise had told him that Cynthia was doing well, and her doctor was on the edge of signing her off to go back to work. He'd waited five years after Gail passed with only the occasional casual dating spree. Until Elise. It was as if he'd been waiting for her.

He could be patient for another week or so.

They walked through Old Town Square, stopping to watch the astronomical clock as its figures danced for the crowd. The chime echoed off the surrounding Gothic towers, blending with the murmur of tourists and the occasional clip-clop of a horse-drawn carriage driving tourists around Old Town. Crossing Charles Bridge, the air smelled faintly of the Vltava River, crisp and cool, mixed with the earthy scent of wet stone. They entered Lesser Town, with its pastel buildings reflecting sunlight in a gentle glow, the red-tiled roofs framed by the early autumn sky.

They bought shrimp salad sandwiches and ate them on a bench overlooking a quiet square that was off the beaten track. The bread was warm and crusty, the shrimp fresh and lightly seasoned, with a hint of dill. Elise laughed as a group of schoolchildren ran past, their scarves trailing behind them like colorful streamers. The sound of their laughter made his chest tighten with thoughts of his grandsons.

For dessert, they picked out a selection of macarons at a small shop. Elise chose lavender and pistachio rosemary, her fingers lingering over the delicate shells. He picked chocolate fudge, maple syrup, and vanilla cream, inhaling the sweet aroma of sugar and butter.

Outside, she grinned at him, brushing a loose strand of

hair from her face. She smelled faintly of the fresh air and her shampoo. "I didn't realize you had such a sweet tooth."

He loved her laugh, the way it lifted her whole face, the light in her eyes. Everything in him ached to tell her how much he'd grown to love her.

Tell her. He felt as if the devil and the angel sat on his shoulders. After the devil's urging, his angel whispered, *Wait for just the right moment.*

Their time together was all he could have hoped for. Without pushing her, without questioning her, without wanting too much too soon, their relationship had blossomed naturally.

They stopped for a sweet kiss beneath a leafy tree. The fallen leaves smelled faintly of earth, and sunlight dappled the surrounding ground. His little devil urged him to deepen the kiss, to take her as if he were making love to her right there. But his angel chastised him, saying, *Don't push. Just leave her with this beautiful feeling for now.*

He backed off, dragging his thumb across her bottom lip —a luscious, inviting brush after the kiss.

AN HOUR LATER, HE RECEIVED A TEXT FROM AMANDA. THE family was on the outskirts of town, heading back. Kent's heart sank, a tight, uneasy weight, but he refused to let it overwhelm him.

They arrived at the house just as the family pulled into the short driveway. They'd been holding hands, but Elise had released him the moment she recognized the car turning the corner, stepping two feet away. He understood completely—Amanda's reaction mattered to Elise—but even as he allowed the space, his chest tightened slightly.

The boys leaped out of the car before the garage door

fully opened. Kent scooped them up one by one, their cheeks flushed and warm. Elise watched, smiling as he gathered them into his arms. His chest swelled with love for these little munchkins who'd captured his heart so thoroughly.

Luca ran to Elise, hugging her legs. She bent to kiss the top of his head. "I'd pick you up, but I think I'd strain my back. You're getting so big, and it's only been a few days."

Luca tilted his head back. "Really? I'm taller?"

She smiled down, stroking his hair, and warmth filled Kent's chest. Elise's smile tugged at him, making his heart flip in that familiar, fierce way.

The boys dashed around, Marek spinning and laughing, their energy echoing off the walls of the house. Amanda approached Kent then, her arms open for a hug. Her motherly smile was wide, radiant, and Kent realized how much she'd needed this time away after the stress of the tour and all the wedding preparations.

Tomás had already opened the trunk, carrying a boy-sized suitcase covered in Marvel characters. He set the case down, shaking Kent's hand with a firm, warm grip. "Welcome back," Kent said.

Tomás rolled his eyes. "Now we have to clean everything out and pack up."

Amanda finger-waved at Elise, who told her, "We went through all the gifts, and as you instructed, we took duplicates of either what's here or at the house in San Francisco over to Hana and Filip. We made up a list of who gave you what. And we shipped what we were sure you would want back home." Then she added, "There are just a few things we couldn't decide on."

"You could've texted me about them," Amanda said gently and with no censure.

Elise smiled, warm and glowing. "We didn't want to disturb your time in the mountains, not even for a moment."

She took Amanda's hand and led her inside, Luca clinging to her other hand. The air in the house smelled faintly of the cleaning products from their morning's work.

"Thank you so much for taking that chore off our hands," Tomás said from the front door.

Amanda echoed him with a soft, "Yes, thank you."

"Come in," Elise urged. "We'll make a cup of tea, and then you can decide what you'd like to do with what's left."

Amanda sighed softly as she surrendered to Elise's nurturing touch. It struck Kent then that though Elise could never fully replace Amanda's mother, she could offer care and warmth, a motherly influence his daughter needed.

The boys scampered after Elise and Amanda, while Kent helped Tomás carry the remaining bags.

"Thank you for taking care of things while we were gone," Tomás said, his accent soft but deliberate.

"You're welcome." Then Kent added, "We packed the suitcases with what we thought you'd like to take home with you." He laughed softly as they carried the bags up the steps. "It was easier for the boys because we knew what they loved. But there's still more to be done."

Setting down the case, Tomás punched Kent lightly on the shoulder. "Knowing Amanda, she'll unpack and repack everything, only to put exactly the same things back in the case."

They laughed together, sharing an understanding of Amanda's precision.

Kent thought about telling Tomás what had happened between him and Elise during their trip, but telling his son-in-law first felt like a betrayal to both his daughter and Elise. Some things he would have to keep to himself for now.

But at the right time, he would tell both Tomás and Amanda. And they would have to understand he wasn't letting Elise go.

Elise would have to understand that too.

IN THE KITCHEN, THE BOYS WERE RESTLESS. "I GAVE THEM snacks on the way here," Amanda said, "but we didn't stop for lunch. I just wanted to get home. So they're a bit jumpy now."

Elise smiled, understanding the urgency. "I'll make them sandwiches." Standing in the open refrigerator door, she said, "I've asked Cook to come back this evening. She'll make a delicious meal for all of us."

Amanda stared open-mouthed for a moment. "You mean Cook wasn't here the whole time?"

After a brief panic, she assured herself that Amanda could know nothing of what had happened with Kent. "Since the boys weren't here, it seemed silly to have her cook just for two."

"Oh." That was all Amanda said.

As Elise worked on the sandwiches, she explained the packing she and Kent had done, mostly because she couldn't stand the awkward silence that fell after telling Amanda about Cook. "We did some packing for the boys. We tried to guess what you'd want to leave and what to take home. But I know their favorite things, so those are all packed."

The boys ran around the table like squirrels chasing one another, the sounds of laughter echoing through the house. Neither Elise nor Amanda reprimanded them. The two little scamps made the home feel alive, warm, and welcoming.

Elise couldn't seem to help chattering away, as if she had something to feel guilty about. And yet, she and Kent were consenting adults. She hadn't even had the children to look after. Still, she felt as if she'd broken the Novaks' trust. Perhaps her lingering shame over the things she'd done as a young woman fueled her guilt. But Nick was just as responsible, since he'd been the one who was married.

But she'd been responsible for what happened to the baby.

Amanda spoke over the boys' antics. "You really didn't need to do all that." Elise couldn't tell whether Amanda was annoyed, even as she went on. "I mean, really, you could've gone home. I don't think we'll need you that much now."

"I don't mind staying," Elise insisted. "While you're closing up, the boys will be demanding your attention. That's what I'm here to help with." She couldn't leave, not yet, even though she'd told Kent they couldn't sneak into each other's rooms now the family was back.

Amanda made a noise like an old lady's harrumph. "You're right. I suppose as soon as I send you home, I'll wish I had you back."

Elise carried the plates to the table and said to the boys, "Wash up, it's time to eat."

Perhaps because they were so famished, they did exactly what she said, washing their hands at the sink—Luca standing on the small step that was there specifically for him. Then they raced each other back to the table.

She poured glasses of milk for each of them, then said to Amanda, "You've had your cup of tea—why don't you have a rest? I'll take care of the boys."

It made her feel useful, almost as if she needed justification to stay. But she had no desire to leave Kent. There was just something about being around him, his scent in the air, his sexy smile, his friendly banter—things she would miss so very much. Things she wasn't ready to let go of yet.

Amanda sighed and pushed herself up from the table. "You're right. I am tired. Thanks for handling the boys."

When she left, it was almost a relief. Elise hadn't felt like that with Amanda before Kent's arrival—only now, after all the passionate nights she'd spent in his bed, knowing that Amanda would disapprove.

Cook arrived to prepare dinner, and Jakub, their driver, returned, washing the cars in the late afternoon. After resting, Amanda did a little packing, then she came to the boys' room, and she and Elise helped them decide what else they wanted to take home that Kent and Elise hadn't already packed.

Of course, they just wanted to play, and very little got done.

They all enjoyed another dinner Cook provided, *kuře na paprice*—chicken in a paprika-cream sauce with noodles. More delicious Czech comfort food.

At bedtime, the boys wanted Kent to read them a story. When he was done, they insisted on one from Elise as well. She smiled at them, brushing her fingers over each of their sweet heads. "You're just trying to finagle more time before you have to sleep," she teased. After ruffling each boy's hair, she left the room, closing the door.

Kent caught her just outside the door in the hallway, running his fingers lightly down her arm and sending a shiver of pleasure through her. Leaning close, his warm breath brushed her ear. "It's been too long since I've kissed you."

When he moved to do just that, she pushed him away and scolded him as if he were a child. "We can't do that," she whispered. Yet the smile she couldn't keep off her lips seemed to invite him.

She knew he would have kissed her if they hadn't heard footsteps on the stairs. Tomás called out, "The boys aren't asleep yet, are they?"

Elise stepped away from Kent. "They're just trying to get me to read them another story. They don't want to sleep. But I'm sure they'll want you to kiss them good night."

She stepped to the other side of the hall, letting Tomás

pass into the boys' room. Even listening to their laughter and squeals of delight, Kent's gaze still felt hot on her skin.

Amanda was just leaving her room. "Dad, do you want a glass of wine on the veranda?"

Elise wondered if it was intentional that Amanda hadn't included her.

"That sounds great." Kent turned to Elise. "You'll join us, won't you?" She saw something seductive flash in his eyes. How could she say no? With Amanda as chaperone, nothing could happen. But she'd be able to look at Kent for the rest of the evening.

After saying good night to the boys—and obviously having read them another story—Tomás joined them on the veranda after half an hour. Amanda had already poured him a glass of wine.

"Bless you both for setting up the espresso machine in the kitchen." Tomás rubbed his hands together. "I've missed my morning espresso while we've been away."

Kent smiled. "You're very welcome. Believe me, we've been enjoying it too." Then he quizzed them about their honeymoon and everything they'd done.

"Lots of hiking," Tomás said. Elise knew he loved to walk but hadn't been able to do much during the tour.

Amanda laughed. "I think I lost five pounds he made me walk so much."

Tomás gave her a seductive laugh. "I don't think it was just the hiking, my darling."

Amanda actually blushed, and Elise wondered how much weight she herself had lost with all the nighttime activity. Glancing at Kent, she knew he was thinking the same thing.

They talked until the astronomical clock tolled ten o'clock in the nearby square. As if on cue, Amanda yawned, stretched, and said, "I think I'll go to bed. I'm tired."

Tomás stood too. "I'll join you, my darling."

Amanda dropped a kiss on her father's head and fluttered her fingers in a goodbye to Elise before they went upstairs.

Kent moved to the chair beside Elise and whispered, "Alone at last."

She put a finger to his lips. "Their room is just above—they can hear us." Through the open balcony door above the veranda, they could hear the faint murmur of voices.

Kent carried his chair to the back of the veranda, beneath the overhang where shadows pooled. Then he signaled Elise. She knew she shouldn't—but she did anyway, carrying her chair to set it beside his.

He kissed her then, a deeply passionate kiss that heated her blood. She felt herself go weak against him, her nipples hard, her body wet. Opening the top buttons on her blouse, he slipped his hand inside to cup her breast. He strummed her nipple, and she was helpless to stop him as he bent his head to lick her. His mouth on her was enough to drive a good woman mad. And she was not a good woman. She was bad, so very, very bad. Especially where he was concerned.

When he went to his knees in front of her and slid his hands up her thighs, pushing her skirt higher, she whispered, "You can't do that. Not here."

"They're upstairs," he answered softly. "No one can see us way back here in the dark." He spread her legs and pulled her panties aside, his fingers delving inside. And she no longer had the capacity to protest. Because she wanted this, the kinkiness of it, out here in the dark, with his family upstairs, and the veranda open to the night. The naughtiness of it turned her on so much she moaned.

Then he put his mouth to her.

This was something they did in the movies. This was something only young people did. But she couldn't help tangling her fingers in his hair, holding him there while he teased all her nerve endings. She covered her mouth to stop herself from crying out when he put two fingers inside her, curling them to find that perfect spot.

She thought of the wanton picture she made, her legs draped over his shoulders, thighs spread wide for him, hands on his head, holding him there, right there.

Tension coiled deep within. Until there was nothing but his fingers inside her, his tongue on her, and the crazy sensations spiraling through her. Then everything inside her shot down to her center, and her orgasm was like a tidal wave crashing over her. Her body, of its own volition, curled over him, holding him close, while she rode it out, his tongue and his fingers making the pleasure last forever.

She realized she'd bitten her lip only when she tasted the blood.

Then Kent sat back, his mouth wet with her, his eyes gleaming in the dim light. And he whispered, "Christ, you taste good."

It was enough to almost make her come again.

HE WANTED TO CARRY HER UPSTAIRS. EVEN BETTER, HE wanted to take her right here on the veranda, just fill her up, and let loose. It was kinky, but having other people in the house somehow ratcheted up all his sexual tension.

He would have done it too if Amanda's voice hadn't suddenly split the night.

"Dad, are you still down there?"

Elise damn near vaulted out of her chair. But he felt sated with her taste on his tongue. Standing, he kept his eyes on Elise as he backed up, until he stepped from beneath the balcony and could see Amanda leaning over the balustrade. "I'm still here," he said.

"I can't remember whether I checked all the doors. Can you please make sure they're locked before you come up?"

He waved a hand. "Of course, honey. I'll make sure everything is locked up tight."

"Thank you." Then he heard Tomás calling Amanda, and she disappeared into the bedroom.

He turned to Elise, but she was already heading toward the veranda door.

He followed her. "Where are you going?" But when he put his hand on her, she pulled away, backing up to the door.

And he knew he'd lost her. If Amanda hadn't…

But Amanda had.

He knew there was a filthy term for what his daughter had done. Whether or not she'd meant to, she had definitely blocked him.

Finally, Elise said, "We shouldn't have done that." Her voice was a harsh whisper in the night.

Yes, he'd lost her. But not for good.

There would be another chance. He would make sure of it.

16

Elise had never been so embarrassed in her life. Even now, half an hour later, her cheeks still burned. What if Amanda had walked downstairs while Kent was doing *that* to her?

Still, she felt awful that she'd left Kent with what was probably a painful erection. But when Amanda called out, she'd freaked. If it had been three minutes earlier, when she was in the throes of orgasm, with Kent's head buried between her thighs?

She couldn't think about it. So she'd run up to her room and hidden herself away. But even a shower hadn't cooled her down. The orgasm had only left her wanting more. After putting on the T-shirt she used as pajamas, she climbed into bed.

She lay awake, despite the incredible climax Kent had given her. Instead of being sated and relaxed, she craved more. More she couldn't have.

But her sleeplessness was the only reason she heard the snick of her door. She opened her eyes to his shadow in the room as he padded to the bed.

"You shouldn't be here," she protested, but only halfheartedly because there was nowhere else she'd rather have him be. She could only hope that Luca slept through without a nightmare, but for now there wasn't a peep out of the baby monitor on the bedside table.

In the moonlight falling through the window, Kent's lips curved in a wicked smile. "Don't you know I can't get enough of you? It hasn't even been a day, but already I miss you in my bed." He trailed a finger softly down her cheek. "And not just for sex," he murmured. "But for the feel of you in my arms, waking up to your scent lingering on my pillow."

His words seemed to turn her heart slowly in her chest. Nick had loved words, and she'd fallen for every single one of them when he was seducing her. Until she understood they were probably the same words he'd used on every woman he wanted to seduce.

By then, it was too late.

But this was Kent. And the sincerity in his smile wrapped around her. He meant every one of his words.

He'd pulled on sweats and a T-shirt, probably in case someone—one of his grandsons, or worse, his daughter—caught him out in the hall. "Let me in," he whispered. "Please."

It was the pleading that got to her. She swept the covers aside for him.

He threw a condom packet on the bed, then tore off his T-shirt and sweats, and she pulled her makeshift nightgown over her head. She wore nothing underneath, not even panties.

Maybe she'd been expecting this. Or hoping.

Once in bed beside her, he didn't immediately jump her. Instead, he gathered her into his arms, held her close, and with his deep breath, she knew he was taking in her scent.

"Christ, you smell so damn good."

She traced her fingers through the hair on his chest and felt him hard against her thigh. But he didn't rush her.

Cupping the side of her face, he lowered his lips to hers, kissing her softly. And she thought of the old song, *Killing Me Softly with His Song*. That's what he did to her, his touch killing every ounce of resistance she might have had, beating down all those thoughts of Nick, strangling the moans that rose up her throat, shooting her pulse rate high into the sky. As he deepened the kiss, he stole her breath with his tongue, almost bringing her to orgasm because it was so like the feel of his tongue between her legs.

Bad thoughts wanted to intrude, like what she'd do when Cynthia finally came back. But they flew away in a flash, and there was only him, only his lips tasting hers, his tongue dueling with hers, his hands drifting over her naked body.

"I want you." His voice came like a phantom calling to her in the night.

He toyed with her breasts, flicked her nipples, pinched until she groaned. Then his fingers did a slow, delicious glide down her abdomen, and her legs spread as if they knew what she wanted even before she did.

Tunneling into her cleft, he stroked that hot, tight bead, so sensitive now she would have cried out if his lips weren't on hers. He took her slowly with his fingers, raising her temperature in increments, until her body flooded for him. She was close, so close, but then he crawled down her abdomen, kissing, licking, tantalizing, until he lay between her legs. The first touch of his tongue set off a tiny explosion. Not quite orgasm, but a pre-shock. When he curled two fingers inside her, her body rose to meet his mouth, and she gasped for more.

She couldn't shout or wail or scream, but the doors were thick, and no one would hear her light gasps or heaving breath. She wanted to come, needed to come.

But again, he didn't let her finish. Rising to his haunches, he draped her legs over his thighs, his erection standing tall, proud, throbbing. She reached down to stroke him, and his soft groan strummed her nerve endings. As she fell back onto the bed, head on the pillow so she could see him, she watched as he rolled on a condom, loving the sight of his hand on himself. Then he stroked her with his crown, setting off tiny fireworks inside her.

When he took her, it was deliberately slow. As he filled her, heat spread through her entire body. And when he moved, he gave her slow, short strokes against that small but powerful spot inside her.

Over and over. Until she wanted to scream. Until her legs trembled, then quaked. He drew her calves up to rest them on his shoulders, closing her body around him, giving himself greater friction, and her too. Her legs kicked gently against him, and she felt the build, first in her core, then reaching out to her limbs, then an avalanche of pleasure slammed into her. She had to bite her knuckle to keep her cries inside.

But oh God, how she wanted to scream for him.

SHE CLAMPED HARD AROUND HIM. CLENCHING, unclenching, holding him in the tight fist of her body. He pounded into her, knowing exactly what she needed. The hard ride wasn't just for him, but for her, each thrust keeping her high on the cliff he'd shot her to. It was only with an iron will and the strength of Hercules that he held back. He wanted her climax to go on and on, needed it. Badly. Wanted to feel her convulse around him, dragging his orgasm from him.

Finally, his will vanquished and his strength depleted by his need for her, he couldn't hold out. It was all he could do not to roar with his climax, his triumph. All he allowed himself was a low rumbling growl. After one last thrust, he pressed his body tight to hers as he pumped into her, every drop draining him.

It was only as he looked down at her again that he realized her fingers had dug half-moon circles in his arms where she held on. The dents in his flesh were like badges of honor.

He fell on her then, kissed her with everything in him, tasted her mouth while she tasted her arousal on his tongue. Then he rolled to his side, bringing her with him, hooking her leg over his, trapping her there. He couldn't pull out, not yet. And he whispered, "Someday, I want to taste you, and I want you to taste me, and then I want to kiss you with our flavors mingling."

She laughed softly. "That's a very naughty desire."

He plundered her mouth the way he'd plundered her body. And she gave as good as she got. Holding her tight against him, he absorbed her heat, wallowed in the feel of their sensual sweat mingling between their bodies.

Because he couldn't stay in her bed, couldn't wake with her in his arms in the morning, he wanted to relish this moment for as long as he could.

ELISE HADN'T WANTED KENT TO LEAVE LAST NIGHT. BUT there was no other way. Now that Amanda, Tomás, and the boys were home, they couldn't go on the way they had. Amanda was her employer, and Elise felt as if she was breaking a bond—even if she was only the substitute nanny.

And if Kent ever learned the truth about her, he would feel the same way, as if she'd broken his trust.

Elise got the boys up in the morning, picked out their clothes for the day, took them downstairs. And found the house in a flurry of activity. Amanda rushed about, barking orders at Cook and Jakub, whom she'd obviously enlisted to help. She even had Tomás on tenterhooks, following her every instruction.

In the kitchen, she waved a hand at Elise. "Thank God you got the boys up. We want to leave in two days."

Behind her, Elise heard Tomás mutter, "Who's *we?*"

This, she learned, was Amanda's way—plans that had to be executed *now*, tasks that couldn't wait another minute. Amanda was a doer, always moving, always ticking items off her list. Though her career as an editor meant long hours at a computer, she rushed about like a tornado.

Amanda pointed a finger at Elise. "We've got so much on the agenda. After breakfast, I just need you to take the boys out somewhere. I don't care where. I just need some space."

Kent entered the kitchen right behind Elise. She caught the low-key, spicy-sweet scent of his cologne laced with his warm musk—or maybe their lovemaking still clung to him.

He took over. "I'll take the boys out for the day." Although he didn't touch her, his body heat enveloped her. "But I'll need Elise—she keeps them calm. Between the two of us, we can handle the boys."

Amanda flicked a hand as if she didn't care. "Fine, fine." Then she stopped, stood still for three whole seconds—an impossibility only a minute ago—then rushed at her father, hugging him. "Thank you, Dad. You know how I get when there's so much to do."

"Then give yourself a couple of extra days," he suggested softly.

But Amanda shook her head, suddenly seeming close to tears. "I don't have time. I've got an edit due at the end of the month for a very important client—a multimillion-dollar author."

The Novaks lived in style, traveled in style, ate in style.

They had housekeepers and drivers and chefs. They didn't need the money—Tomás was a world-famous pianist—and they had all they could ever want. But Elise understood Amanda's need for a career of her own, for independence, for the esteem that came from her work.

"Go on, get busy." Kent shooed Amanda out of the kitchen. "We'll take care of the boys."

Cook sighed in relief, almost sagging against the counter, and Tomás clapped Kent on the back. "Thank you. I can usually handle her, but she didn't do any work while we were away on the honeymoon—just like we agreed. But now she's manic about it."

Kent slapped Tomás's shoulder, then propelled him out of the kitchen too. "Go help your wife." Then he turned to Cook, hands on his hips. "Has Amanda given you tasks too?"

"Yes, sir. She wants me to do the shopping."

Kent huffed. "Why would she need you to shop when we're leaving in two days?"

"She had invited Mr. Novak's parents for dinner and wants something special."

Kent rolled his eyes and waved a hand. "Then please make your lists and do your shopping. Elise and I can make the boys' breakfast."

Cook put her hands together, almost in prayer. "Thank you so much, Mr. Kent."

He smiled. "You know I can't say no."

She bowed again, then pulled a piece of paper from her pocket. "I have made my list. I will go now."

Kent added, "You must have Jakub drive you. If Amanda complains, I'll explain why you need him."

The boys sat quietly at the table, as if they'd seen their mother's feverish episodes before. Elise felt guilty even for thinking that. Amanda had a lot on her plate, a world-famous husband, two lively boys, months of travel, and a career neglected for over two weeks. She surely couldn't have been editing during wedding preparations. Elise wasn't even sure how much work she'd been able to do during the entire concert tour since they'd been almost constantly on the go.

Once Cook was gone, Kent stepped behind Elise, dropping a kiss on her nape. Luckily, the boys were busy with plastic dinosaurs and didn't notice. Kent whispered the same thing he had last night, "Alone at last."

But they weren't alone. Little boys had big ears and eyes. She'd have to keep Kent in check—though a huge part of her didn't want to, even knowing how dangerous that was.

THE DAY OUT WITH THE BOYS AND ELISE WAS EVERYTHING Kent could have hoped for. People looked at them as if they were grandparents taking the kids out for the day—and he loved it. He swung Luca into the air, then Marek wanted the same, and as he did it, Elise called just loud enough for only him to hear, "Don't hurt yourself."

When he was with her—whether playing with the boys or making love to her—it was hard to remember he was sixty-five, though sometimes a stitch in his back or a twinge in his knee reminded him.

But not today. Today was perfect.

They took the boys to an Exploratorium-style museum, much like the one in San Francisco, full of hands-on games and science exhibits. Marek and Luca wanted to try everything, to talk to every docent, to learn all they could.

Kent was so proud of them—proud of his daughter for raising such amazing children, proud of Tomás, whose calm steadiness balanced Amanda's volatility. Marek took more after Amanda, while Luca leaned toward his father's placid nature. And he loved them both equally.

When an experiment engrossed the boys, Kent curled his fingers around Elise's. She let him hold her hand, but only until the boys finished.

While they were spinning tops to learn about centrifugal force, he whispered that they wouldn't even notice if he kissed her.

She stepped away, brows lifted. "Haven't you ever heard the saying about little pitchers having big ears?"

"They're not even looking." Still, he let her go. It became a game; he, the seeker, she, the hider. But there would be tonight, when he could sneak into her room again.

For just a moment, the ache of that thought hit him. Why did they have to sneak around? They were consenting adults. Her stint as the boys' nanny was almost over. But she'd need a reference if she wanted another job like this, and now that she'd sampled travel in luxury as a nanny, she'd likely want to do it again.

So he kept himself in check with a little handholding, a peck on the cheek when the boys' backs were turned, a full-blown kiss only when a docent led them to a new experiment and all their attention was elsewhere.

For just that moment, she would lean in, offering him the sweetness of her mouth, the lusciousness of her kiss—before she pulled away.

HIS TIME WITH ELISE FELT GLORIOUS, ENHANCED BY THE boys' antics, their laughter ringing through the air, their bright eyes sparkling with delight. He admired how good she was with his grandsons. She would have made a wonderful mother, an amazing grandmother. Her patience was endless, her adoration of the boys evident in every word she spoke to them, every ruffle of their hair, every look she gave them. He heard the warmth in her voice, saw the soft brush of her hand against theirs, and felt a swell of wonder in his chest.

They treated the boys to chicken nuggets, though why children thought compressed, processed food could ever taste better than a proper Czech goulash, he couldn't say. The crisp, golden nuggets vanished in an instant, their small hands eager, crumbs dotting the table. Amanda would have had his head, and probably the boys would prattle on about it when they returned to the house. But that's what grandfathers did —they spoiled their grandchildren.

He called Amanda around five o'clock to ask if they could come home.

"Where have you been?" she almost screeched over the phone.

Kent answered calmly, "We took the kids out to enjoy the day, to get them out of your hair the way you asked."

"But I didn't expect you to be gone all freaking day, Dad. Hana and Filip and everyone else will be here in half an hour, and there's so much to do."

"Then you should've called me earlier and let me know you wanted us to come home," he said reasonably.

From a distance, he heard Tomás's voice calling out, "Everything's fine, Amanda. Cook has dinner well underway. No worries."

But that was Amanda—she wanted everything perfect, fretting over details as if the family would notice whether or not the hors d'oeuvres were precisely aligned on a platter. Kent simply said, "We're on our way, sweetheart. We'll be there in just a few minutes." He hung up before she could shriek again.

Elise gave him a small shake of her head. "I'm sorry. I should've said something earlier."

With the boys' hands in theirs, they walked back to where Kent had parked the car. Amanda had so many things she wanted Jakub to handle, besides taking Cook out to do the shopping, that Kent had driven them.

"No worries," he repeated Tomás's words over the boys' heads. "Amanda sometimes panics when there's absolutely no reason."

If Amanda were truly as worried as she'd appeared, she would have told them about the family gathering herself, instead of leaving it to Cook to mention the party when discussing the meal she had to prepare. And Amanda could have texted him far earlier.

The family had already arrived when they reached the house. Laughter and the scent of Cook's delicious concoction mingled in the air. Amanda, amid the hugs and greetings, seemed perfectly fine now. The boys dashed off to play with their cousins, their squeals of delight filling the house. The adults gathered for drinks on the veranda, the amber glow of bistro lights reflecting in the crystal snifters of cognac, while the night air carried the faint perfume of jasmine and the distant buzz of voices on the street below. Cook had prepared some appetizers, the aroma of fresh herbs and pastry making Kent's stomach rumble.

Elise hung back, murmuring softly, "This is family time. I'm just the nanny."

He took her hand, the warmth of her palm pressing into his, and pulled her with him. "Elise is trying to escape to her room, claiming she's just the nanny," he said to Tomás.

Tomás laughed, his eyes warm and inclusive, taking her hand and leading her out onto the veranda. "Don't be silly. You're part of the family. You've been with us for the past three months, and you've done an amazing job with the boys. Thank you. Have a drink with us to celebrate the last family party."

Elise couldn't get out of it—which had been Kent's plan.

Despite Amanda's earlier panic, the evening was

marvelous. Tomás regaled them with tales of their ten days in the mountains—the crisp air, the scent of pine, the sound of birds and streams, all the hikes, and the games played as a family in the evenings.

Amanda rolled her eyes. "Right, and then there were the two times we got lost in the forest."

Tomás waved a hand. "We weren't lost. We just took a couple of wrong turns, ended up on a different path, and went a little farther than we planned."

Amanda slapped a hand on his arm lovingly. "You're such a man. You never ask for directions and refuse to look at a map." She leaned over to kiss him.

Everyone laughed, and Hana added, "He gets that from his father. Filip will never ask for directions either. Thank goodness we now have GPS on our phones, or we would get nowhere on time."

Again, the family laughed, the air warm with camaraderie and the scent of blooming jasmine from the veranda planters

They dined on crispy *bramboráky*, potato pancakes, which Cook had topped with caramelized onions and fried eggs. Hana told Kent that potato pancakes often accompanied a lovely stew, or were eaten on their own with sour cream or crème fraiche.

With children present, the evening ended at ten o'clock, well past their bedtimes. Kent hugged Hana, then Filip, happy he'd gotten to know Tomas's parents better over the two weeks he'd been in Prague. When he would have shaken hands with Tomas's siblings, they pulled him in for firm hugs.

Elise took the boys upstairs to bed, and Kent anticipated the night ahead, when the house was silent, when he could sneak into her room.

He would have done it if she hadn't caught him in the hallway and whispered, "Don't come to my room again. It makes me too nervous with everyone in the house. Please?"

She looked up at him with such a pleading expression that he agreed—but it took only a second for him to decide what he absolutely had to have in return. "Only if you agree to see me once we're back home." He didn't care about the timing, whether it was right or wrong, whether he was pushing or not. He simply couldn't wait.

Doubt flickered in her eyes, and her mouth turned down. "That's really not—"

He cut her off. "If you don't agree, I'm going to kiss you right here in the hallway. Let anyone walk by who wants."

The threat made her smile. "You are such a wicked man. All right. I'll see you." Then she marched into her room, closing the door. He waited to hear the click of the lock, but the sound didn't come.

He wondered if he should ignore her protests and come to her room when the house was quiet. He might have done just that if Tomás hadn't topped the head of the stairs and waved him over. "Join me on the veranda for a cognac, Kent."

And Kent had no choice but to follow his son-in-law downstairs.

17

"Where's Amanda?" Kent asked.

Tomás waved a nonchalant hand. "She was tired after the drive. She just wants to go to sleep."

They stepped onto the veranda, where the evening air was cool and scented faintly with jasmine, and the bistro lights threw a mellow, golden glow across the chairs and low table.

Tomás poured two fingers of cognac into crystal snifters, the amber liquid catching the light. Kent accepted his glass, letting the warmth seep into his palms. He swirled it, watching the ribbon of caramel and oak drift upward, and breathed in the fragrant, slightly spicy scent that made the air seem heavy and intimate. It made him wish Elise sat beside him.

They sipped their drinks, watching the shadows deepen across the river. Somewhere in the house a door closed softly, and the hum of quiet voices—Cook and Jakub finishing the party's cleanup—floated from the kitchen.

Finally, Tomás spoke. "I'm worried about her."

Kent cocked his head, the fire of the brandy lingering on his tongue. "Why?"

"It seems as if she worries about everything these days," Tomás said. "She manufactures it—like today, when you didn't come home in the early afternoon, even though she's the one who asked you to take the boys out of her hair."

"She's always been a perfectionist," Kent said, thinking of Gail, who had instilled in Amanda such focus and precision. He admitted to a touch of perfectionism in his own work—always wanting his architectural creations to be perfect, sometimes adding a flourish that the client didn't request, simply because he knew it would enhance the building.

Tomás was shaking his head. "She was so worked up the first couple of days in the mountains, crying about how much she missed the boys, that she was afraid they would forget her while we were gone, that they'd start preferring Elise to her."

"I had no idea. I'm sorry, Tomás," Kent commiserated, feeling a twinge of guilt that he'd enjoyed himself so much while they were away.

"She wanted to go back to Prague. Which is why I decided to have you bring the boys to use." He grimaced. "Even if it was our honeymoon. It seemed the only way to calm her down."

"I wish you'd told me." His chest hurt thinking about his daughter's distress.

"You could have done nothing, Kent. And please, don't think I'm complaining about my wife. I just want you to understand the things that have me worried." Then he added softly, "She misses her mother."

Kent agreed. "We all miss her. Gail always knew how to calm her down."

"That is true," Tomás said. "When Amanda got worked up, your wife could immediately pinpoint the cause and calm her daughter. I've never had that knack—but I've always known you do, Kent. I've seen you handle her perfectly."

Kent gave a soft snort. "Don't be silly. You're her rock. You keep her steady."

Tomás leaned forward, elbows on his knees, the glass cradled in his hands. "But this is the thing—these episodes are happening more often. When she gets herself in a frenzy, she will storm, cry, and finally break down, saying she needs her mother. It's been five years, Kent, and I no longer know how to help her grieving."

"We should've insisted she go to grief counseling."

Tomás shook his head. "You cannot force someone. We both suggested it many times. But she must decide to seek help. So far, she hasn't."

"I haven't been helping things. I never cleared out Gail's belongings. Every time I say something about it, Amanda pleads with me not to do it."

"You have to do what's right for you, Kent. If you wish to clean out Gail's things, you must do it. Amanda can take what she wants, but the rest is your decision."

Kent shook his head. "If I offered her anything, she'd take it all. Dresses, shoes, skirts, blouses, pants, belts, scarves, coats, sweaters—and none are Amanda's style. She took some of her mother's scarves but never used them with her own outfits. Makeup, perfume, hairbrushes with strands of Gail's hair, nail polish, purses—Gail loved shoes and purses."

He made a decision, one that had been a long time coming. "Let's get her home and settled. Let her finish this job she's so worked up about. Then I'll let her know I'm cleaning out her mother's things and tell her she can pick what she wants."

Tomás said smoothly, "I don't look forward to her total freak-out."

Kent agreed. "Neither do I, but perhaps it will help her

let go. If it doesn't, if she truly freaks out, then it's time to bring up counseling much more forcefully. It's time for that anyway."

Tomás sipped his cognac. "Then we have a plan."

"We do," Kent said, finishing the last of his drink.

He could only hope the plan worked. His heart hurt for his daughter, but he had no solutions he knew for sure would work. Maybe Elise would know what to do. She'd agreed to see him when they were home, and maybe that would be the time to talk to her. He couldn't do it here when she was worried about Amanda's reaction to their relationship.

More than anything, he longed to climb the stairs, open Elise's door, touch her, kiss her, hold her. Just to be near her. But he'd promised he would wait.

When they got home, though, he wouldn't let her stonewall him. Now he needed her not only for himself, but for Amanda too.

THE FOLLOWING DAY, AMANDA'S MOOD WAS MUCH THE same as it had been the day before—manic, even bordering on frantic. Today, however, she sent Kent out with the boys and kept Elise with her, insisting she needed Elise's help. No entreaty from Kent, saying he needed Elise's calming influence with the boys, did any good.

He took them to the zoo again—because they'd loved it so much the other day and there were never too many animals for little boys to see—and let them wander the winding paths, pointing out the polar bears and cheeky lemurs.

Afterward they went to Kampa, and he bought them each an ice cream cone, which they ate in Kampa Park—or the crazy baby park, as Marek called it.

Luca, the more sensitive of the two, licked a thin ribbon of strawberry ice cream from his cone, then looked up at Kent with worried eyes.

"What's wrong with Mama?" he asked.

The boys had seen their mother in all moods, but it was a testament to how badly things had become over the last few days that little Luca had noticed something amiss.

As Marek licked his chocolate ice cream, Luca's gaze kept flicking between him and Kent. Kent crouched down to meet their eyes and offered as much of the truth as he could. "You know how hectic the tour has been? And all the while your mother had to prepare for the wedding too. She's also behind on work. All of that is weighing on her." He stroked Luca's downy cheek, then reached over to ruffle Marek's hair. "That means we have to be extra understanding. Things will go back to normal once we're all home again."

Marek's face was solemn despite the smears of chocolate on his cheek and at the corners of his mouth. "But when we get home," he said quietly, "Elise will leave us. And Cynthia will come back."

It was the first Kent had heard that it could be a problem. "Don't you like Cynthia?"

The little boy, looking far too adult for the moment, shook his head quickly. "Oh no, Cynthia is really nice."

Luca chimed in. "But Elise tells us the best stories."

Marek added, "And when we build with LEGO, she helps us."

"And Cynthia doesn't?" Kent asked.

"She just sits there and reads the directions," Luca said, nose wrinkling.

"That sounds like she's helping," Kent teased.

Marek shook his head so hard his soft hair flew. "Elise makes us figure it out on our own. Sometimes she even does things wrong, so we have to read the directions ourselves and fix it."

Kent wanted to laugh at their seriousness. "It sounds like Cynthia's doing a good job too—just a different one."

A bright green zoo parrot swooped down and landed on the head of a nearby bronze statue, squawking at either the sculpture or the boys—Kent couldn't tell which. Luca, still determined, declared, "We like it the way Elise does it better. She says making mistakes is a good way to learn."

Kent understood once again the marvel that Elise was. "Maybe you could ask Cynthia to do it Elise's way. I'm sure she'd be happy to."

The boys grumbled but finally agreed.

After lunch he called Elise, mostly to hear her voice, even if only over the phone. "How are things going?" he asked.

He couldn't tell if her sigh was exasperation or exhaustion. "We're moving along. How are the boys?"

He laughed softly as Marek and Luca chased each other through the park, shuffling piles of fallen autumn leaves. Another boy, dark-haired and grinning, joined them, and they all tumbled together, the boys speaking surprisingly good Czech with the other child—or at least as far as Kent could tell. A young mother laughed, watching them, then turned and winked at him.

"Well, we've colonized the crazy baby park," he said, grinning. "And they seem to have made a new friend."

"That's wonderful," Elise said warmly. "I have to run—I hear Amanda calling."

She was gone far too soon, and Kent stood for a moment, phone still warm in his hand, basking in the delicious echo of her voice.

He let the boys play until the young mother called her son to her. They hugged and waved like only small boys could, the Czech woman flashing Kent a friendly smile.

By two o'clock, he deemed it time to head home. The boys were getting tired and clamoring for a snack. And he needed to check what kind of help Amanda and Tomás still needed in order to be ready for tomorrow's departure.

In the kitchen, the boys' childish chatter filled the air as they devoured *linecké cukroví*, buttery sandwich cookies with red currant jam and a dusting of sugar, and *perníčky*, fragrant ginger cookies shaped like stars and hearts. Crumbs dotted their fingers and lips as they hummed their delight over the special Czech cookies Cook had made for them.

Kent left them to their feast and went to look for his daughter, but he found Elise first, standing amid half-packed boxes in the boys' room. His heart, his mind, his whole body responded to her presence.

"They had a great time," he said, moving closer. "We met another little boy in the park. I've never seen three kids have so much fun kicking leaves into piles, then racing through them."

Her smile reached deep inside him, lighting every dark corner. "That's what little boys do," she quipped.

He wanted to pull her into his arms and kiss her. "They love the way you build LEGO with them."

She snorted as she tucked Luca's Bumble the Abominable Snowman into a box beside Marek's prized pterodactyl, along with their identical sloths. "They just like it when I make mistakes so they can feel smarter than I am."

Kent wagged a finger at her. "Oh no, they know exactly what you're doing—you're teaching them."

She tipped her head, as though she hadn't realized they'd figured out her tactic. "No kidding?"

"No kidding," he murmured, eyes lingering on her lips as she smiled.

"Where's Amanda?" he asked.

"She was in the garage with Jakub last I saw—something about boxes for storage," Elise replied lightly.

Kent stepped closer, sliding a hand around her hips, drawing her nearer as he dipped his head for a kiss. "I've missed this all day long."

Her palm came up to his chest but didn't push. "We shouldn't."

"Just one more," he whispered, brushing his mouth against hers.

Elise melted into him, letting him seduce her. He tasted of chocolate and warm autumn air, of everything that was delicious and dangerous. Heat pooled deep in her belly—need, hot and urgent. She clutched his shoulders, giving herself up to him for this one moment, devouring him as he consumed her. Tangling her fingers in his hair, she pressed closer, molding her body to his. She'd missed his touch the night before, missed sharing the day with him. If this kiss was all she could have, she would let it fill her senses.

The gasp from the open doorway wasn't enough to make her let him go—until Amanda's voice swept in like an Arctic wind.

"What the hell is going on?"

Kent stiffened, only now realizing Amanda was there. Slowly he pulled back, his eyes shuttered, his body retreating even as Elise ached for him to stay.

Amanda stood rigid, shock and anger twisting her face. "What is going on here?" she demanded again, her teeth snapping on each word.

Kent brushed her question aside. "Nothing important, Amanda. Just a small show of affection."

His blithe tone struck Elise like a blow—cold, sharp, an

iceberg cracking the fragile hull of hope she hadn't meant to build. Had he been playing with her last night when he'd made her promise she'd see him again once they were home? Was she just a lonely man's casual distraction, the nanny caught in a foolish crush? The thought stung all the more because she knew she'd run headlong past casual into something that looked an awful lot like caring.

And yet, a quieter part of her wondered if Kent had meant his words only for Amanda, to soothe the storm. She couldn't tell.

"That's not what it looked like to me," Amanda snapped.

"Looks can be deceiving," Kent replied, calm and steady.

Then, true to form, he stepped forward, placing a gentle hand on Amanda's arm. "Let's go have a cup of tea—or better yet, a glass of wine."

Amanda yanked free. "I don't need wine." She backed away from her father, eyes bright with unshed tears.

The sight tore at Elise. She'd never wanted to come between Kent and his daughter, yet that was exactly where she stood. The tension was a living thing, sticky and heavy, holding her fast.

Amanda's chest heaved. Then she spun and fled down the hall.

Kent lingered in the doorway, eyes dark with heartbreak, storm clouds gathering there.

This was what Elise had feared—the shadow she'd felt hovering just out of reach. It was as if Kent's late wife had stepped into the room, reminding her of boundaries she could never quite see but always felt pressing against her.

If he touched her now, she'd splinter. Before he could say a word, she eased the door shut, pressing her palms flat against the wood as if that barrier could hold everything at bay. She half expected him to knock, maybe even pound, but he did neither.

Maybe what he'd said to Amanda was the truth. That what they'd shared was nothing at all.

※

Kent hadn't wanted to leave Elise. She'd appeared so devastated, so lost. But she'd shut him out. He could have beaten the door down, maybe he should have. But he feared what she would say. He was afraid that in the aftermath of Amanda's anger, Elise would tell him everything between them was over. She needed time to calm down. So instead, he'd gone in search of his daughter.

He entered the kitchen to find the two boys hunched over a kids' puzzle on the kitchen table. The warm sunlight streaming through the windows made the scattered puzzle pieces glitter in the afternoon light. This wasn't the normal place for puzzles, which were often assembled on the lesser-used dining room table. He assumed the boys were working here because the rest of the house was being packed up and drop-clothed, the faint scent of cleaning solution and furniture polish hanging in the air.

Cook bustled around the kitchen, her hands raised in the air to flutter uselessly, then returning to whatever task she had been working on. The clatter of utensils, the gentle hum of the refrigerator, mixed with the lingering scent of baked cookies.

"Where's Amanda?" Kent asked, his voice calm, yet threaded with quiet urgency.

"Out," she said, waving a hand vaguely toward the veranda.

The boys now saw him, and Marek was already bouncing in his seat, impatience and excitement written all over his small face. "Děda! Will you help us with the puzzle? Luca doesn't get it!"

Luca, more methodical, placed another piece in the quarter-finished puzzle, his brow furrowed in concentration. Kent knew that Marek's cheekiness wasn't just mischief—it was about one-upping his brother. He was the older child, and he wanted to be better at everything. And yet, even in their playful competitiveness, the boys worked well together.

In a soft, almost pleading voice, Luca said, "Please, Děda."

At any other time, Kent would have dived in, letting the boys do most of the work while he subtly guided them. The faint sweet scent of the ginger cookies would have made the moment even cozier. But he said, "I have to talk to your mama first. Then I can help you."

Marek groaned, "But, Děda—"

Kent cut him off gently but firmly. "I'll be back."

With that, he left, ensuring no further argument could stall him from talking to his daughter.

His hand hovered over the veranda doorknob when he saw Tomás standing outside with Amanda. She gesticulated wildly, the sun catching the coppery tones in her hair. Though Kent couldn't make out the words, her voice carried across the veranda in animated waves. He guessed Tomás was absorbing every detail of her indignation—or what she thought she'd seen.

Of course, she had seen exactly what she thought, his desire and need for Elise.

As he opened the door, Amanda froze, deer-like eyes wide, uncertainty etched across her face, the breeze from the veranda ruffling her hair.

Kent had braced for her fury, but she held her head high as she stalked toward him, refusing to look at him. Stopping by the door until he moved out of the way, she stepped inside, then shut it with a force that made the glass panes rattle. The sound echoed through the otherwise quiet afternoon.

Tomás sighed, his shoulders slumping as if carrying the

weight of the world. For a man who always seemed cheerful and in command, his face was a study in fatigue and worry, mirrored in the faint crease between his brows.

Waiting, Kent expected his son-in-law to lash out. But Tomás walked to him, placed a hand on his elbow and guided him toward the door. "Let's go out for coffee."

Kent remained momentarily immovable. "I have to talk to Amanda." He didn't need to explain that he wanted to discuss his feelings about the kiss Amanda had witnessed.

But Tomás's hand on Kent's elbow was unrelenting. Kent suspected the younger man would drag him out if he didn't go willingly.

❧ 18 ☙

Ten minutes later, Tomás and Kent sat across from each other at a café a block away, the smell of espresso mingling with the faint crispness of autumn outside. Their drinks—espresso for Tomás, Americano for Kent—sent up gentle tendrils of steam.

Rather than immediately addressing the issue, Tomás said, "I knew it would be a difficult transition when I decided to leave Prague. I'd already been gone for those years I spent at Cambridge, but when I returned, my parents thought I would settle permanently near the family. You might imagine they were quite upset that I would choose to live in America—and worse on the West Coast rather than the East Coast. It was so far away, my mother said. She bemoaned the fact that I would not be nearby. I tried to explain that I thought San Francisco would be the best place to move my career forward. My father was stoic and said nothing, but I felt his censure for hurting my mother this way."

"I'm sorry," Kent commiserated. "I didn't know that. But I should have realized how hard it was for you."

Tomás waved away his platitude, his fingers tapping

lightly on his cup. "Isn't that what all families do—have a hard time letting go?"

Kent realized where he was going with this. "Yes. It's hard."

"Coupled with my parents' disappointment, I was thrust into a battlefield within the Symphony. They did not want an outside pianist. They wanted one of their own. They certainly didn't want a foreigner and thought it was some sort of takeover. For a while, the Symphony was in turmoil. But you know what turned them around?"

Kent felt as if he didn't know this man as well as he'd thought. He'd had no idea about Tomás's struggles. "I'm sorry I never asked."

Tomás waved it away. "That's not necessary. You were also a very busy man. But let me tell you what changed things for me."

Kent waited, letting the man tell his story, the ambient hum of conversation and the clink of cups around them fading into the background.

"It was your daughter."

Kent couldn't say why the man's words suddenly brought tears to his eyes. Perhaps it was knowing that Tomás loved Amanda with everything in him—just as he loved his sons.

He prompted, "How did she do that?"

"She was editing a book about the most important pianists, past, present, and future. The author had chosen me as one of those future pianists."

Kent remembered the book and knew that was how the two had met.

"She wanted to check her author's authenticity. And it was she who suggested that Marcus O'Malley, the American pianist I had supposedly supplanted, should be included in the book. I made the introductions. And that book helped propel both of our careers forward into the limelight."

"I think you were born for the limelight, Tomás."

The younger man nodded his head, completely without ego. "I had a goal. I would have risked everything to have the life I have today. But from that moment, I always knew that Amanda would be part of that life."

"So did her mother and I," Kent agreed.

"She is everything to me. And seeing her so upset wounds me." Tomás put his hand on his heart. The gesture was almost palpable, the warmth of emotion radiating off him. "I blame myself," Tomás continued, "for Amanda's current confusion."

The admission floored Kent. "Why on earth would you think that?"

"I have babied her," Tomás said with a well-used American phrase. "When she said she didn't want to get married because Gail was ill, I agreed we would put the wedding plans on hold. When, after Gail died, she said she couldn't possibly think about marrying and having a ceremony without her mother, I conceded."

Kent wanted to interrupt. "We both did that."

"Maybe she needed it then. But I have let this go on too long." Tomás rushed on, in case Kent might misunderstand. "I'm not saying she should ever stop missing Gail. We will all forever miss Gail. You especially."

And yet Amanda had just found Kent kissing another woman. For the first time, guilt about his actions overwhelmed him.

Tomás leaned forward, laying his hand on top of Kent's in a manly yet comforting gesture. Seeming to read Kent's thoughts, he said, "You have every right to move on. In fact, my friend, you *should* move on. You're still a young man in spirit."

Kent chuckled softly without any humor. "Not so much in body."

Tomás smiled with him. "With Elise Martin, you're like a man twenty years younger." After holding Kent's gaze for a long moment, he added, "And she's a beautiful woman."

"You should know that I'm in love with her." Getting the words out felt cathartic, as if he'd been holding them in forever.

Tomás nodded. "I have watched you together. I understand completely."

Where earlier Kent hadn't thought he needed to explain, he now did. "She's awakened something in me I thought was long gone. She's made me feel young again. As much as I'll always miss Gail, Elise has made me realize that I still have a life to live."

Tomás added, "Your wife was a lovely woman. And selfless in so many ways. She would never have wanted you to make a martyr of yourself to her memory."

Kent felt himself choking up. "No. She wouldn't. Just as I wouldn't have wanted her to do that if our roles were reversed." He breathed deeply, then said, "But I can't help worrying how this will affect my relationship with Amanda. As we talked the other day, she's never fully processed her mother's death. And I'm afraid she'll see my having a new relationship as a betrayal of her mother's memory."

"I agree. That's exactly how she's feeling now." Tomás sat back in his chair after another sip of his espresso. "In fact, she told me that Elise had masterminded the entire scenario of having the boys come stay with us during the honeymoon."

When Kent opened his mouth, but Tomás forestalled him. "I know Amanda and I made that decision, but she's in such a state now that she's rewriting history and blaming Elise."

Kent closed his eyes, and his gut wrenched. "That's so she doesn't have to blame me." Then he looked at Tomás. "Do you see my dilemma? I can't force this. Amanda is still struggling so deeply with her grief."

Tomás waved a hand. "You realize it's not just about you moving on with Elise. Amanda has been under stress for months now. And that—" Once again he put his hand to his chest. "—I blame myself for. I thought it would be lovely to combine the tour with our wedding at the end, that it would make things easier. But I was terribly wrong. All I did was add extra pressure. This was my fault. We could have come earlier this year to be married. Or next year. But doing it now was easier for me."

Kent let out a soft snort. "And now we're each blaming ourselves."

Tomás leaned forward, his elbow on the table, hand circling in the air. "The truth is, it is no one's fault. No one is to blame. God took your wife, for which we're all so sorry. And it happened during a difficult time in Amanda's life, as she became a new mother. But now I feel it is up to us to help her heal."

Kent felt that wrench in his gut once more. "When we get back, we should contact a family therapist and talk it out."

But Tomás shook his head. "Oh no, my friend. What we need to do is address our beloved Amanda's feelings now."

"But she's unlikely to listen right now."

"If we allow her to go on this way, she'll only become more entrenched. No, we must confront the issue now. You need to have a long talk with your daughter and tell her everything you feel. Amanda doesn't recognize that *you* are the one who has been alone these past five years. She has had me and the boys. You must make her understand you're not an old man. That you loved your wife so much that you want to experience love again. That it's because of how special Gail was, how beautiful, how kind, that you're willing to put your heart out there. That you want to fully embrace life again. And that you wish Amanda to embrace it as well. She can't do that if she hangs on to her grief so tightly that it's choking her."

Kent stared at this man—his son-in-law, the love of his daughter's life, a famous man with an incredible talent and skill. This man, Tomás, had an old soul. Perhaps even older than Kent's. "How did you get to be so smart?"

Tomás sat back and laughed. "I'm just saying the things I wish I could've said to Amanda. But for five years, I haven't had the courage."

Kent chuckled with him. "So you want *me* to do it."

Tomás shot him with a finger gun like any American would do. "Bull's-eye."

Yet Kent knew that wasn't Tomás's real reason. The problem of the moment was between him and his daughter. He was the one who needed Amanda to understand his feelings for Elise, his everlasting love for Gail, and his desire to help Amanda move past her grief. It was his job as Gail's husband. And as Amanda's father.

His coffee had gone cold. Tomás's small espresso cup was empty.

Without another word between them, they both stood, and Kent hugged his son-in-law. Then, pulling back, hands on Tomás's shoulders, he said, "Thank you."

ELISE STAYED WHERE SHE WAS, HER BACK TO THE DOOR, until she heard Kent's soft footsteps fade away down the hall. The quiet pressed against her ears, broken only by the faint ticking of a clock and the muted hum of voices from somewhere in the house.

Had she wanted him to push past her resistance, pound on the door, make her open up to him? It was hard to say. Part of her wanted him to hold her in his arms and tell her that everything would be okay. That same part of her didn't want to let him go. But there was the other part that couldn't face the consequences—having to deal with Amanda and Tomás, needing to tell Kent about the terrible things she'd done in the past, admitting to the kind of woman she'd once been.

Maybe she should go down to the boys and act as their nanny, pretend nothing had happened. But the door was closed, the brass handle cool under her palm, and it seemed somehow to be a metaphor. *Just shut it all out.* So she went back to packing the boys' things, folding small shirts scented faintly of sunshine and soap.

Even if it felt like she was hiding out.

Perhaps twenty minutes later, the door opened. No knock. Kent would have knocked.

Amanda stood in the doorway, a sharp silhouette against the hallway light.

Elise's heart dropped. Despite being a mature woman—older than Amanda—her heart still seemed to plummet, heavy as a stone.

Then Amanda advanced on her, her citrus lotion trailing faintly like bitter orange peel. "I won't let you get away with taking advantage of a vulnerable old man like that."

There was so much to unpack in that one sentence. She tackled the first, the most important. "Your father isn't an old man."

But Amanda didn't listen. "You had one job, and that was to look after my boys. But you set out to entrap my father. And you've been neglecting my boys."

"I haven't neglected them," she said calmly. Though she was guilty of other things, that she hadn't done.

But Amanda was on a roll, ignoring anything Elise said. "What about the way you left them with Tomás's parents for a whole day? You should've been there with them. And then you palmed them off on me, wanting me to take them on my honeymoon, for God's sake." Her voice rose, sharp and brittle, as if the concept itself was incomprehensible.

As much guilt as Elise felt, she wouldn't take on neglecting the boys. "Your parents requested a day with them. Since the boys were only going to be here for a couple of weeks, I thought that would be the right thing to do. And may I remind you that you were the one who asked for the boys to come up to the mountains."

"Only because I was afraid of leaving them alone with you."

Amanda wasn't making sense. She didn't want Elise to be with her father, but she'd taken the boys up to the cabin because she felt they were being neglected? And thus left Kent alone with Elise? No, it didn't make sense.

But Amanda moved on to the worst of Elise's supposed crimes. "I know you're only interested in my father for his money. Being widowed, he's in a vulnerable place. You're just a gold digger, trying to take him away because this very lucrative nanny position you've held for three months is almost over."

Her stomach seemed to cramp. It all reminded Elise of that horrible time when Nick's wife had accused her of being a home-wrecker, of all the awful things she'd said. Of all the guilt Elise felt. The situation was different but the guilt was the same.

Amanda continued to hound her relentlessly. "You know my father will never love you. He'll always love my mother. You'll never be able to replace her."

The words were brutal, reaching all the way to the deepest, darkest part of her, where guilt and shame lived—but also where, for the last few days, a small kernel of hope had grown. Kent had said he wanted to move on, that he was ready. But could he really be ready to leave his wife behind?

And even if he was—even if Amanda was wrong—once he learned about Elise's past, he would realize she wasn't the right woman to move on with.

"How could you do this to our family? How could you take advantage of us like this? The boys adored you, and all you wanted was to get your grubby little hands on my father's money."

It wasn't true. None of it. She had planned nothing. But somehow it all went back to what she'd done with Nick. She'd been a home-wrecker. And she hadn't given a damn about the people she hurt because she wanted what she wanted.

Nick's wife had hammered that home to her. And in the same way, Amanda hammered it home that Elise had swept aside all her duties and slept with Kent—not just once, but over and over for the past week—even knowing that her actual employer, Amanda, would have hated it.

She hadn't cared. She'd done it because she'd wanted it.

How did that make her any different from what she'd been thirty-five years ago?

She wanted to put her hands over her ears and scream at Amanda to stop.

It was almost a relief when Amanda said, "I want you to pack your bags and leave."

Yes, it was a relief. She wouldn't have to listen to any more of this. She wouldn't have to remember the past.

Then Amanda added, "I'll book you a flight—the first one out. I want you gone."

God, how it hurt. Leaving Kent. Leaving the boys. Running away in disgrace. It felt like thirty-five years ago, when her parents had disowned her, when she'd lost the baby and had nowhere to go, when she'd felt helpless and hopeless.

Amanda stomped out of the room and left her by herself.

That should have been a relief too. But all she wanted to

do was leave this anguish behind—and leave her memories of Nick behind too.

She crossed the hall to her room, throwing everything into the two suitcases she'd brought with her. She didn't even repack her sundries, just tossed everything into the case, along with a bag of dirty laundry.

That metaphor struck her too—all her dirty laundry. Isn't that what she'd been hiding? All her dirty little secrets.

She should have told Kent that very first night at the reception, when she'd told him she'd been married and her husband cheated on her. He would have walked away then, and none of this would have happened.

But oh God, she would have missed his touch, his kiss, his loving.

And maybe having those memories to keep was worth it all.

Pulling her bags off the bed, she let them land on the floor with a thunk. Then she saw the little shepherd girl on the dresser, the tangible reminder of her time with Kent. The ache in her heart seemed almost unbearable. Should she leave it behind? But Kent had wanted to give her that gift. If she took it with her, she could hold it while she closed her eyes and remembered that lovely day. All the lovely days.

In the end, she packed the figurine back in its box and put it in her carry-on. She couldn't trust the delicate figurine to the baggage handlers.

Her two roller bags clunked along the upper hallway, wheels echoing faintly against the high ceiling. The big one was heavy, and she carried it down first, then went back for the smaller case and her carry-on. Then she rolled them to the front door.

Kent was probably with the boys. She'd have to see him, and he would ask what was going on. She had no clue what she'd say to him. But she couldn't leave without saying goodbye to the boys.

The sound of their voices and their bright, innocent laughter spilled from the kitchen and brought tears to her eyes. Yes, it would hurt to leave them. It would hurt so much.

She turned toward the kitchen just as Amanda stalked down the stairs, heels slapping each step. She held out sheets of paper. "Here, I booked your flight. Jakub can take you to the airport. Your plane leaves in two hours."

Amanda's closeness backed Elise up against her suitcases. But she couldn't let this go. "I need to say goodbye to the boys."

Anger stained Amanda's beautiful face. "I'll tell them you said goodbye."

Elise wouldn't let it go. "They'll think I abandoned them. That won't be good for them. No matter what you say, they'll think it's their fault."

As anguished as Amanda was, Elise knew she loved her boys and wouldn't want Elise's departure to have any lasting effect.

"Fine. Just go. Get it over with. I'll have Jakub get the car out."

Elise didn't give her a chance to change her mind, heading quickly to the kitchen. The warm scent of spices drifted from the stove where Cook was working. Only the boys and Cook were in the room. She couldn't help asking, "Where's Dědeček?"

Marek piped up, "He and Papa went out. I think they went for coffee. Will you help us with our puzzle?"

How badly she wanted to stay, to help them with the cardboard pieces scattered like fragments of a story across the table. How badly she wanted to talk to Kent before she left. But there was no time—not for anything but a quick explanation.

She bent down between the boys' chairs so that she was on their level. "I can't help you with the puzzle, sweetheart. I'm sorry, but I have an emergency back home, and I have to leave."

Marek wailed. "Nooo!"

Luca, even though being younger, was more dogged. "Why?"

"A family emergency."

Of course he had to say, "I thought you didn't have any family back home."

Children remembered everything, despite what adults thought. They heard; they remembered. "This is a friend who needs me." She hated to lie.

Though busy at the stove, Cook shot her a sideways glance. Maybe she knew something was up.

Elise turned back to the boys. "I'm sorry. I have to go. My flight leaves in a couple of hours. Give me a hug. I loved being with you both. I'm going to miss you very, very much."

Marek threw his arms around her, hugged her, and for a moment Elise held him tight, breathing in his little-boy scent. Then Luca jumped down from his chair and threw himself at her. She knew she was going to cry; she just hoped the tears wouldn't come until she was gone.

On her way out, she blew kisses from the doorway.

She left the boys. She left the house. She left Amanda and Tomás. She left the life she'd enjoyed for the last three months.

And she left Kent.

19

Kent and Tomás walked back from the café. As a car passed, Kent almost didn't look up. Maybe it was a sixth sense that made him raise his head. He recognized the car, then Jakub in the front seat, and finally Elise seated behind Jakub.

Where was she going? Kent had a bad feeling. So bad it choked the words out of him. "What the hell?" He turned, frantic, waving his arms as the car pulled away. He started to run, but Tomás caught his sleeve.

"You'll never catch up with her," Tomás said, voice steady, his faint Czech accent rounding the words.

"But didn't you see? That was Elise. Where is Jakub taking her?"

"I don't know," Tomás answered quietly. "But our best course of action is to talk to my wife."

Amanda had seen that kiss. She'd been angry. And he'd left her alone with too much time to think when he should have gone straight to her and talked it through.

And now Elise was leaving. He knew it in his gut. This wasn't a trip to the store.

Kent speed-walked—almost running—back to the row house, Tomás close on his heels. He bounded up the front steps and nearly battered the door down, though it was unlocked.

Voices drifted from the kitchen. He followed them and burst into the cozy room.

The boys sat at the table, bent over the jigsaw puzzle they'd been working on when he left. At the counter, Cook simply stared at Kent, mouth open, a paring knife frozen in her hand.

Amanda sat across from the boys, fiddling with puzzle pieces but not placing them inside the frame. Her look was placid—too placid—and Kent knew in his gut she'd been up to something.

He advanced into the kitchen, feeling Tomás just behind him. "Where's Elise?" he asked.

Amanda met his gaze serenely and blew his world apart. "I fired her and booked her a flight home. In two hours, she'll fly to Zürich, then back to San Francisco from there. And good riddance."

For a heartbeat, Kent didn't see his daughter, the mother of his grandchildren, Tomás's wife. He saw the little girl she'd once been, the child who enjoyed getting her own way. He loved her no less, but anger welled up inside him. "Why would you do that?"

Then he caught sight of the boys' startled faces, mouths open, eyes wide. He turned to Tomás. "Can you take the boys out onto the veranda?"

Tomás shook his head gently. "Cook, would you mind? We have things to discuss."

"Of course." Cook hustled the boys toward the French doors, ushering them onto the veranda despite their protests. A breeze stirred the kitchen air as the door clicked shut behind them.

Kent faced Amanda again. "Well?" He didn't need to repeat the question.

Her serene facade melted. She leapt to her feet, finger stabbing the air. "You can actually ask me that?" She swung toward her husband. "I told you I found them in our boys' bedroom kissing. The boys' bedroom, for God's sake. And it wasn't just some friendly peck on the cheek the way he—" Without looking at Kent, she jabbed a finger at him. "—says was totally benign. I know what they've been doing behind our backs while we were away." She turned back to Kent. "You were sleeping with her, weren't you?"

He wanted to explain and began, "Yes, but—"

She didn't let him finish. "You betrayed my mother's memory with our nanny. How could you do that?" Confusion and tears clouded her eyes, misery tightening her face, her lips drooping as tears slid down her cheeks.

"What I feel for Elise doesn't diminish my love for your mother—or for you," Kent said quietly.

Amanda balled her fists, trembling. "So you admit it."

He longed to run after Elise, to catch her, to tell her how he felt, to beg her to stay. But he couldn't leave his daughter like this. Not now. This had been a long time coming, and they needed to air everything between them right now. Or they might never find their way back to each other.

"This isn't about Elise." He kept his tone gentle. "Or about her being your nanny. This is about you and me. About losing your mother."

Amanda stamped her foot. "It is most definitely about you screwing our nanny." Her voice wobbled with grief. If anyone else had spoken about Elise like that, Kent would have ripped them a new one—but this was Amanda's sorrow speaking. And it was the closest they'd come to talking over their feelings about Gail's loss.

Somehow that brought a calmness to him and a softness

to his voice. "She's not just your nanny. She's a beautiful woman, and I'm drawn to her. I want to spend time with her." He may very well want to spend the rest of his life with Elise.

Amanda's tears fell unchecked. "But what about Mom? She was the love of your life. How can you suddenly choose someone else?"

Kent spread his hands, palms open. "Because your mother is gone. She's been gone for five years. I loved her with all my heart. But I have to move on."

"Move *on*?" she cried. "How can you move on after thirty-five years with her? You shouldn't be able to move on from that!"

He answered in the calmest voice he owned, laced with love. "We both have to move on. We both loved your mother and mourned her death, and we'll always grieve her, always miss her. But you have a life—your husband, your sons. Don't let grief steal what you have right in front of you."

As she took a menacing step toward him, he held his ground. He'd feared her anger for five years, letting it grow—and fester—between them.

"You won't even let me clear out her clothes," he said, pain sharpening his tone. "Do you know how that feels every time I walk into the closet and see everything hanging there? It wrenches my heart."

Tomás shifted, hovering like a referee, his own face etched with sympathy as he reached out to Amanda. Kent understood his feelings. He was caught between supporting his wife, wanting to help her heal, and understanding Kent's perspective after their talk in the café.

But Amanda brushed Tomás off, focusing completely on Kent. "Those things *shouldn't* change. We should remember her every day. But you even talked about selling the house a couple of years ago. How could you ever consider that? It was Mom's dream home. It's where I grew up."

This time Tomás didn't let Amanda silence him. "My love," he said softly, "we've spoken about this. Those are just things—reminders. They aren't your mother. I know how it hurts. But she is truly gone."

Amanda pressed her fists to her eyes like a child. When she lowered them, her face was blotchy, raw—a mirror of Kent's heart.

He spoke to the core issue. "Your mother will always hold a place in my heart. And finding someone new doesn't mean I'll forget her. It doesn't erase her."

"But, Daddy..." she whispered, slipping into her childhood name for him.

He shook his head gently. "You're not a little girl anymore. And I'm a widower. I'm done hiding my feelings from you. I've dated since your mother passed, but I never told you—because I feared this reaction. I can't keep living this way. I want to be honest with you. None of those women were special, but Elise is. She makes me feel alive again, young again. She reminds me of how good my life with your mother was. I want that kind of happiness again." His voice thickened. "Your mother and I had so many plans. We would have done them all if she hadn't gotten sick. But I know in my heart she wouldn't want me to be alone. She wouldn't want our life together turned into a shrine I could never leave—just as I wouldn't want that for her. It doesn't mean I never loved her, or that I won't always love her. It doesn't mean I don't love you. It means that I want to know love again—and I've found the woman I want to love. Elise."

Amanda sagged back down into her chair, face buried in her hands.

Tomás crouched beside her, stroking her hair and back, murmuring quiet words of love.

A tear slid down Kent's cheek. "I love you so much,

Amanda. I love the boys. I love your husband. Please don't let my feelings for Elise come between us."

Amanda's dam burst. Tears streaked her face; sobs shook her shoulders. "I miss her so much, Daddy. There are so many times I want to run to her for advice, but she's just not there. Sometimes I go to the house and sit in her closet, touch her things, trying to feel close to her. But it never works." She gulped a breath.

Kent's heart twisted. He hadn't realized how truly bad things had become. He whispered, "I love you, sweetheart. Tell me how can I help you?"

"I don't think you can," she murmured. Then she turned to Tomás. "Call the boys in. I just need to hold them."

Tomás rose, one hand still on her shoulder. He pressed a kiss on the top of her head. "Go find Elise," he said softly to Kent. "It's my turn to take care of my family."

Kent backed out of the kitchen, leaving them together. That was what they needed for now.

He'd said what needed to be said, but it wasn't over—he and Amanda still had to find a way forward for themselves, for the whole family. But right now, Amanda and Tomás needed time. And he had to find Elise.

He hoped it wasn't too late.

Kent stopped only long enough to run up to his room for his passport, in case he needed to get past security to find her. As he raced out of the house, he heard Amanda and Tomás in the kitchen, their voices too soft for him to hear what they were saying.

Jakub hadn't returned from the airport, and if Kent took the other car, he was sure he couldn't navigate the Prague streets well enough to get there in time. Jogging to the nearest crossroads a block away, he hailed a cab, paying the man extra to get him to Prague Airport as fast as possible.

"Running late?" the man asked in a thick Czech accent.

Thinking of himself as a hero in a romance movie, Kent said, "I'm trying to catch my girlfriend before she takes off without me." There were any number of movies with airport scenes of lovers racing to find each other again.

The driver—whose name badge read something unpronounceable—grinned. "When does her flight leave?" His English was flawless despite the heavy accent.

Kent checked his watch. "About an hour and a half."

Centrifugal force pushed him back in his seat as the man punched the accelerator, dodging cars, barely missing pedestrians. "I will get you there on time."

Kent thought about saying he'd like to get there alive, or at least uninjured. But his taxi driver was an expert. They didn't even have what Kent would have called a near miss.

He tried calling Elise, but her phone was off. Because she didn't want to talk to him? He left a message anyway, saying he was on his way and begging her not to get on that flight.

Entering the airport departures lane, the man took it at breakneck speed, pulling into a spot and slamming on the brakes, pitching Kent forward. Luckily, he managed to brace himself against the seat.

"You're the best," Kent told him, looking at his watch and seeing he still had over an hour. He threw some extra bills to the man. As he climbed out, the driver said, "Good luck. Just remember, Prague is the city of romance. You will find your lady love."

The car door shut on its own as the driver took off like he was in a race.

Inside the terminal, Kent jogged first to the security line, scanning faces. Elise was a relatively tall woman, and he figured he could spot her. But she was nowhere in sight—until he saw her figure on the other side of security, walking away with her roller case. He shouted her name. Heads turned, but hers wasn't one of them. He tried her phone, and again it went straight to voicemail.

He needed a new plan and raced back to the ticketing counter. He and both Amanda and Tomás always flew the same airline. That's what she would have chosen for Elise.

His heart dropped, as if smashed on the floor like a bug on a windshield. The lines were enormous, people with two and three bags inching forward. A caterpillar would move faster.

Then he remembered. Taking out his credit card with priority status, he entered the much shorter line. Thankfully, he made it to the front in less than five minutes—far faster than the inchworm line.

"I'd like to get on the next flight out to Zürich. It leaves in an hour." He was sure that's what Amanda had said, Zürich, then San Francisco.

The woman didn't bat an eyelash as she tapped on her keys. "Do you have luggage, sir? Because I don't believe your bag will make it onto the plane on time."

"I don't have any baggage. Just the ticket, please." Then he asked, "Can you tell me what seat another passenger is in? She's a friend of mine. Maybe you can seat us together."

She looked at him for the first time, her dark brown eyes assessing. "I'm sorry, sir, but we can't give out that information." Then she gave him a boarding pass and pointed to another short line a few steps from the ticket counter. "Our priority guests can use that special line to get through security."

He thanked her before he dashed off, grateful for the line that took only another five minutes. He didn't even have to take off his shoes or belt and had nothing to be scanned but himself.

It was getting close to boarding time when he found the gate. And he felt the second calamitous stomach drop since arriving. Elise wasn't there. He checked the people sitting, standing, or hunkered down on the floor.

She could be in the restroom. He wasted several critical minutes standing outside the women's restroom. She never emerged.

What the hell did he do now? There was nothing for it but to get on the flight and hope he found her there. He turned back toward the gate.

Then he saw her, seated in the gate opposite, where there were empty chairs. She seemed to be staring into space.

Thank God he'd found her.

"Elise?"

The male voice pulled her out of her daze. Elise looked up at the apparition, light from the windows turning him into nothing more than a silhouette.

A security guard? She wondered what she'd done wrong. But he'd used only her first name. "Yes?" she asked.

"Don't go." His breathless voice gave him away.

Kent. It felt like a miracle. All she could ask was, "How did you get through security without a ticket?"

He held up a passport in one hand and a boarding pass in the other. "I bought a ticket to Zürich."

"But you're supposed to be leaving tomorrow."

He swept her bag off the chair next to her, set it on the floor, and sat beside her. "It was the only way I could get through the security gate." He smiled, the most delicious, beautiful smile. "I miss the days before nine-eleven when we could walk all the way to the gate and meet someone right at the plane."

"Your grandchildren will never know that experience."

Then she ended the silly banter. "You bought a ticket just to find me?"

"Of course." He took her hand. "Please don't leave. I want you to stay. We have so much to talk about."

She could do nothing more than shake her head.

"I talked to Amanda," he said. "I told her how I feel about you. We can work this out."

She wanted to ask exactly how he felt, but fear tightened her vocal cords.

Then it was as if every emotion inside him poured out. "I loved Gail for so long. She was the light of my life. And because I loved her, it made me realize I want another love in my life. I don't want to spend the rest of my days alone, clinging to her memory. She wanted me to find love again too. She even told me that."

Kent allowed her only one startled, "But—" before he interrupted. "You are my second chance." He smoothed a thumb over the back of her hand. "Haven't you already guessed I'm in love with you?"

As much as she wanted that to be true, she couldn't help saying, "But we've only known each other for two weeks." Had it even been that long?

"And they've been the best two weeks I've known since Gail died. I've dated other women. Maybe I was even searching for a replacement."

Softly, her heart aching, she said, "I don't want to be a replacement."

He raised her hand to his lips, kissed her knuckles. "That's what I'm trying to tell you. I feel for you—things I can't remember feeling before. I loved Gail, but you've sparked something inside me I've never felt. Maybe it's because my mind is clogged with memories of the last three years of her life, when she was so sick, when I felt so helpless to do anything for her. Or maybe it's because Gail taught me how extraordinary marriage to a woman you care deeply for can be. I don't know why. I was married for thirty-five years, and love morphs in all that time. You don't stop loving, but it changes, because now there are children and bills and work and all the pressures of life." He closed his eyes and tipped his head back. Finally, his voice slightly choked, he said, "And then you experience such an immense loss."

She wanted so badly to hold him in her arms, to offer him comfort, to soothe him. But doing that would bring so many complications when she knew she had to leave.

"That's why I know I love you," he said. "Because I've known love before. I know what it feels like—" He laid his hand on his chest. "—in here. I'm not some lustful young man." For just a moment, a twinkle skittered through his eyes. "Although I am lustful for you. But what I feel is so much more. I'm asking you to stay so that we can explore this. So that you can decide if you feel the same way."

Her heart wanted to burst, and yet it seemed to shrink inside her. Because he was in love with a phantom. He didn't know all the things she'd done. And when he did, he would run back down the wide terminal hallway and leave her all alone again.

She said softly, "I know you think you feel—"

Again, he cut her off. "I don't just *feel* it. I *know* it. Let me help you discover if you feel it too."

Her flight began boarding, passengers lining up even before their zones were called. She whispered, "People are getting on the plane now. I really have to go."

But he didn't let her go. He held her hand, inescapable. "I've got a ticket. If you board, I'm going with you." He gave a small, self-deprecating laugh. "At least as far as Zürich."

Determination edged his features. There was only one way he would let her leave.

By giving him the truth. "I have to tell you something."

20

Kent was suddenly terrified of what Elise had to say—that she was actually married, or she had a live-in lover, or, worst of all, that she'd never felt anything close to love for him, and never would.

His voice came out as little more than a croak. "Whatever you have to tell me won't change my mind."

But he was afraid it would change everything—not that he loved her, but that she would strip away any chance they had of being together.

She pulled her hand from his, and he let her go, understanding the momentousness of whatever she had to tell him.

As the line of passengers waiting to board lengthened, the crowd encroached on them until Kent looked up, and a nearby man and woman backed off.

"Tell me," he urged.

She took a deep breath as if she had to fortify herself. "I told you I had an affair with my professor, that we got married when I found out I was pregnant, and that I lost the baby."

He nodded. "Yes. But that all happened a long time ago."

Then he thought—maybe she hadn't lost the baby. Maybe she was still in contact with the professor. Maybe the man wanted her back after all these years. His mind raced.

But she went on. "What I didn't tell you was that he was married already."

He said quickly, jumping to her defense, "He was the one who was married, not you." But he knew it took two.

"I knew he was married. But I was so infatuated, I didn't care."

Again, he had to defend her. "But you were young. People do a lot of things they regret later on." He'd never cheated on Gail, but he couldn't say he'd *never* entertained a brief thought. But he never would have acted on it.

"I took precautions," she said. "But I got pregnant anyway. And when I told him, Nick wanted me to have an abortion."

Christ. She hadn't just *lost* the baby. But he refused to judge her.

"I told him I wouldn't do it, that I'd have the baby. And I wanted him to divorce his wife. He didn't have any children." Her words spilled out now, unstoppable. "His wife couldn't have any. But now I could make him a father. I thought that justified everything." She closed her eyes, and a single tear slipped from her lashes as she whispered, "I was relentless."

He suddenly saw her as a pregnant young woman, little more than a girl. Because what were you at twenty? You thought you were an adult, and yet you were barely out of high school. You knew nothing of life, nothing of consequences. And he ached for her.

"Before I was even showing, he agreed to a quickie divorce. Because I'd pounded into him how his wife could never give him children. But I could. I was horrible," she whispered so softly that he had to read her lips to understand. She looked at him with eyes so wounded he felt her pain—the pain of the young woman she'd been, the pain of the woman she was now.

"You were young," he murmured.

She shook her head. "I was old enough to have an affair with my married professor. I was old enough to get pregnant when I didn't mean to. I was old enough to know exactly what I was doing when I hounded him into getting a divorce."

"We all do things we regret." He tried to console her. "Even things we find abhorrent once we grow up."

The boarding queue dwindled, but she didn't look at it.

She simply continued her story. "We went to Nevada for the divorce, but you have to remain in the state as a resident. And Nick had to go back to the university. So I stayed, which allowed him to still have an address there." Now she met his gaze head-on. "His wife came to see me—his ex-wife." Her voice trembled, her hands spreading as if to encompass it all. "I'd never wanted to think about her—that was the problem. But now I could see what I'd done to her. She was so angry, so broken." She didn't reach up to wipe away a tear leaking from each eye. "And she told me that Nick was having an affair with another of his students."

He wanted to take her into his arms, to hold the young woman she'd been, to ease the heartache she must have felt. But he only whispered, "I'm so sorry."

But she couldn't seem to stop. "I raced back to Berkeley. His wife was right. I mean, really, *she* was his wife. I was just a stopgap, a nothing. He was with a student just like me. Because that's what he did. He was addicted to his affairs with students. I was just one more."

Kent couldn't help himself then. He cupped her cheeks, wiping away her tears with his thumbs. "You have to forgive yourself."

"But you haven't heard the rest."

He wondered how much worse it could get.

"I ran out. I didn't want to hear his excuses, his reasons. And I especially didn't want him to tell me he regretted marrying me."

Kent couldn't help himself. He leaned in, kissed her softly, gently, soothingly.

She let him, but then she pulled back. "I got in my car, and I was crying so hard I could barely see. I ran a stop sign, and a car broadsided me."

"Oh God." He said it so she wouldn't have to. "And you lost the baby."

Of course, she said it anyway. "I didn't *lose* her. I *killed* her."

His insides cramped. Her pain was like nothing he could have imagined. He'd loved his wife, lost her, grieved for her. He wished he'd spent more time at home, wished he'd retired earlier, wished they'd traveled more. Wished for so many things.

But he'd never blamed himself for Gail's death.

Elise looked at him. "So now you know the real Elise Martin. The terrible things I've done." She glanced at her gate as the agent called for all passengers to board.

Standing, she gathered her bag. She was still going to leave.

He rose beside her and took her hand. "Please don't leave me alone."

Yet he was terrified he'd already lost her—that he'd lost her thirty-five years ago when she ran a stop sign and lost her baby.

TELLING KENT HER STORY TORE OUT CHUNKS OF HER heart. It almost surprised her it could still be beating. And yet, it felt as if a great weight had lifted from her soul, allowing it to float free. She had nothing left to fear, having told the truth to the only man she'd allowed herself to care for after Nick.

The only thing left was to face the look in his eyes when he gazed at her with all his new knowledge.

That was why she'd jumped up to board before the plane closed its doors.

But there was his voice behind her, carrying so much weight it seemed to glue her feet to the terminal floor.

"Please don't leave me alone."

She wanted to flee, craved escape, but those words struck deeper than she could have imagined. *Please don't leave me alone.*

Her body moved before her mind could argue, and she turned to look at him.

His eyes glistened, leaking sorrow like a wounded hound's, the faint creases at the corners deepening, betraying the weight of his worry and longing.

Then, as if hope had lifted his spirit, his shoulders straightened, and the corners of his mouth turned up in the faintest smile.

"That was thirty-five years ago," he said softly, stepping closer. "You made a terrible mistake, and there were catastrophic consequences." He closed the distance between them—just a few more steps—but it felt like miles. He reached for her, and she dropped her bag to the floor so he could hold both her hands. "Tell me," he said, "that you're the same woman you were then. Tell me you've learned nothing since then. Tell me you would do it all exactly the same way, without making a single different choice."

God, if only she could have a do-over.

"You know the answer is that I never would have started my affair with Nick," she whispered, shutting her eyes so she couldn't see his beautiful face. "But I snuck around with you behind Amanda's back. I'm still all about sneaking around."

"You're not the same woman. And what we've been doing isn't the same thing at all. It's time to forgive yourself. To stop punishing yourself by being alone."

Had she been punishing herself all these years? Is that why she'd never had a serious relationship? How often had she thought that she didn't deserve happiness?

Their final boarding call echoed over the terminal speakers. She opened her eyes. "I have to go."

He didn't release her hands. His grip was firm, grounding her. His voice strengthened, commanding attention. "Neither of us is married. Neither of us has an attachment back home. Your stint as a nanny is almost over. We gave the boys the best time of their lives. When Amanda asked them to stay at the cabin, we did exactly as she asked."

"But she never told us it was just fine if we slept together," she protested, her voice a fragile whisper.

He moved quickly to cup her cheeks. She barely registered the warmth of his palms before he spoke. "We don't need her permission to fall in love."

She felt her eyes widen as his did, mirrored reflections of longing and certainty. He punctuated his next words with a slow, deliberate nod. "I love you, Elise Martin. Amanda has only made that a problem because she hasn't finished grieving."

"You can never stop missing those you love," she said softly.

"I know," he said. "And I told you I'll never stop loving Gail. I'll miss her forever. But I can also accept new love into my life."

"My flight is about to lock me out," she whispered, the metallic echo of the terminal loudspeaker amplifying her fear.

"I don't care," he said firmly. "Get another flight."

She heard their names called since they'd already checked in. Last chance.

Finally, his voice low and steady, he said, "There's only one thing that really matters. I love you." He kissed her gently, brushing his lips against hers with the tenderness of a promise. Pulling back just enough to meet her gaze, he let her see the certainty there. "Do you love me?"

This was it. If she told him she wasn't in love with him, he'd let her go. She could get on that plane, fly to Zürich, then board another flight to San Francisco. She could return to her life as it was before this trip.

All she had to do was tell him she didn't love him.

All she had to do was lie.

But she couldn't.

"Yes, I love you. But—"

He cut off her protest with another kiss, soothing and sweet, grounding her with the sheer certainty of his presence.

Then he whispered against her lips, "Thank God."

Suddenly, he was all business, picking up her bag and heading them over to the gate agent. "I know we have so many things to work out," he told her as hustled her along. "Especially how Amanda feels about us being together. But I can't let her emotions control my life. I need to live it the way I want." He glanced down at her. "That means I don't want to live alone. I want to live my life with you."

Elise's breath caught in her throat. "I don't think she'll ever understand."

"She needs to let go of her own guilt and grief. She has to do it for the boys. And for Tomás."

At the counter, Kent's control never wavered. "This is Elise Martin, and I'm Kent Woodward. We were supposed to be on that flight, but we had a family emergency. We need to cancel. Can you help us?"

The agent acted swiftly after closing the boarding gate.

The roar of engines firing up carried through the thick glass windows, shaking the terminal with its vibration. Only a few minutes later, the plane backed away, disappearing down the runway.

In the end, the gate agent rebooked Elise on the original flights leaving tomorrow with the rest of the family. Kent had never canceled his booking and received a voucher for the Zürich flight to use another time. As they walked away, Elise whispered, "You're a miracle worker."

He stopped her in the middle of the terminal. Departing passengers skirted around them, arriving passengers maneuvering like a river flowing past a dock. He pulled back to look down at her. "Say it again."

"What?"

"Tell me you love me."

She whispered with all the truth in her heart, "I love you."

"I don't care about anything you've done in the past. I care only about the woman you are now. You are good, beautiful, accomplished, and caring. That's all that matters to me. And I love everything about you."

Could it be true? Could he forgive her? And if he could, did she have the courage to forgive herself and reach for happiness with him?

"I love you," she whispered. "Thank you for still caring about me even after hearing my story."

He rubbed his cheek against hers. "You don't have to thank me. I'll always care about you. I'll always see you as the beautiful person you are."

Maybe she could too, with his help and his love.

Then he smiled, warm and steady. "So let's go fix this thing with my daughter."

As he walked her down the long terminal hallway, his arm around her shoulders, Elise breathed in his subtle male scent and savored his comforting warmth. She suddenly knew he could fix anything. That's the kind of man he was.

And he'd helped her face her guilt and fears after all these years.

❦

Back at the house, Kent braced himself for another confrontation with Amanda. Elise's suitcase was still on the flight, heading to Zürich. If all went well, she'd get it back tomorrow, just in time for them to leave again.

For now, his concern was Amanda. He loved his daughter with all his being. He didn't want to alienate her, but he could no longer let her emotions control his life.

With Elise's carry-on in hand and his arm around her, they mounted the steps to the front porch, the crisp evening air brushing past them. Before he opened the door, he said, "Everything's going to be okay."

Elise answered, "I know it will be."

Opening the door, he braced for Amanda's yelling, but there was only the distant chatter of little boys' voices drifting from the kitchen, mingled with the faint clatter of dishes.

Setting Elise's case down in the foyer, he put his hand beneath her elbow and guided her forward. His jaw nearly dropped as he took in the scene in the kitchen.

Cook stood at the counter, busily preparing dinner. The smell of sautéed vegetables and baked bread filled the room. His family sat across from one another: Luca next to Tomás, Marek beside Amanda, the colorful puzzle—almost completed—spread across the table.

Kent felt as if he'd stepped into an alternate universe.

Then Luca saw him and Elise. "Děda—" he cried. "Look how much we've done on our puzzle!"

Marek clapped his hands lightly, excitement lighting his features. "We're almost done! We have to get another puzzle. I want to buy something here to take home with us."

"Of course," Kent said. "We'll find something."

But he was watching Amanda. Finally, she looked up at him. He'd been gone only two hours, yet his daughter seemed like a new person. She rose from the table and said, "Can I talk to you?" Then she looked at Elise. "I'd like to talk to both of you."

She led them into the living room, with Tomás following. The warmth of the room wrapped around them, the faint scent of vanilla candles mingling with the aroma of the dinner Cook was preparing.

Amanda turned, greeting them with a tentative smile. "I want to apologize for my behavior."

Kent began, "You don't have to—"

She held up her hand. "Yes, I do. Elise, I said some terrible things to you. I'm so sorry. I hope you can forgive me."

"I know you're under a lot of pressure," Elise said, her voice soft in contrast with the tension in the room.

"Tomás has made me see that's no excuse."

"I never said that, my darling," Tomás interrupted.

But Amanda waved him off. "I know you didn't. But it's the truth. I said some awful things." She gazed at Elise, her eyes slightly teary. "And you and my father have a perfect right to be together."

Finally, she looked at Kent. "You were right. I've been holding on to my mother's memories too tightly. It prevented me from moving on, and it hurt you too. If Elise makes you happy, Mom would've wanted that. It was wrong of me to say you couldn't be together."

She held out her hand to Elise, who took it, squeezing back. "You stepped in when we were in a bind. We would've had to bring someone we hadn't properly vetted when Cynthia had to go in for that surgery. You saved us. You've been so good with the boys. I couldn't ask for a better nanny." She laughed softly, a sound like warm sunlight. "Unless it's Cynthia, of course. But you saved us, and I treated you abominably. My bad." She widened her eyes. "My *so*-bad."

Then she focused on Kent again. "I should never have made you feel like you needed to hide parts of your life from me. That was so wrong." She held out her hand to Tomás, who took it, raising her knuckles to his lips.

"My wonderful husband has talked some sense into me," Amanda said. "He's made me realize how badly I need grief counseling." To Elise, she added, "I know you make my father happy. That makes me happy, and it would make my mother happy."

Then she held out her arms to Kent, and he gathered her into his embrace. Instead of apologizing again, she said, "I love you. I'm so glad you're my father, and that you're still with me. And I want you to be happy."

He hugged her tightly. "I'm so happy you've done this for me today. I never want us to be angry with each other. If we are, I want us to talk it out."

She nodded. "I will, Daddy, I promise. I love you so much."

His emotions shifted inside him—relief, love, hope. He didn't fool himself. There would be relapses on all their parts. But this family could rebuild their relationships.

And Elise would be part of it. He felt the soft brush of her hand on his, the warmth of Amanda's embrace, the gentle laughter of the boys, and knew that this new life was real, possible, and theirs to share.

21

Joy filled Elise's body. Happiness for Kent, for Amanda, for the Novak family. They could move past the anger. They would be whole again.

Elise just wasn't sure how she fit into it.

She couldn't forget all the things Amanda had said after she found Elise with Kent, and the memories her words had dredged up. Kent had forgiven her, and with his help, she knew she could forgive herself. But despite what she'd said, Amanda was a whole different story. She'd apologized, said all the right things, but did she truly mean them?

Elise wanted to step back, to look from afar as Kent reunited with his daughter.

She'd even taken a few steps toward the hallway when a timer dinged on the oven, and Cook appeared in the doorway.

It was as if she too had melted into the background until this moment. "Dinner is ready," she said with a smile. "I have made *pečená kachna se zelím a knedlíky*, roast duck with red cabbage and dumplings. It is a meal we have for celebrations."

She looked at them all, her eyes sparkling. "Shall I open champagne?"

Perhaps she *had* listened to everything said—and yelled—this day.

Tomás clapped his hands. "Absolutely. This is a time to celebrate."

When Kent moved to Elise's side and folded his arm across her shoulders, she wanted to believe that everything would be all right.

THEY SHARED ANOTHER OF COOK'S DELICIOUS CZECH meals, the duck tender, the cabbage slightly spicy. And an hour later, Jakub drove Kent and Elise away from the house.

Kent had told Amanda that he wanted to give them some family time. But he also needed some Elise time. He wanted to make love to her, to hold her in his arms, to wake up beside her in the morning. Despite everything he and Amanda had moved past, his daughter wasn't quite ready for that. He didn't think Elise was either.

So he'd booked a hotel room, and the boys had given both of them hugs and kisses before they left. Tomás had also hugged Elise, but Amanda, though she held both Elise's hands in hers, didn't seem quite ready for a hug yet. He knew in his heart it would come with time.

In the car, he asked, "Do we need to stop and get you anything along the way, since your suitcase is probably still in Zürich?"

Seated close together in the back seat, they clasped hands. "After all the travel I've done over the past three months," Elise said, "I learned to pack a change of clothes and a few essentials in my carry-on just in case. So I'm fine."

Kent had run upstairs before they left and packed a few things for the night.

Now Jakub pulled up in front of the Dancing House.

Elise gasped, looking up at the lighted facade. "Oh my God, don't tell me you got us a room here."

He loved her delight. "I most certainly did."

The lobby was small, but the reception clerk was as helpful as he could be. "Would you like me to make a reservation at the restaurant for dinner?"

Kent shook his head. "No, thank you. But we'd like a bottle of champagne sent up to the room."

The man winked. Champagne, the universal sign of romance.

A bellboy carried their small bags, ushered them into the elevator, and finally opened the door to a spacious room with a view. "Welcome to the Ginger Suite."

Hand to her mouth, Elise gasped. After he'd tipped the bellboy and they were alone, she wandered to the windows of the round room. The view of the river, lights sparkling on its surface, and the backdrop of Prague Castle and Charles Bridge, felt like a fairytale. They'd seen this view from the veranda every night. But here in the Ginger Suite of the Dancing Hotel, it was as if they'd entered a picture postcard.

When she turned into his arms, he realized she was crying. Cupping her face, he lifted her chin to look at him. "What's wrong?"

She shook her head slightly. "Nothing's wrong. It's just that only hours ago, I thought I'd never see you again. I thought you couldn't possibly forgive me for my past, and that Amanda would never forgive me for falling in love with you. My life seemed like an endless, lonely road." She gazed up at him as he wiped tears from her face. "And now I'm here with you. And you love me." Her voice rose, as if in incredulity.

He brushed his lips across hers. "I do love you. I've been waiting for you for five years. I'm sure that's why none of the other women I dated seemed to fit. Because somehow my heart knew you were out there waiting for me."

"And my heart has been waiting for you for thirty-five years."

He kissed her then, the longest, deepest, sweetest kiss. It might have gone on forever but for the knock on the door.

The bellboy had returned with champagne in a bucket of ice, and two glasses. Kent gestured for him to enter. The dark-haired young man set the bucket between the two chairs by the window. "Shall I uncork it for you, sir?"

But Kent, as he handed the young man a tip, shook his head. "No. We'll take care of it. Thank you."

When he was gone, Kent gestured toward the champagne. "We can have a glass now. Or we can save it for later and go up to the bar for a drink. That will give us a chance to walk around the observation deck too." He tucked a stray lock of hair behind her ear. "Then we'll have our champagne when we get back, and I'll beg you to let me ravish you."

She laughed, and the last of her tears, even if they were of happiness, vanished. "A drink in the bar would be fabulous before you ravish me."

The Glass Bar offered a breathtaking view of Prague. Per their waiter's recommendation, they both ordered a *Beton*, a drink made with tonic water and a traditional Czech liqueur called *Becherovka*, then garnished with a lemon twist.

The young man smiled as he delivered the drinks and waited for them to taste, the question in his raised eyebrows.

"Ginger?" Elise said.

"Cinnamon?" Kent asked.

"Both. A little bit sweet and a little bit bitter," the man said just like an American.

Elise declared, "I like it," and Kent nodded in agreement.

"Then enjoy."

After the waiter left, Elise leaned close. "I think we're right above our suite."

"Does that mean I can't make you scream tonight because someone might hear?"

She laughed. Oh, how he loved her sexy laugh. "No. I intend to scream loudly."

After finishing their drinks, they passed through a glass atrium to the observation deck. From there, as they walked around the deck, they were given a magnificent view of the most romantic city on earth.

Prague would always be that for him. Because it was where he'd found Elise. It was where he'd fallen more deeply in love with her every day they'd roamed the city together.

As the wind chilled her, Elise took Kent's hand. "Our room might feel a little cozier now." Involuntarily, she punctuated the sentence with a shiver.

With his arm around her, Kent led her back down. As he opened the door to the Ginger Suite, she said, "Did you see the size of that bathtub?"

He laughed, a deep, beautiful, sexy sound. "I did. And I saw those plush robes to wrap ourselves in too."

Standing in the middle of the room, she twirled around to look at him. "Thank you."

With two steps closer, he asked, "You're always thanking me. For what this time?"

She spread her arms wide. "For booking this room. For all the wonderful things you've done for me this week." After a pause she added, "And for loving me."

He closed the last few steps between them and wrapped

her in his arms. She had never felt so desired, so cared for, so loved.

"I'll pour the champagne," he said. "You run the bath."

She pulled out a few necessities from her carry-on. And saw the box she'd added at the last minute.

His voice came at the same moment she felt him behind her. "What do you have there?" he asked.

Picking it up gingerly, she unwrapped the little shepherd girl with her lambs.

"You kept it," he whispered.

She turned her head to look at him over her shoulder. "It was the only thing I had to remind me of you. I thought I *should* leave it behind. But then I just couldn't."

Dropping a kiss on her nape, he murmured, "If I'd noticed it was gone, I would have known there was hope. But I rushed through the house too fast."

"I'm glad you rushed." She put her arm back to wrap around his neck. "I'm glad the plane hadn't left." Then she whispered. "I'm glad you're here with me. And that you love me."

"Always."

Then she stroked a finger along the pretty dress of the shepherd girl. "I'll always treasure her because of everything she means." Placing the figurine back in the box, she laid it in the carry-on, then turned into his arms. "I love you."

He kissed her sweetly, then hotly, until her heart was beating frantically.

Stepping back, he smiled. "Now run that bath. I'll be right there with your champagne." He kissed her on the tip of her nose and swatted her bottom, sending her off to the bathroom with a laugh.

She had never felt joy like this before.

Finding a small bottle of bubble bath, she added it as the water ran. Then she dropped her clothes to the floor, not caring that she hadn't folded them, and stepped into the deliciously hot water, sinking down as the bubbles rose.

Kent entered with two glasses. "Hey, no fair. I didn't get to watch you undress."

She splashed a hand in the rapidly rising bubbles. "But I get to watch you." She gave him her most wicked wink.

And oh, did he ever give her a show.

Unbuttoning his shirt, he kept it closed until the last moment before throwing it aside, revealing his gorgeous chest. Sixty-five was definitely the new forty-five. He toed off his shoes and kicked them across the room. Then he turned his back to her, slid his slacks down and stepped out of them, his boxer briefs outlining his beautiful behind.

Still with his back to her, he hooked his thumbs in the waistband and slowly tugged on them, spreading his legs slightly, bending over to give her the best view as he pushed them down. Fingertips braced on the floor, he looked back at her and winked.

She laughed. "You are shameless."

But God, how utterly beautiful he was. Then he climbed into the tub with her, and the water rose almost to the top as she twisted off the taps.

Picking up the two champagne glasses he'd set on the side, he handed one to her. "To the sexiest woman alive."

She tapped her glass to his. "To the naughtiest man I can't wait to get my hands on."

They each drank to the other's toast. Then he pulled her between his legs, settling her back against him, his hardness along her spine. She couldn't resist moving subtly, stroking him with her body.

His lips at her ear, he whispered, "If you want to play..." He cupped her breasts, tweaked her nipples, then he hooked his feet around her ankles and spread her legs. "Then let's see how wet you are."

She giggled. "I'm in the water, so I'm extremely wet."

But he tunneled his hand beneath the bubbles, between her legs, and stroked her. And she moaned for him. They teased and played, kissed and touched. Until the bathwater grew lukewarm.

Then he lifted her out of the tub, rubbed her down with the luxurious thick towel, and finally wrapped the robe around her.

It was her turn to watch him dry off. She enjoyed seeing his hands on himself. She enjoyed watching how hard he got. Because they both knew what was to come.

Instead of taking her into the bedroom, he pushed her down on the edge of the tub, parted her robe, and whispered, "First, I want this."

When he bent his head and put his tongue to her, she cried out with all the pleasure and all the love flooding her body.

NOTHING COULD BE MORE GLORIOUS THAN GIVING HER pleasure. Kent held her as she climaxed, using his mouth and his tongue and his fingers to keep her on the edge for as long as he could. The faint salt of her skin, the heated silk of her thighs against his cheeks, the trembling clutch of her fingers in his hair—it all filled his senses and made him drunk on her.

When she curled over him, wrapping her arms around his head and whispered, "I think I'm going to fall," he drew her down to the thick bath rug, the soft pile cushioning them, the steam from their bath still clinging faintly in the air. He covered her with his body, peppering kisses over her damp face, tasting both water and the salt of her tears of release.

Then he kissed her, a long, luscious tangle of tongues, a kiss that bound them tighter than any spoken promise could.

When he drew back, she said, "I taste myself on your lips. And I want to taste you in my mouth."

"We have time enough for that." In his heart he added, they had a lifetime for that.

Rising, he helped her to her feet, her body warm and pliant against his. Then he scooped her up in his arms—her wet hair brushing his bare chest, her breath soft on his neck—and carried her to the bed. Having closed the curtains before he joined her in the bath, the room now felt cocooned in shadows and intimacy, wrapped in the scent of soap and the lingering musk of her climax.

After laying her on the bed, he climbed on top of her, framed her face in his hands, and kissed her again—a slow, intense kiss that spoke of everything in his heart, every vow he hadn't yet said aloud.

Then, bracing himself on his elbows above her, he whispered, "I love you."

She stroked her hands up and down his arms. "And I love you."

When he reached for the condom he'd left on the nightstand, she held his hand. "I've always been careful. I go to my doctor regularly and there's nothing wrong with me. Do you trust me?"

"More than anything. And I've always been careful too."

"Then I don't think we need the condom."

His heart seemed to soar, and he kissed her then, with all the love in his heart. Falling into the vee of her legs, he entered her slowly, with reverence. The caress of her flesh surrounding him was like silk.

She gasped, her body clenching, her breath catching on a note of surprise and joy, her pleasure still so close to the surface. Braced on his elbows, he took her slowly, meeting her gaze for gaze, feeling himself fall into the endless pool of her eyes.

"It's never been like this," she murmured.

"It's never been like this for me either." He didn't believe Gail would hear that as a betrayal. She would be glad, he thought, glad he'd found this amazing woman.

Spreading her legs, Elise took him deeper. Her feet pressed against his butt, urging him to a slightly faster pace. Still, the slowness was maddening to him. His body wanted to plunge, conquer, drive deep until he shattered. But he knew the ecstasy would be even greater if he was patient, if he took her to the edge, then nudged her over. And fell with her.

She gasped, and he felt her inner muscles working him, drawing him in, holding him captive. She closed her eyes, no longer seeing him, lost in sensation, lost to the pleasure, bliss shimmering just over her horizon.

He felt the hard clamp of her body around him, and just as she cried out, he took her hard. Together, they rode the wave she'd just crested, his deep thrusts keeping her suspended in that rapture for what seemed like forever.

Then, try as he might, he couldn't hold out a moment longer. He filled her with everything in him, crying out her name, crying out his love. Until they both lay wrecked on the bed, arms wrapped around each other, his body still filling her, pulsing, their breaths mingling in ragged gasps. They held onto each other as the aftershocks of their pleasure faded into a trembling quiet.

But the memory would always remain in his mind, in his heart. As he feathered her hair back behind her ear, he whispered the words he wanted to say for the rest of his life. "I will always love you."

She echoed him, filling him up, "I will never stop loving you."

They'd awoken to pleasure in the night, as the moonlight poured over them even through the curtains. As he lay sleeping, Elise took him in her mouth, tasted him, loved him. Though he wasn't a young man anymore, he was still virile. And he was hers. She gave him pleasure with all her heart, reveling in the gift of his body. This time he let her finish him in her mouth, and his taste was ambrosia.

Not to be outdone, as soon as his tremors stopped, as soon as he came back to her, Kent brought her the same pleasure with his mouth. After the ecstasy, when they kissed, their tastes mingled, as they would for the rest of their lives.

He made love to her again before the dawn broke, then they slept late, with the morning sun slipping around the edges of the curtains. It was a luxury to wake up in his arms, his warmth anchoring her, his breath stirring her hair. To know that she could do this every morning. And every night.

She couldn't get enough of him.

As she lay in his arms, he echoed her thoughts. "I'll never get enough of you."

She wanted this to go on forever. No matter how old they were.

They ate breakfast in the seventh-floor restaurant surrounded by the beautiful views of Prague—the city glistening in the morning sun, the red rooftops stretching across the horizon. Trying a bit of everything, they enjoyed meats, cereals, fruit, pastries, fresh-baked bread—including a full English breakfast.

Over coffee, Kent raised her hand to his lips. "Are you ready to return to the house? Or we could change our flights and stay here another night?"

Elise wanted to remain cocooned with him in that beautiful suite, making love all night long. But they had to face his daughter, his son-in-law, and his grandchildren.

"We should keep our flights." Maybe she shouldn't worry

him, but she wouldn't hide her feelings from him, not anymore. "Do you think Amanda is still okay with us? I hope she hasn't changed her mind overnight."

He held her hand, his fingers wrapped around hers, steady and warm. "Yes, I think she'll be okay."

She wished he'd said he was *sure*.

THEY RETURNED MIDMORNING, KENT WITH THE LAZY, satisfied look of a man at peace, Elise with nerves fluttering in her belly like caged birds.

As soon as they opened the door, the boys raced down the stairs and threw themselves at Kent, their laughter filling the house. Then Luca came to Elise, hugged her leg, and whispered, "I missed you."

Marek wrapped his arms around her waist. She melted with love for these two boys—the grandchildren she'd never had. Over their heads, she looked at Kent, and his gaze told her he knew what she was thinking. He smiled back at her, his eyes soft with understanding.

Tomás came down first. Elise just wished Amanda would appear so she could get this over with.

He man-hugged Kent, then opened his arms to Elise. She went into his embrace gladly, relieved by the warmth of his welcome. "Have you had breakfast?" he asked.

Kent answered for them. "We had breakfast at the Dancing House."

Tomás raised an eyebrow. "I've never stayed there. There was such a conflict over the supposed travesty. But I love the Dancing House."

"It was amazing," Elise said, thinking not just of the views and the restaurant, but of the lovemaking. Which had been the best part.

"We're almost packed." Tomás flipped his wrist to look at his watch. He still wore one, though many people had thrown theirs away in favor of phones. "We've got an overnight flight." Then he said to Elise, "I'm not sure about your flight since we changed everything around yesterday."

Kent said, "The airline was gracious enough to change Elise's flights to the same as ours."

Tomás clapped his hands. "Then all is perfect." He looked at Elise. "Amanda wondered if you could help her finish her packing when you arrived."

Her stomach sank. Kent gave her a gentle nod and a smile, his gaze reassuring, but she couldn't help feeling there was another sea change coming.

Still, she smiled. "Of course." And she climbed the stairs to her fate. She heard Kent behind her say, "I just need to pull the rest of my things together."

In her bedroom, Amanda was haphazardly shoving clothes into a suitcase, her movements jerky with suppressed emotion.

Elise went to her. "Here, let me fold for you."

Amanda said, "Thank you." And Elise could hear nothing in her voice, not a single sign of her mood.

They worked in tandem for a few minutes, the only sounds being the whisper of fabric and the zippers on packing cubes.

Finally, Amanda turned, surprising Elise by taking her hands and squeezing her fingers. Elise felt a teardrop fall on her skin.

Amanda's voice quavered only slightly. "I'm happy for you. I really am. It's just that I've always felt as if my mom would be truly gone if my father ever found another woman to love."

Elise didn't say that her mother *was* truly gone, that she had been for five years. But that wasn't what Amanda needed to hear. "It doesn't mean your father will ever stop loving your mother. She'll always be in his heart. He loved her with everything in him."

Amanda raised her chin, meeting Elise's gaze. "But doesn't it mean he loves my mother less now?"

Elise couldn't help reaching out to tuck a straight lock of hair behind Amanda's ear. "Never. What it means is that he loved your mother so much and their marriage was so good that he wants to have that kind of happiness again." She hoped that what she said was true. "Do you think your mother would want to look down from heaven and know he was happy?"

Amanda blinked away another tear, but said nothing. Elise wasn't sure her words had meaning for the younger woman, but she plowed on. "I know it's self-serving to say that, because I'm the other woman. But your father often talks about your mother. He tells me how much he loved her."

"Doesn't that hurt your feelings?"

Elise shook her head. "No. Because it means he knows how to love and how to be happy. Your mother taught him that. Which is why I have faith that he and I will find happiness too." She squeezed Amanda's hands. "I never want to come between you and him. You and the boys are the most important people in his life. If it comes to a choice, I want him to choose all of you."

Amanda's eyes turned cloudy all over again. "I don't want to make him choose. I can't bring my mother back, and I can't make him as happy as he was with her. Because there will always be something missing for him." She swiped her cheek as a tear rolled down. After a deep breath, followed by a shaky exhale, she added, "I want you to make him happy. The boys already love you. Tomás thinks you're wonderful." She took another breath and ended with a hiccup. "And you've been so good to me too. You're good for our whole family." She squeezed Elise's hands. "Please make my father as happy as he once was."

Elise answered in a husky whisper. "I will."

Then Amanda threw her arms around Elise and hugged her tightly.

With Kent's love and Amanda's acceptance, Elise suddenly had everything she could ever hope for.

After thirty-five years, her life was finally complete.

EPILOGUE

T*wo months later*

THE HOLIDAYS WERE UPON THEM, STARTING WITH Thanksgiving. That morning, they'd all gone to the cemetery to honor Gail—Amanda's mother, Kent's wife. She had died five years ago, just before Thanksgiving, and it felt right to remember her on this day of gratitude, when they were all so thankful to be together.

Back at the house, the turkey filled the air with its succulent, buttery aroma. Amanda and Elise had prepared side dishes of roast potatoes crisping at the edges, caramelized yams glazed with brown sugar, bright green beans tossed with slivered almonds, and savory sausage stuffing rich with sage. Kent had tried to help, but laughing, they'd both shooed him out of the kitchen. For dessert, they'd even made Czech *kremrole*—rolled pastries filled with cream—to add a little taste of Prague.

At eleven o'clock—eight at night back in Prague—they video-chatted with Hana and Filip. The screen had flickered with smiles and laughter, bridging thousands of miles. Now, the adults relaxed in the cushioned chairs of Kent's Hillsborough home, the warmth of the fire crackling in the hearth. Amanda, wearing one of her mother's favorite sweaters, stroked the knit as if she could still feel Gail's touch in the yarn.

The house itself had shifted over the last two months. Many of Gail's belongings had been given away, though Amanda kept the most cherished pieces, like that sweater. The yearly family portraits still hung on the walls, Amanda growing from baby to teenager to woman, snapshots of milestones, vacations, and laughter. There were pictures of the grandkids, of course, and now, Kent had added new ones. Photos from Prague, the boys grinning with Elise, the start of a fresh chapter.

In the middle of the living room, the boys bent over a new LEGO set, a replica of the Empire State Building. There was even a small King Kong they could add. Elise smiled, thinking one of them might become an architect like their grandfather. Though lately, Luca had taken to the piano, his small fingers moving across the keys with startling ease. His father called him a prodigy, and Elise had to admit the boy had a gift.

Since she'd moved in with Kent a month ago, Elise's touch was everywhere in his home. A framed print from Prague now graced the wall, and on the coffee table lay the book she'd bought on the life of art nouveau artist Alphonse Mucha. The delicate Meissen shepherdess she'd carried across the ocean gleamed behind glass in the china cabinet, always there to remind her of Kent's love. And she wore the moldavite necklace she hadn't let him buy her in Český Krumlov. It was still a beautiful reminder.

Gail's china service sat on the buffet in the dining room, paired with its serving dishes. Elise believed Gail would have wanted her beautiful things woven back into family life.

Elise's clothes now hung in the bedroom closet, and her toiletries rested in the bathroom. Each night, she curled into Kent's arms, their bed warm and welcoming. She felt as if she'd finally come home.

The kitchen timer dinged. Both she and Amanda rose, but Elise waved her away. "No worries. I'll get it."

She opened the oven door for the last basting of the turkey, and a wave of heat wrapped around her, golden and rich with butter and herbs. It was exactly how she felt whenever Kent touched her.

As if her thought summoned him, he was there—his warmth at her back, his familiar, masculine scent surrounding her, the solid weight of his arms sliding around her waist.

"I love you," he whispered against her hair.

"And I love you." She kissed him quickly, mindful of the turkey, but her heart lingered in the moment.

It was Thanksgiving, and she was thankful beyond words. She had never believed she could have another love, never thought she deserved one. But Kent had taught her how to forgive herself, how to step into a new life with grace. He had given her love, and a family too—something she'd thought she'd never have.

She loved him for himself, but also for all that he'd brought to her world. He was right. They were meant to be. And she would love him forever.

KENT'S HEART WAS SO FULL HE THOUGHT IT MIGHT BURST with happiness. When he'd lost Gail, he never imagined he could feel this way again.

Elise finished basting the turkey, checked the meat thermometer poked into the breast, and when she closed the oven with a soft thud, she said, "Almost ready."

The rest of the dishes were warming in the second oven. Gail had been a wonderful cook, and when they'd remodeled the kitchen, she'd insisted on two ovens. Just months ago, that thought would have ached. Now it warmed him. He would always miss her, but he could be grateful, too, that at the end, she had loved him enough to set him free to love again.

He couldn't resist pulling Elise close, their hearts pressed together. "Thank you," he murmured into her hair.

She tipped her head back, catching his gaze. "For what?" They often played this loving game, one of them doing the thanking, the other asking what for.

And there was so much to thank her for. "For being you. For loving me. For embracing my family and falling in love with them, too."

"I loved them even before I loved you."

His chest tightened. "If you hadn't been here that day I brought Amanda to help clear out her mother's things, I don't know what would've happened. Tomás and I both feared Amanda would shatter."

"She might have," Elise said gently, cupping his cheek, her thumb warm against his lips. "But you and Tomás had already arranged for her to see that grief counselor. You gave her the tools. I just... showed up."

He covered her hand with his own. "You're a calming influence. Even the boys are calmer with you around."

He could list every gift she'd brought into his life after five barren years of grief. But he knew, too, that he had given her something precious—helping her forgive herself, giving her the joy she'd believed she didn't deserve.

So instead, he kissed her temple and said softly, "Shall we let the boys know it's their turn?"

Her smile was radiant. They had purposely left the duty of setting the table to Marek and Luca. Boys needed responsibilities.

"Yes, it's time."

Kent stepped out of the kitchen and clapped his hands. "Nana Elise says it's time to set the table," he called, voice ringing through the open rooms. He grinned and clapped again. "Boys—that's your job!"

The two leapt up, eager to please their Nana Elise, as they'd taken to calling her without prompting. He saw how it touched her every time.

They rushed into the dining room, where Elise and Amanda had already lined up everything ready to be set out, cutlery, decorative placemats, shining wineglasses, water goblets, and lace napkins delicate as cobwebs. Gail had crocheted each one by hand, embroidering a tiny flower in the corner. Gail had thrived on her domesticity, and now Elise thrived on bringing it back to life.

"Is this right, Nana Elise?" Luca asked, carefully placing a fork beside a neatly folded napkin.

Her smile lit the room, and Kent's heart. Elise wasn't a replacement for Gail, and the boys would always see their grandmother's face in the photos on the wall. But now they had the gift of Elise's joy, her gentleness, her love.

He glanced toward Amanda, curled on the couch in her mother's sweater. Little of the anguish of two months ago lingered in her eyes. His daughter would always love her mother, always wish Gail were still alive. But today she was open to the future. Their future.

While the turkey rested on the counter, Elise and Amanda carried out the side dishes, setting them on warming trays along the buffet. Kent brought the steaming golden bird to the head of the table, then offered the carving knife to Tomás.

"Would you like the honor?"

Tomás shook his head, smiling. "Oh no. This is your house. You must carve. But you'll be helping me with the dishes afterward."

Laughter rippled around the table. Women had cooked; men would clean—it was tradition enough.

Once turkey and sides loaded their plates, Kent carried the rest of the bird back to the kitchen. Then they all settled around the table, Kent at one end with Elise beside him, Tomás at the other, Amanda next to him, the boys in the two remaining seats. Wine glowed in the adults' glasses, and grape juice sparkled in the boys'.

Before they began, Amanda lifted her glass, her voice hushed with emotion as she met Elise's eyes. "Thank you for bringing new life into our family."

Glasses clinked softly. Elise's eyes glistened as she raised her glass once more. "Thank you for bringing me into your family."

The meal unfolded in a glow of joy and unity. Kent twined his fingers with Elise's beneath the table, the secret pressure of skin on skin grounding him.

"I love you," he whispered.

He loved her with everything he had. He'd almost forgotten how happiness felt, how love could fill every crack in his heart. Elise had brought it back.

As laughter rippled around the table and candlelight flickered across the crystal and china, Kent brushed his thumb over Elise's hand, their fingers twined beneath the linen cloth. Her touch was still a spark in his blood, a reminder of Prague's passion and the promise of all the nights to come. But here, with Amanda's smile easing the ache of the past and the boys' chatter filling the room, their passion deepened into something richer—love that wrapped them in belonging.

Surrounded by family, by warmth, by the flavors of tradition and the sweetness of new beginnings, Kent knew he would never stop hungering for Elise, never stop being grateful that he had found her. And she had found him.

The *Once Again* series, where love always gets a second chance.
Skinny Dipping in Lake Como, Book 14
They've known each other since they were teenagers. Now they'll finally discover what they've been missing all these years. A scorching friends-to-lovers mature romance!

The Once Again Series

Dreaming of Provence | Wishing in Rome
Dancing in Ireland | Under the Northern Lights
Stargazing on the Orient Express | Memories of Santorini
Siesta in Spain | Top Down to California
Cruising the Danube | Margaritas in Mexico
Beachcombing in the Bahamas
Love Affair in London
Holiday in Paradise, Boxed Set Books 1 - 3
Love on Vacation, Boxed Set Books 4 - 6
Escape to Romance- Once Again Series, Books 7-9

ABOUT THE AUTHOR

NY Times and USA Today bestselling author Jennifer Skully is a lover of contemporary romance, bringing you poignant tales peopled with characters that will make you laugh and make you cry. Look for *The Maverick Billionaires* written with Bella Andre, starting with *Breathless in Love*, along with Jennifer's new later-in-life holiday romance series, *Once Again*, where readers can travel with her to fabulous faraway locales. Up first is a trip to Provence in *Dreaming of Provence*. Writing as Jasmine Haynes, Jennifer authors classy, sensual romance tales about real issues such as growing older, facing divorce, starting over. Her books have passion and heart and humor and happy endings, even if they aren't always traditional. She also writes gritty, paranormal mysteries in the Max Starr series. Having penned stories since the moment she learned to write, Jennifer now lives in the Redwoods of Northern California with her husband and their adorable nuisance of a cat who totally runs the household.

Learn more about Jennifer/Jasmine and join her newsletter for free books, exclusive contests and excerpts, plus updates on sales and new releases at **https://jenniferskully.com/newsletter/**

ALSO BY JENNIFER SKULLY/JASMINE HAYNES

Books by *Jennifer Skully*

The Maverick Billionaires by Jennifer Skully & Bella Andre

Breathless in Love | Reckless in Love

Fearless in Love | Irresistible in Love

Wild In Love | Captivating In Love

Unforgettable in Love | Endless In Love

Reunited In Love | Painted In Love

Tempted in Love

Once Again

Dreaming of Provence | Wishing in Rome

Dancing in Ireland | Under the Northern Lights

Stargazing on the Orient Express | Memories of Santorini

Siesta in Spain | Top Down to California

Cruising the Danube | Margaritas in Mexico

Beachcombing in the Bahamas

Love Affair in London | Passion in Prague

Holiday in Paradise, Boxed Set Books 1 - 3

Love on Vacation, Boxed Set Books 4 - 6

Escape to Romance- Once Again Series, Books 7 - 9

Mystery of Love

Drop Dead Gorgeous | Sheer Dynamite

It Must be Magic | One Crazy Kiss

You Make Me Crazy | One Crazy Fling

Crazy for Baby

Return to Love
She's Gotta Be Mine | Fool's Gold | Can't Forget You
Return to Love: 3-Book Bundle

Love After Hours
Desire Actually | Love Affair To Remember
Pretty In Pink Slip

Stand-alone
Baby, I'll Find You | Twisted by Love
Be My Other Valentine

Books by Jasmine Haynes

Naughty After Hours
Revenge | Submitting to the Boss
The Boss's Daughter
The Only One for Her | Pleasing Mr. Sutton
Any Way She Wants It
More than a Night
A Very Naughty Christmas
Show Me How to Leave You
Show Me How to Love You
Show Me How to Tempt You

The Max Starr Series
Dead to the Max | Evil to the Max
Desperate to the Max
Power to the Max | Vengeance to the Max

Courtesans Tales

The Girlfriend Experience | Payback

Triple Play | Three's a Crowd | The Stand In

Surrender to Me | The Only Way Out

The Wrong Kind of Man | No Second Chances

Courtesans Tales, Boxed Set Books 1 - 3

Courtesans Tales, Boxed Set Books 4 - 6

Courtesans Tales, Boxed Set Books 7 - 9

The Jackson Brothers

Somebody's Lover | Somebody's Ex

Somebody's Wife

The Jackson Brothers: 3-Book Bundle

Castle Inc

The Fortune Hunter | Show and Tell

Fair Game

Open Invitation

Invitation to Seduction | Invitation to Pleasure

Invitation to Passion

Open Invitation: 3-Book Bundle

Wives & Neighbors

Wives & Neighbors: The Complete Story

Prescott Twins

Double the Pleasure | Skin Deep

Prescott Twins Complete Set

Lessons After Hours

Past Midnight | What Happens After Dark
The Principal's Office | The Naughty Corner
The Lesson Plan

Stand-alone

Take Your Pleasure | Take Your Pick
Take Your Pleasure Take Your Pick Duo
Anthology: Beauty or the Bitch & Free Fall

Printed in Dunstable, United Kingdom